SALT & HONEY

In a southern Africa violently split during Apartheid, Koba is taken away from her Kalahari desert-tribe after witnessing her parents being murdered by a party of white hunters. She slowly learns to adapt and survive in a dangerous but beautiful environment. However, she is plagued by the knowledge that unless she leaves those who have grown to love her, she faces exile from her own people. The only answer may be to risk all through the brutal laws that condemn her.

CANDI MILLER

◆

SALT & HONEY

Complete and Unabridged

ULVERSCROFT
Leicester

First published in Great Britain in 2006 by
Legend Press Limited
London

First Large Print Edition
published 2007
by arrangement with
Legend Press Limited
London

All characters, places and events, other than those
clearly established in the public domain, are fictitious
and any resemblance is purely coincidental.

British Library CIP Data

Miller, Candi
  Salt & honey.—Large print ed.—
  Ulverscroft large print series: general fiction
  1. San (African people)—Fiction
  2. Apartheid—South Africa—Fiction
  3. Large type books
  I. Title
  823.9'2 [F]

  ISBN 978–1–84617–784–2

Published by
F. A. Thorpe (Publishing)
Anstey, Leicestershire

Set by Words & Graphics Ltd.
Anstey, Leicestershire
Printed and bound in Great Britain by
T. J. International Ltd., Padstow, Cornwall

This book is printed on acid-free paper

TO YIANNO. WHO ALWAYS BELIEVED

Contents

Map of southern Africa — mid–1900s

Map illustrates where Koba begins and ends her journey, a distance of approximately 3,000 kilometres. (Note: South-West Africa is current-day Namibia.)

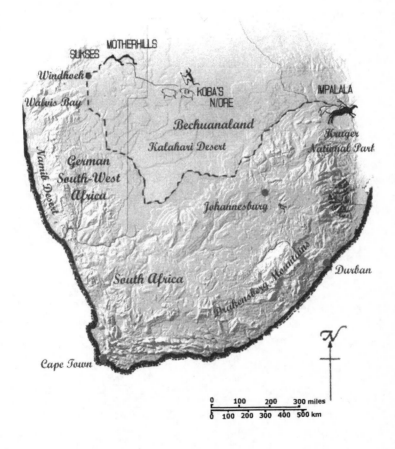

Prologue

South-West Africa, 1958

The guard dogs began to bark, so insistently that Marta got out of bed and hurried to the window.

Unremitting blackness, not even the Southern Cross visible on the horizon. Must be cloudy, she thought. With a bit of luck, tomorrow will be cooler. She'd forgotten how hot it could be here in December. Bad for her feet, already swollen by pregnancy.

She heard frenzy in the doberman's barking now; even the ridgeback's usually token accompaniment sounded urgent. Not one of the ubiquitous jackals then, patrolling the farmyard fence in the hope of finding a way into the hen house. And it wouldn't be one of the servants. They wouldn't dare enter the yard until the dogs had been chained up for the day by their master, Etienne Marais.

1

But Etienne and all the other men were away for the night — out in the veld somewhere, hunting. Marta looked at the shotgun propped up next to the window. Etienne, her brother-in-law, had insisted she take charge of it in the men's absence.

'Lettie's likely to pepper one of her Parisian pink toenails if I leave it with her,' he'd said, winking in the direction of his wife.

'I want nothing to do with guns,' Marta had told him.

★ ★ ★

She left the room now without it, feeling her way down the dark passage towards the growing cacophony. As she struggled with the screen door she heard the doberman yelp. Then a familiar voice, cursing it, 'Shut up, you blerry brak.'

'Etienne? André? Is that you-lot out there?' Surer now, she hastened down the verandah steps, aware of shapes — animal and human. Impossible to distinguish anyone in the moonless night.

'Deon,' she called out to her husband as a man, limping worse than usual, came into view. He held a torch and in its shaky umbra she saw a horse with two small figures astride it. Behind plodded an ox, something massive

2

and inert lying across its broad back. The dogs capered around it, the ridgeback whining.

'Voetsek, jou focken brakke,' she heard her nephew, André, swear.

Marta whistled for the dogs and grabbed each one by its collar, making them sit.

'Why are you back so soon?' she asked Deon.

'Beenah accident,' he mumbled, drunkenly. Marta's hands flew to the open neck of her nightdress, clutching it closed. The dogs bounded away.

'Mannie?' she whispered.

'Boy's awright.' Deon waved the torch vaguely in the direction of the horse.

Marta snatched it from him and stumbled over to her son. Her hand roved across the child's body, trying to discover what the weak beam could not.

'Are you alright, my boy?' He seemed it — cool, no fever, no wounds, no obviously broken bones. Thank God. She trained the beam on his fright-stricken face.

'For pity's sake, what's the matter?'

'Ma, Ma.' He was gulping back sobs. 'It's not me, Ma. Check Uncle Etienne. Save him, Ma, please, Ma, 'cos it's my fault,' he choked. Baffled, she turned from her son.

Suddenly there was lamplight from the

house, candlelight coming from the servants' compound, and above, on the verandah, the shrill tones of her sister-in-law, 'Liewe Magies, what's going on?'

Marta trained the beam on the ox and gasped. Etienne lay completely still, a maroon stain spread across his chest.

What the . . . ? She should feel for a pulse. She couldn't move.

'Ma, please! You must do something quick. I think . . . '

She spun back to her son, spotlighting him. In the wider arc of light she now saw he was propping up a small body — slim yellow limbs, wide oriental eyes. A Khoisan child. But not from around here, that she could see from the child's traditional dress — a pubic apron and a cloak made of animal skin. It must be from a Kalahari desert tribe. What on earth was it doing so far from home? And alone? 'Someone, help me get these children down,' she shouted, dropping the torch and running back to the horse.

As she reached up for the Khoisan child, it recoiled in terror and raised bound hands to fend her off. Marta stopped, horror-struck. 'Why is this child tied up?'

★　★　★

4

As soon as André had secured the dogs, servants began to pour into the yard in various stages of dress. Housemaids, never before seen bareheaded this side of the fence, looked unfamiliar and naked despite having blankets or shawls draped modestly around them. Some carried bleary-eyed children while their men milled about bare-chested with knobkieries or lengths of metal pipe held at the ready. As the elders tried to establish who should be in charge now that the whites and Twi, the boss boy, were preoccupied, two youths with initiation cuts still healing on their chests set off to patrol the perimeter fence, burning logs held aloft. The dogs strained at their chains, barking rabidly.

The anxious human susurrus built until Marta could feel it down the back of her neck, like the rasping breath of a leopard.

'Give me a lamp, get a torch,' she shouted into the throng. 'And for God's sake, someone go start the generator.' She heard footsteps fly to do her bidding, then Lettie shrieking at the sight of Etienne, followed by André's voice as he tried to soothe his mother. Marta kept her attention on Deon. 'Where did you find this child?'

'Out there; Mother Hills way.' His blood-shot eyes flicked towards a pair of hills whose stone summits had been eroded into nipples by the lascivious desert wind. Veiled by the night, they still held an allure. When the morning sun reached the cleavage of the hills, it would fall on the jewel nestled there, a dazzling aquamarine pool set in red-gold rock, surface evidence of the abundant artesian wealth beneath the soil.

South-West African farmers had learnt how to plunder this hidden horde. None better than Etienne Marais. He, of the banknote green cornfields that stretched around the farmhouse as far as the eye could see. Big, blond, broad Etienne Marais, an Afrikaner success story, master of all in the area and parliamentary representative of those whose skin colour entitled them to vote.

Now he lay dying as Marta struggled with the knots tying the child to the pommel.

She was aware of André pushing past, carrying his father with the help of three black servants. Lettie skittered alongside in kitten-heeled slippers, whimpering. She was wringing the lifeless hand that fell over the side of the makeshift stretcher.

'Marta, Marta, for pity's sake, come help, man. Make some muti or something. My Etienne's bad. Liewe Magies, leave the damn child. It's only a kaffir.'

* * * * *

6

Kalahari Desert, 1950

Meat. Piles of it. Strips skewered on thorny branches drying in the doorways of grass-domed huts, slabs sizzling on every cooking fire. People laughed, called across the camp, teased one another. Excitement flared like fat in a flame as the hunters hacked at the giraffe carcass, slipping and sliding in a slush of sand and blood.

Zuma sat straight-legged on sand pinkened by the evening sun. In a gourd, she mixed giraffe fat with ground bark. It made a thick paste, satisfyingly red. Grinning, she began working it into her skin, determined she should look her best for the dance that would follow the feast. After all, she would be on show. She was the owner of the first arrow to hit the old bull.

Mmm, the first cut of Tall Elegant Person's meat is mine. Tami's arrow-arm is strong — a good son-in-law. But my arrow, yau, a fine food-bringer, a meat-maker. People will remember I am a rain season child. I must shine tonight. My skin must glow like the coat of a red buck.

Zuma sensed a wind tapping at her shoulder and knew immediately what it was. She determined to ignore it. Being a medium was a nuisance. The spirits always chose

7

inconvenient times to speak. Couldn't they wait until she took part in a trance dance? She shook her head to clear her ears of their whisperings. Her ornaments jiggled. She touched her cropped hair. Was the grey showing in her regrowth yet? Maybe she should ask N#aisa to shave her head again.

The spirit wind eddied around her, insistently. She ignored it, massaging away the goosebumps that had formed on her arms. The wind spiralled around her, collecting a cargo of sand. Too late Zuma closed her eyes against the dust devil.

Coughing, eyes an angry red, she capitulated, cocking her head to one side and listening to the message.

★ ★ ★

So, there were /Ton at their tree-water. She would tell Kh//an, her husband and a more experienced shaman, but he was old now for such a long journey. And what match were his arrows for /Ton thundersticks? There'd been enough fighting between her people and others. She shrugged. Perhaps it was her duty to add this episode to the Ju/'hoansi story. Make sure the children knew.

She rose, smoothed the hide apron that covered her groin and strolled over to the nearby fires. She chatted to a couple of women, flirted with a man in passing, all the while assessing receptiveness. Tonight the young ones wanted meat. They could smell it — everywhere. Who could begrudge them, after months of roots and berries, Zuma thought? But the meat wasn't ready yet. A story might distract them.

She fixed two feathers to the back of her head and with arms bent backwards like folded wings she began her kori bustard impression, pacing ponderously about the camp.

A big-bellied tot pointed at her, tugged at his mother's kaross, eyebrows quizzical.

'Kori woman has an egg she wants to lay,' his mother laughed.

His older sister scooped him up. 'Come, we'll follow her. She'll have a story to crack open.'

Other children joined them, trotting after Zuma as she high-stepped to a bower under a baobab tree.

'Wum, wum, wum, wummmmm,' she cried.

Hearing, older children abandoned games and ran to join the group. Zuma n!a'an was a fine storyteller.

Zuma let them settle, then, drawing her three-year old granddaughter, Koba, onto her lap, she said casually, 'There's a new story, but you probably don't want to hear it.'

Her granddaughter cocked her head to one side, inclining a tiny cowrie shell of an ear to the wind. 'I *can* hear,' she whispered, big-eyed. Her small voice was drowned out by the chorus of the other children clamouring for Zuma to tell them her tale.

'Well, it's new but it begins long-back, after the time of the Early Race but before our time, when groups of Harmless People lived all over this land, towards sun's-rising-place where the mountains have teeth.' Zuma bared her own, ground down by years of softening hide. 'Towards sun's-resting-place where the sand shines with diamonds.'

'Where's that?' a little girl with shining eyes breathed. Zuma pointed west and patiently explained the route between the camp and the Skeleton Coast, mentioning as many dunes, watering holes and other landmarks as she could remember. No child listened more intently than the long-eyed one on Zuma's lap. Koba was mesmerised by this hint of a world beyond the camp.

Zuma's tone became mysterious. 'Then, into this land came strangers. They drove herds of tame animals before them and suffer-suffered when they found no water or grazing.

10

'Our people showed them where the water was and took their herds deep into the valleys to find grass. When the Ju/'hoansi returned with the herds full fattened, they were given tobacco and were glad. 'Come and be our herdsmen,' these Herero and Tswana tribesmen said to our people, 'and we will give you plenty of milk'. But the Ju/'hoansi did not want to. They preferred to follow the meat animals they loved.'

While the group nodded, Zuma felt for the beaded pouch at her waist and withdrew a pipe. She pushed tobacco into the bowl and dispatched a boy to fetch a light from the nearest fire. The children waited politely. All except Koba.

'More, more,' she pleaded, chubby fingers reaching to remove the pipe that stopped the story.

'Yau,' Zuma laughed, holding it out of reach. 'This granddaughter of mine is dry. She thirsts for stories like a root for water.'

The older children distracted Koba — pulling faces, tickling her, passing her from lap to lap. Once Zuma had a good draw going on the pipe, she continued. 'After the herdsmen came, the Ju/'hoansi moved away. Game gone, you see. The farmers' herds were eating all the grass.'

She closed her eyes as she began the

beloved litany, 'Eland, gemsbok, kudu, wilde-beest, hartebeest, tsessebe, roan . . . ' The children chanted along, many with their eyes closed, almost tasting the great meat animals. Zuma puffed contentedly. 'Now all these, eland-gemsbok-kudu-wildebeest-hartebeest-tsessebe-roan, had to move off to find new food.' Zuma shook her head so the feathers wafted sadly. 'Ju/'hoansi and farmers became enemies.'

'How did they become enemies?'

The old woman removed the pipe from her mouth and sighed. 'They fought each other for things — for grass, for tree-water, for the tame meat animals. The strangers had many things our people wanted. The Ju/'hoansi took them with their arrows, but were chased off when the /Ton arrived,' Zuma paused, rolled her eyes, 'with their thundersticks.'

Fear snaked through the older children in the group. Younger ones sensed the mood change. Koba demanded an explanation.

A boy jumped up, extended his arm at shoulder height and pulled an invisible trigger. The fire-fetcher joined him. Soon they were 'shooting' at each other, competing to reproduce the perfect rifle report.

Koba began to cry. Zuma gathered her granddaughter and pressed the bobbled head to her red chest. 'Hush-hush. No thunder-sticks will find you here.'

'Dere, dere,' Koba insisted, pointing towards the distant hills.

Zuma's face clouded as she recalled the whispering of the wind. But Koba was too young to have The Ear. Time to abandon the story. The new part might only confirm what frightened them both.

'Yau,' she exclaimed, clapping her hand over her nose, 'my what's-up-front, something's in it. Koba, Koba, can you see?' She thrust her wiggling nose close to the child's astonished face. 'It's pulling me, calling me.' She leaned away from the bemused group. 'A smell has got me by the nose. I must follow. Come Koba.'

The older children caught on. Getting up they sniffed the air. The smell of grilled meat was irresistible. 'It's ready,' they shouted as they dashed to their family fires.

Zuma came more slowly, cradling Koba and blowing softly into her ears to disperse any sounds there.

Chapter 1

South-West Africa, 1958

Koba stood at the Mother Hills, mesmerised by the water. She'd never seen anything like it. A pool of permanent drink, glowing yellow-green like a cat's eye seen in the firelight. At home, deep in the Kalahari Desert, water collected only after a rare downpour. It lay briefly in shallow, brown sheets, then vanished. 'Sipped by the sun,' said her mother. 'Swallowed by the sand,' said her grandmother.

Koba believed Zuma. Sometimes the old woman could find her a drink of cool water when she stuck a straw into the burning sand. No need now, not with all of this.

Koba trailed pink-padded fingers in the water, then dabbed at a graze above her anklet of ostrich eggshell beads. Balm for her barbed-wire graze.

'I left a piece of my skin hanging in the claws of the /Ton fence,' Koba said to Zuma, who was crouched nearby.

15

Her grandmother shook her head. 'Sorry-sorry for it.' Zuma flapped at the flies paddling in the mucous of her infected eye. 'This tree-water belonged to us, long before the /Ton came. Now, uh-uhn-uhn . . . ' The old woman hawked and spat. Green sputum spotted with blood stayed on her chin. Koba darted forward and wiped it with a corner of her hide apron. She hovered as her grandmother hacked out coughs.

Anxiously she studied the bowed grey head, remembering that her grandmother hadn't asked her to shave it for a while. Strange, Koba thought, Grandmother used to be so vain about not showing age ashes.

Now Zuma dipped a whisk of bustard feathers into the pool. Koba watched her shake water drops onto her skin. They looked strange, like stars on the hide of an elephant. Zuma rubbed the droplets into her skin, giving careful attention to the tired leather of her concave breasts. Still vain, Koba grinned, as she stepped into the pool to begin her own ablutions.

She scooped up the water with a minimum of splash. This place, where the sound of heat stored in rocks was the loudest noise, unnerved her. Koba bent to rinse her face, raising her buttocks to the afternoon rays. Then she waded ashore and flopped down on a rock to dry off. Her skin warmed but she kept shivering. She didn't like this place,

16

despite the surfeit of water and plant food.

'And why have Father and Mother gone for more food? Already we have enough meat to make our bellies swell like a snake that's swallowed a buck, yet they collect more.' She scowled at the pile of nuts her father had instructed her to clean. 'Are we termites trying to stock a nest?'

Zuma said nothing, just rubbed water into the folds of her shrunken belly. Koba waited. Her grandmother had an answer; she could tell from her feigned deafness. The old woman's hearing was as sharp as a meerkat's. But no words came.

Koba stood up angrily. 'Yau, adults! Always-always ignore me.'

She kicked out at the pile of nuts. Several shot into the pool with plops that amplified as the sound echoed around the stone enclosure. A cloud of blue waxbills rose with a whirr of wings to settle in the safety of a thronbush.

Koba gazed fearfully about, but nothing else moved except the creeping shadow of the afternoon. Behind, she heard Zuma suck her few remaining teeth.

'You are like a calf butting the wrong end of its mother. Put your heart in the right place and your mouth will find milk.'

Koba sulked. Grandmother was her favourite relative, but trying to understand her was

17

like trying to see the sun behind clouds. Something bright up there, a person could feel it, almost see it, but it bothered the eyes to look. After a while she squatted down, slightly behind Zuma.

'Grandmother n!a'an,' she asked respectfully, 'are there evil spirits in this place?' Zuma manoeuvred a stiff turn towards her. Her expression was grave.

'Uhn-hn, I don't feel them, child.'

'I feel something — like lions walking,' Koba whispered.

Zuma looked about agitatedly. 'Yau, do not mention clawed things. Not here. Not now.' Her bead and brass hair ornaments swung in front of her face as she shook her head.

Koba knew she'd done wrong. A person shouldn't speak directly of danger. It might awaken. But it wasn't her fault she'd been born as sensitive as a springhare's whisker. She tried to be like the other children, tried to play catch-clap and feather flight out in the bush without hearing whisperings on the wind, but she did hear the voices of people who weren't there. Not distinctly, just as mumblings that she didn't understand.

When she'd first told her father he'd become cross and forbade her to speak of it again. Her mother had referred her questions to Zuma.

'She has The Ear,' she said proudly. But

18

Zuma muttered that it wasn't time to concern herself with such things. Anything she heard in the wind was not a message for her.

It's good that I'm deaf to them, Koba shivered. Feelings are easier to ignore than whisperings.

'What about your nut work?' Zuma reminded her. 'Your father had his fierce face-front when he told you to clean them.'

'Too many to crack open and it takes too long with the hammering stone wrapped up,' Koba said sulkily. 'A mongongo won't open unless we're sharp with it.'

'Muzzle the stone,' her father had insisted before he'd left the camp to go hunting. 'No one must hear it talk or they will know we are in the Mother Hills.'

Koba knew people were afraid of this n/ore. She'd heard it spoken of in hushed tones around campfires. Was it because of its closeness to /Ton, she wondered?

She had never seen whites, let alone their homes. And even here they were so far from a /Ton house that no smoke was visible.

Perhaps /Ton don't use fire to cook, Koba mused. People said they had machines to do their work — and their walking. The machines were wondrous, people said, but the /Ton were ugly — chameleon skin, first white then turning red in the sun. Coming off, like a snake's. Did that hurt, she wondered? And did /Ton truly have hair like winter grass — pale and straight? She wanted to see them, just a small look, but her father said they should leave as soon as possible.

To Koba's surprise, Zuma now spoke. '/Ton say if we walk on this ground or take even one springhare from it, we can be killed. !Khui!' She reproduced the report of a rifle. The sound sent a lizard scurrying for cover and left Zuma coughing. Koba hesitated in offering help — it served her grandmother right for making such a disturbance. When Zuma began scrabbling feebly for her pipe, Koba relented. Just sucking on it could soothe the old woman. Koba fished it out from the beaded pouch. The stem was long-gone and the wooden bowl had two dark indentations where Zuma's fingers had gripped it for as long as Koba could remember. She handed it to her grandmother.

She waited while Zuma sucked her cough into submission, then pleaded, 'Why-why have we come? It's safer in the desert — a person can hear things. Should we not begin to pack the food, Grandmother n!a'an? Then when Mother and Father return, we can leave. Be away from here before night.'

'Child, child,' Zuma replied as she brushed off Koba's beseeching hand, 'do not worry me like a bee around a honey badger. I sit here until I die.'

'Die, *die* — yes, you will!' Koba gripped the twig-like limb as hard as she dared. 'Haven't you seen the gemsbok Father shot and the duiker hanging in the gai tree? The /Ton will come with his gun and kill us all!'

'Koba, Koba,' Zuma tsk-ed, 'be still. You are like a tumbling weed — fast-fast going nowhere. Sit. Sit! There is a story I will crack open to tell you.'

For Koba the words worked like a lullaby. She felt safe, secure as a seed encased in a nut. It was almost as though she was little again and being cradled in her grandmother's lap. If she was relaxed enough to tell tales, there was nothing to fear, Koba thought. Grandmother could see beyond. Spirits talked to Zuma even when she wasn't in a trance. She heard them clearly so she would know about any imminent danger.

The old woman reached for a peeled mongongo and sucked on it, her milky eyes focused on the distant horizon. Koba moved the bag out of reach. They hadn't peeled enough yet.

Zuma squirreled the nut away in one cheek and smiled, lopsided. 'Your grandfather, Kha//'an, was very fond of this place. It was here that we first saw each other. There,' she gestured to where a beach arched over the eye of the pool like a blonde brow, 'where medicine dances would be held when all the

Ju/'hoansi came. We women sat there, singing. The men answered from beyond the circle. Slowly, slowly they moved in, stamping, singing, the rattles on their ankles going so.' The old woman rotated her wrist. Bangle jangle approximated the sound of jiggling shells and beads.

'In the middle of the line I saw a young man, taller than the others.' Zuma reached for her feather bushel and began to trace dreamily along her leg. 'He had muscles like an eland, long and strong-strong. His chest. Yau! Bright in the firelight, golden like metal. When I saw his head, bent so as not to be boastful of his view above others, I knew him to be Kha/'an, whose mother was Koba — she for whom you are named.'

The old woman removed the slimy kernel from her cheek and nibbled at it. Between swallows she spoke. 'Koba had the water rights to this hole, from when it was called /Kae/kae, before it was Mother.'

Her granddaughter began to fidget. Perhaps Zuma was no longer kori-woman, best storyteller in the tribe?

'Koba had them from her mother, old Be, who was married . . . '

'Grandmother,' Koba blurted out. 'What happened when you saw Grandfather?'

'Eh? Oh, Kh//'an . . . Kh//'an felt the interest of my eyes and I looked away.'

Koba nodded. It was proper behaviour. Zuma chortled. 'But when everyone was asleep, I met Kh//'an up there.' She gestured with difficulty to the ledge high above their heads. Koba craned her neck to see but was blinded by the sun's rays refracted off the rocks.

'I shall show you . . . when you have finished your work.'

'But Grandmother . . .'

Zuma ran arthritic fingers around her gums to clear nut debris. 'Auck, child, it is too hot now to climb so high . . . and the way is heavy with unfinished work to carry on one's conscience. Come, finish the nuts. We will look tomorrow.'

'But . . .'

'There is time.'

Zuma hummed while Koba sighed elaborately but to no avail. She resumed her work peeling the nuts, trying to conjure up the face of her dead grandfather. All she could remember were his fingers, feathered it seemed to her. Later she realised it was because he was always plucking birds. Kh//'an had been the best trapper in the village, adept at setting snares for gamebirds — guinea fowl, sandgrouse, even large kori bustards.

One day he'd disturbed an adder and been bitten on the ankle. Zuma had bound the area with clean strips of hide, but still the leg had ballooned. After a few days it looked taut and shapeless, as massive as the branch of a baobab tree.

Zuma had managed to control Kh//'an's fever with infusions of medicinal plants, but the skin on the limb had begun to break down, splitting into oozing sores which ate deeper and deeper into his flesh. No amount of poulticing had kept the rot at bay, and finally maggots set to work, eating the wound clean but exposing the bone.

It was relief when the leg eventually fell off below the knee. They'd buried it, as if it were a full corpse, moved away as custom dictated, and the wound had healed.

But Kh//'an had lost his will to live. He lay in their hut day after day, his face turned from the door.

Zuma had discussed with her son-in-law, Tami, her wish to carry Kh//'an to the rock painting. But without help from others in their group they could not manage it. And they couldn't insist that their kinfolk come too. A pilgrimage to what had become known to the tribe as the Mother Hills was just too dangerous.

Many medicine dances had been held for the healing of Kh//'an, with Zuma entering a trance herself so she could plead with the spirits to leave Kh//'an with her for a while longer. But they told her he wished to die, so

Zuma had sat beside him as he wasted away, refusing on his behalf the choice meat young hunters brought to tempt him.

As though she sensed Koba's thoughts had made the same journey as hers, the old woman sighed. 'Uh-uh-uhn. I have lived too long without him. It's my time to die. Kh//'an's spirit will come here to meet mine.'

Koba frowned her incomprehension but Zuma was looking at her emaciated arm. 'I long to feel him stroking me, but bah,' she sneered at her limb, 'this ugly thing. Once it was a python — smooth, shining, with beautiful markings. Many men wanted to stroke it.'

Her granddaughter shuddered. Everyone knew that Zuma had eaten food with many men. Her appetite was still big-talk around the campfires.

Zuma guffawed at Koba's prim expression. 'Don't worry, tomorrow you leave me on the ledge.'

★ ★ ★

Koba flung herself at Tami as he stepped into the camp. 'Father, Father, will we leave Grandmother here when we go?'

Tami's shoulders were red from the gemsbok embryo he carried.

'Yes,' he said, gesturing for her to gather some branches so he could lay down the carcass.

This meat he would cook tonight. It was so tender his mother-in-law might be able to chew it.

Koba was still at his elbow. 'What about the hyenas and baboons? I've seen their spoor.'

'That's why we'll leave Grandmother up on that ledge.' Holding the buck by its toy-sized back hooves, he slit along the belly. Fluid gushed out, falling onto the beach. Immediately, flies fell onto the gore and began to lap at it. 'Rock at her back and a fire at her feet, she'll be safe until she chooses to let her spirit leave her body.'

'Safe perhaps from the hyena — but the baboon? That Tearing-tooth will douse her fire to get at her.'

'Koba, Koba!' Tami slipped the knife carefully into the sheath at his waist. Its blade was badly chipped but he didn't dare sharpen it — it was eggshell-thin already from all the filing. He needed metal to make a new one but the only place to get it was at the trading store. He was reluctant to go there. /Ton frequented it.

He set the buck down on a rock and pulled his daughter towards him. Looking into her eyes, he asked, 'What's the matter with you? You've seen old people sit down to die, or lie in their huts waiting. If a hyena hurries Grandmother . . . ' He shrugged and stood up. 'If Zuma has spoken to you of her coming death, then she must also have told you how dangerous this place is for us. But not for her. We must go. She has chosen to stay.'

⋆ ⋆ ⋆

It was miserable around the campfire that night. Insidious currents curled under karosses, crêping flesh and fraying tempers.

'Animal hide is no good for such nights,' Koba's mother, N#aisa, said. 'The cold stabs through into one's back.'

'Eh-ha,' Zuma nodded. Her back was full of scars, burn marks from years of lying almost in the fire in the search for warm sleep.

Tami looked up from the thumb piano he was strumming. 'Turn your backs to the fire, women. They will soon be warm.'

'And then our fronts will be frozen.' N#aisa looked tired, the smooth of her brow ruffled with resentment. 'If we had proper clothes, wrap-right-round ones like the /Ton's, we could be warm all over.'

'You do not need /Ton clothes!' Tami snapped, pushing the crude keyboard away from him and dangerously close to the fire. 'Every time we come within a day's walk of the /Ton, you become long-lipped.' He stared at them all, firelight blazing in his brown eyes. The women dropped their gaze and he dropped his voice. 'Your karosses are as thick

27

and soft as I could make them. Your aprons are beautiful with the many beads I have sewn onto them.'

Koba was surprised at her father's words. Almost boastful. Lucky they weren't in the village. People might think Tami was strutting.

'An apron takes a long time to dry after rain-soaking,' N#aisa replied. '/Ton clothes dry much quicker.'

Tami tore at his hair. 'Leave it alone. You're like a fly on a wet wound.'

The females stared. It was seldom the man that people called 'Quiet Tami' became so irascible. 'Yes, it's cold . . . ' N#aisa and Koba rolled their eyes at each other. 'Bone-biting,' he admitted, his neck corded with the effort of control, 'but tomorrow the sun will shine. We'll walk away from here . . . with nothing to slow us down.'

He jabbed a finger at the women ranged around the fire opposite him. 'For too long our people have thought that /Ton ways are better than ours. They are not!' Tami banged his fist onto his knee. 'You must learn this, Koba, teach it to your children!'

Koba nodded solemnly. It was the first time her father had made a marriageable-age remark to her. Did this mean she had a suitor? She tried to catch her mother's eye but N#aisa was furiously mashing up the inside of the small green melon she gripped between her knees.

Tami walked around the fire and hissed at his wife, 'Yes, the /Ton have many machines — lorries, guns . . . but they are slaves to their animals! They cannot move away fast.' He glared, and then walked off into the darkness.

Koba stared at the fire, flames now sputtering because her mother had placed the moist melon into it. What was going on? Everyone was so careless.

'Bah,' N#aisa grumbled, 'what do /Ton need to walk away from? They have freedom. We are prevented from hunting animals that we've always eaten; we have wires across our paths . . . ' The moisture in the melon was burning away. N#aisa ranted on regardless. Koba drifted off. Her mother was always grumbling. Being with her grandmother was better. But Grandmother was dozing again, or pretending to.

She walked in the direction her father had taken and found him picking leaves from an acacia tree. Irritably he shoved them into his pipe.

'My heart longs for tobacco.'

'I know.' She laid her hand on his knee as she squatted down next to him in the mauve moon-shadow of the tree. The night was noisy with the 'nyaaaa' of the jackal, a tremulous sound but comfortingly familiar.

Koba waited for her father to speak. Instead he stood, smiled, and swung her up and over one shoulder, as he'd done when she was little.

Koba felt foolish, riding high into camp. She was too big; too much of her torso protruded above her father's head. She felt unsteady. And she hated the sight of her grandmother from this vantage point. She looked too small in her blankets, like a worm that couldn't fill its skin.

★ ★ ★

Koba scraped a little hollow for herself in the sand and lay down, curled up as close to the glowing fire as she dared. Above her the night sky dulled, the glittering banner of the Milky Way cloaked by clouds driven in by a violent wind. When the moon peeked briefly from behind the billowing black, baboon sentries were visible on the ridges above them. One began to bark.

'You have offended the People Who Sit on their Heels,' Koba's father teased, reminding her of their earlier conversation.

Koba rolled over irritably. She didn't feel like jokes. How could her father not understand what was in her heart?

Seeing her tense back, he threw an extra log onto the fire and, despite his better judgment, blew it into flame. Koba relaxed.

Later, when her parents were asleep, a cold-shouldered width apart on their sleeping mat, Koba crept across to Zuma. The old woman lay propped up on one elbow, face pillowed in her palm. Her cloudy eyes were open.

'Grandmother, I feel a tapping in here.' Koba touched her chest.

Zuma looked long at her granddaughter. Finally, she whispered, 'I have known that tapping.'

'You have?' Koba leaned forward. 'What is it? Do you feel it now?'

Zuma shook her head. 'No. Those powers and my Ear have gone.'

Koba slumped. In a small voice she said, 'But can you tell me what the tapping means?'

'The tapping is a signal for you.'

'A signal?'

'To tell you to open to the message.'

'What message?'

'The one from those who have no voice to warn with.'

Koba's skin prickled with fear. More Faceless Ones. Why was she tormented so? Her breathing quickened until she felt the flutter of her grandmother's hands around her face. They settled as lightly as leaves on her cheeks. 'Poor, plagued little one. Your power steals your childhood from you.'

'I haven't got any power,' Koba was close

to tears. 'No one listens when I say we should leave this place.'

'Child, there is power in patience, in endurance. We Ju/'hoansi have that kind of power.' She stared into the darkness above Koba's head and sighed.

I don't want any of this, Koba felt like screaming. I don't want to feel things, to hear things others can't. I don't want to be here. But she felt Zuma pulling her downwards, towards the mat, indicating that she should curl up against her. Zuma began to croon an old lullaby and instantly Koba felt calmer.

She lay down and wriggled into the curve of her grandmother's body. She felt Zuma's legs creak up to cradle her. The lullaby was purring through her. She felt soothed — it was yawn-warm with the fire at the front and a familiar body at the back. Good, the way Grandmother was sheltering her from the sand-spraying wind.

Once the song stopped and was replaced by the rhythmic rasp of Zuma's sleep-breathing, Koba felt alone again. She lay watching for a break in the clouds so she could see the baboon sentries on the summit. While they watch, I can sleep, she told herself. Tomorrow, perhaps, my heart will be done with this. But when she thought of leaving Zuma, she began to cry. Her sorrow grew and shook sobs from her that she was sure would wake her grandmother. She didn't want that. The old woman should have her last family night in peace. She should be comforting Zuma, not the other way around.

Koba stifled her sobs, wiped her eyes, stood up and stepped over her grandmother. She then lay down again, behind the old woman. She felt the sand spatter against her back, felt her skin contract against the cold, but her heart was warm pressed against her grandmother.

*   *   *

Cold at my front, Koba thought when she woke up. Aah, that was why — her mother was raking away the warm ashes. Auck, Koba sucked her teeth, the sun's not up yet. But where was her grandmother?

She sat up and was relieved to see her nearby, shoving things into her kaross. Zuma n!a'an looked a little stronger this morning.

Then she saw her grandmother shoulder a small bundle, with difficulty, and turn towards the summit path.

'Wait!' Koba scrambled up. 'I want to come with you.' She picked up the sack of nuts, grabbed a fistful of meat strips drying in a tree and headed for the steep path. Quickly, she caught up. The old woman was breathless, but merry.

'Wipe the worry from your what's-up-front. Look around you. See what the birds see.'

Koba leaned against a boulder and gazed out over the dawn landscape. Grass tousled by wind, dunes as pink as the eyelids of newly hatched birds. The land looked soft from sleep. In a tree, truncated from this perspective, the hunched shapes of roosting vultures. With the first updraft of warm air they'd take flight, riding the thermals until they were spiralling well beyond sight. There to keep an eye on the day's dying.

'Mother,' N#aisa appeared and took Zuma's bundle from her, 'walk carefully or you will kill yourself falling off this path.'

Zuma began to laugh, at first a wheezy snigger then with hacking, howling mirth. N#aisa looked mortified. Koba gave her arm a squeeze while she tried to hide her giggles. Her mother grinned sheepishly. They linked arms and continued up the path.

Once out of the gully they found them-selves in sunshine. N#aisa allowed herself a tentative smile while Zuma exulted. 'Aiee-eeeee-aaaaa!' she shouted, flinging her arms above her head towards the gold and guava sky.

The vultures shifted on their perch as if appalled at the woman's vitality.

'Hush, Mother n!a'an!' Tami pleaded as he

34

came into view carrying armloads of meat and utensils, 'your voice will carry.'

'Let it,' Zuma wheezed. 'Let everyone know I'm home!' She scuttled forward. 'And here are the Early People.' She pointed to a rock wall, off to one side. It was covered in drawings, reddish-brown and black, human figures and animals.

They all stepped forward, transfixed. Reverently, they peered at the rock painting. 'Did the great god make this, Mother n!a'an?'

'Some say so, but others say it was the Ju/'hoansi, long-long-long ago.'

'Our people have never painted,' Tami said emphatically. He put his bundles on the ground and stepped closer. 'Hau, I see hunters. Didn't know them at first — so flat. But look, look how they stalk. N#aisa, see, this one's ready with a spear should his friend's arrow fail.'

'And see this woman clapping,' N#aisa traced around a figure with raised arms. 'They'll feast tonight!' She and Tami drifted off, chattering and pointing as they drew each other's attention to new wonders in the teeming mural.

Zuma tapped the rock in the vicinity of a crowded scene. 'A trance dance, child. Full of power.'

Koba frowned. She saw figures in a line but could they be people? They had the heads of buck and elephant-size penises. The female ones had tails. They leaked from their faces and were bent low like the old. 'I see no power.'

'You must feel it. Put your hand on that eland.'

Koba cupped her hand over the ochre line drawing of a powerful buck. The rock felt cold and hard. Only her back was warm with the sun shining on it.

'No, no, you must press skin with the eland. Use your head to learn his wisdom,' Zuma urged.

Gingerly, Koba leaned her forehead against the sandstone. It felt warm, as though the sun were now shining on her front. But that couldn't be. She was up against night-chilled rock. Yet there was something yielding against her forehead; she could have sworn it was covered in animal skin. She could smell a musty male antelope. Koba pulled back from the mural and stared at the eland. He wasn't meat and blood. She turned her incredulous face to her grandmother.

Zuma clapped her hands with joy. Though dim now, her inner eye discerned the mark of the eland on her granddaughter's forehead. The child would now have a powerful spirit guide. She beamed, then drew her granddaughter towards her and blew over her face. Best if the experience was forgotten for the time being.

Koba opened her eyes a few seconds later when Zuma clapped again. 'Come. Put my sleeping mat here, son-in-law; this is where I shall lie.'

36

For the next hour Koba and her parents prepared Zuma's final camp. They stacked firewood and water containers, checked flints and food supplies, scraped out a sleeping hollow and swept the rock floor. They piled extra karosses onto her sleeping mat and arranged her essentials close to hand: tobacco pouch, fire fan and a digging stick to use as a poker or weapon.

Then there was nothing more to do, nowhere to look but at the faint footpath that led away from the Mother Hills back towards the desert. They all saw the wraith of smoke curled on the horizon.

'The /Ton's home-fire?' Koba asked.

'No, that is towards the west.'

Koba read anxiety in the set of her father's shoulders. 'It could be our own people, Father.'

'No, too big.'

'Maybe it's just a veld fire. Now is the time for them.'

Tami shook his head. 'The sun is not yet hot enough.' Then, seeing the strained expressions on his family's faces, he smiled. 'But perhaps it's yesterday's fire, walked this way in the night. Don't worry — far off.'

Koba was worried. She'd seen how soot stuck to the undersides of their feet and left a trail across blackened bush. Even the /Ton would have no trouble seeing such a sign.

They had to leave, quick-quick.

She flung her arms around her grand-mother and held on, trembling.

'What's this I feel?' Zuma held the child at arm's length. She lifted the small chin in her shaky claw. 'A person who can shelter another in the night has nothing to fear.' Koba sniffed but felt gratified. 'And you will have a guide. Now you will find your answers.'

'Not without you.'

'I'll be there, beyond the circle of firelight.'

Koba whispered, 'Something bad is going to happen. I can feel it.'

Zuma made to whisper back but Tami rushed forward. 'Stop feeding these notions of hers, Mother-in-law!'

'I say nothing she doesn't already feel.'

'No!' he put a hand on each of Koba's shoulders. 'These are feelings beyond her years. Come.' He turned Koba away. She felt a wrench that tore at her insides like a tree uprooting. She stood in agony, arms clutching her middle. Tami had to pick her up.

N#aisa pushed past and knelt down to Zuma. She clasped her mother's hands and blew on them. Zuma pressed her daughter's head into her lap and murmured something Koba could not hear. Then, 'Go, go quickly.' N#aisa jumped up and ran, head down. Hearing her sobs stopped Koba's. She'd never seen her mother cry.

Tami saluted hurriedly and set off with Koba. She twisted in his grasp, stretching her arms out to Zuma. Tami forced her to turn. 'We must hurry.' They ran. Near the bottom, Koba halted and looked back. High up, indistinct, she saw something. But it wasn't bright, like the sun behind cloud. It was black and beetle-sized — Zuma, arms raised to wave, her kaross flapping about like shredded wings.

Chapter 2

Mannie sat on the stallion like a Crown Prince. He knew that even André, six years older than him, wasn't allowed up on Bliksem, though Etienne was behind him, an arm firmly around his middle. Mannie hoped it was only a matter of time before his uncle would ignore Pa's warning about him being too young, and allow him to take the reins.

The ride to the furthest reaches of the farm had been exhilarating. Etienne had given the huge horse its head and they'd galloped at full tilt across the land, powdering labourers working by the wayside with an imperial cloud of red-brown dust.

Now the horse stood halted and heaving at the game fence, its coat damasked with sweat stains. Even at seventeen hands high, Bliksem's head did not reach the top barbed-wire strand of the massive construct that kept Etienne's kudu and other antelope out of his cornfields and cattle pastures.

The land beyond the fence was Etienne's too. Recently acquired for game, it was hundreds of hectares of uncultivated bush-veld, hock-high grass dotted with thornscrub and occasional trees, and it stretched all the way to the distant Mother Hills.

He had another game farm too, hundreds of miles away in South Africa. His brother, Deon, managed it for him.

Or mismanaged it, Etienne had grumbled last time he visited and found even common impala buck too scarce to hunt. He'd been planning to write to Deon and give him an ultimatum — sober up and do the job properly or move off the farm. But now that his boet-and-brood had turned up at Sukses, he'd have it out with the bugger face-to-face — just as soon as the opportunity arose.

Right now though, there were too many other things that needed seeing to in his constituency and around the farm. And to top it all, Twi said there was a poaching problem.

He glared down at his foreman. Twi was a wizened little man whose slanting eyes suggested a Bushman heritage. Now they were downcast as he nudged a dead gemsbok with his splayed toes. She was sprawled against the fence, her soft, white stomach slashed, her uterus burgled of its calf.

Blue-black flies fizzed around the mess of mucus and blood.

'Butchering abortionist bastards,' Etienne spat.

'What's a 'bortionistbastard'?' Mannie asked, not missing the warning look his father gave his uncle.

He was thrilled when Etienne ignored it and kept on shouting and swearing, using words Mannie desperately wanted to remember so he could repeat them to the boys at school.

Etienne lowered his nephew to the ground and then jumped off the horse. He bent over the buck. 'Didn't even want the horns or the hide, the bastards. Killed her for an embryo — a little scrap with hardly any meat on it! It's muti-murder, man. Some focken witch-doctor's responsible for this.' The big Boer straightened up, inflated with indignation.

Twi was studying a small wound in the buck's chest. 'Not the witchdoctor, Baas,' he said, 'Ju/'hoansi. One shot. Here, heart-near.' He nodded. 'A good arrow, good hunter.'

Mannie thought his uncle was going to explode with rage. Etienne's face looked purple, his eyes bulged like ping-pong balls, and he was dancing around in the dust like a horse that didn't want to be saddled.

'Take it easy, Boet,' he heard his father say.

'Overwrought and overweight is bad for your heart, hey.'

Etienne's big boot lashed out, connecting with the mesh of the enormous fence. It twanged, the reverberation rousing the veld from its afternoon torpor. A butcher bird flew from the topmost wire with a tearing protest, displaying a blood-red chest, and a snake slithered away towards some scrub. The stallion shied but Etienne held onto it, all the while waving his free hand about, shouting at Twi, 'You're telling me it's those wild cousins of yours? Trespassing? I'll kill the bastards when I catch them. They got no right to be here, let alone helping themselves. Do they think I'm keeping a blerry larder for them?'

Twi remained silent, staring down at the sand. Mannie had the impression the little man wasn't as worried about his master's temper as he and Pa were.

Mannie backed away from the group. Turning, he picked up a twig and began drawing circles in the dun-coloured sand. Pa never got that cross, the ten-year-old thought. It was ugly. Ma got cross but then she did have reddish hair. She got cross about stupid things, like the police sjambokking natives or him playing marbles in the passage. Or not eating his cabbage.

Pa said that was because she was German

and Germans loved cabbage. When she was cross enough to make her lips look like she'd been sucking on a lemon, Pa called her 'Sauerkraut'. Ma didn't laugh about that, but he thought it was moerova funny.

He spied a column of big, black ants marching towards their hole. He placed his twig across their path, knowing they'd soon surge over it to get to the nest. Just like a Panzer division, he thought.

He supposed his Ma felt a bit shy about being German. Not so much here, in South-West, where there were lots of people with funny accents, but back at Impalala. Every time they showed a war movie at the bioscope in Nelspruit, he had to fight in the playground the next day when a boy said his Ma was a 'Nazi'. No good saying she grew up in Africa nowhere near any Tommies or Jews. Easier to fight.

★   ★   ★

Several yards away, Etienne was still shouting, 'Bliksemse Bushmen, they must work for food, just like everyone else, or go back to the focken desert.' A pulse pummelled visibly on his neck. 'We can't have people helping themselves to another man's stuff like they're entitled or

44

something,' he fumed. 'Hell man, what are they? A bunch of Bolsheviks?'

Deon snorted. 'Here it comes — red peril propaganda. I tell you, Boet, ever since you became the MP for Onderwater, you've become a cliché.'

Etienne whitened under his tan. Through clenched teeth, he said, 'Use all the big words you like, Boetie, but I'll tell you one thing, I didn't make all of this,' he waved his arm across the endless horizon, 'by sitting on the stoep dopping all day.'

Deon looked away. Ja, Etienne had given him a job when the hotel laid him off, but did he have to be reminded of it every time they met? Jissus, his leg hurt; he needed a drink. He shouldn't have come on the ride, shouldn't have come back to Sukses. He was only there because Marta wanted to visit her father's grave.

It had been more than ten years since old man Hoffman died — during the war, in an internment camp for enemy aliens. Enemy alien, Manfred Hoffman? That was a laugh. The old goat had lived in Africa for longer than he'd ever lived in Germany. The mission station, deep in Damaraland, was the only home Marta had known.

★   ★   ★

45

Deon had met her when she turned up at Sukses collecting for the mission. Her dusty donkeys needed resting and she herself must have been dying for a bath, Lettie said, ushering the sunburnt, wind-swept young woman inside.

'My dear, you must stay the night. I can make up a bed in two ticks, run you a nice, cool bath and . . . ' Deon had known what was coming. Sure enough, it was a Lettie-foot-in-the-mouth classic, 'I can find you a pretty blouse to wear.'

He kicked his sister-in-law under the table. She turned guileless blue eyes to him, then registered, 'Not that your blouse isn't very nice. It looks very, er, hard-wearing . . . ' she flustered.

Marta looked taken aback at the turn the meeting had taken but she did her best. 'Um, yes, it is hard-wearing. Hemp, I think. One of my father's,' she trailed off.

'And I'm sure it looks very nice on him,' Lettie hastened to reassure her guest.

Marta looked more astonished than offended. Deon groaned audibly but relaxed when the glowing young woman started to laugh. It was a sound he found as refreshing as rain falling on parched earth.

Soon the blushing Lettie was tittering too and promising that she'd get a handsome donation for the mission station from her husband if Miss Hoffman would forgive her and accept her hospitality.

Marta Hoffman appeared that night still in her father's shirt but it had been washed, ironed and neatly buttoned up. A shame, Deon thought. He'd have liked another glimpse of the delicate freckles at the base of Marta's throat.

'See how nice we did Miss Hoffman's hair,' Lettie said, showing how she'd tamed the red-gold Marta mane into braids and looped it up, fraulein-style. Marta and Deon smiled at each other over Lettie's head.

That night Etienne's supporters gathered for a braai. They were celebrating some rugby success or other. Deon remembered how Marta had scandalised the women by leaving them to talk about jam-making while she joined the men out on the verandah.

They'd been drinking brandy and coke, and talking the usual nonsense, 'Hey, you-ous. Heard what the kaffirmeid said to the bishop?'

'Faster Master, here comes the Miesies,' the men chorused. They stopped guffawing when Marta appeared.

'Correct me if I'm wrong but would that be about the Afrikaans dominee, a Dutch Reformed minister from the government's

47

church of choice? And wasn't he the first person to be prosecuted under our wonderful new Immorality Act?' she asked innocently.

Deon chuckled from the shadows. 'Ja, I read about that one. Ironic.' Marta threw him a grateful green gaze, then watched with amusement as a few men stood up saying nature called and others busied themselves refilling their pipes or topping up their drinks from a trolley manned by a uniformed servant.

Etienne stood his hallowed ground. 'Ja-well, the law is the law, Miss Hoffman,' he replied.

'Ja, and a wonderfully flexible thing it is under the National Party, Mr Marais.'

'What do you mean?'

'Again, correct me if I'm wrong, but didn't the reverend gentleman receive a suspended sentence for his heinous crime?'

★   ★   ★

Deon kept in touch with the intriguing Miss Hoffman after that, using quiet duty-manager nights at the hotel to write her letters. When she wrote saying that her father had died, he took leave and went to Damaraland to support her.

However, that was all before the accident

which left him crippled and an alcoholic. The booze helped the pain, he explained to her, but they both knew that was just an excuse. He'd always been a drinker. Being around Etienne just made him worse.

But what could he do? He had to come. Marta wouldn't hear of delaying the trip and she couldn't travel on her own, not on a seven-night train journey in her condition, and with carriage changes too. So he'd gone to the bar while she pawned her mother's jewellery to pay for their train tickets to Onderwater.

★ ★ ★

Tired out from the long gallop across the veld, the stallion ambled up the incline to the house. At the gate, tiny black children, vibrating with excitement, orchestrated the opening of the heavy cross-barred gate. Some pulled, some pushed, most just rode the arc of its high, wide swing, squeaking with delight. Etienne threw down a sixpence as they passed. Dive, scramble, dust. When Mannie looked back, the picannins were back on the gate, chirruping and rocking like birds on a telegraph wire.

The farmhouse was a tin-roofed stone building, with a wide verandah that jutted out in front like a stubborn chin. An adolescent stood there, feet wide apart, arms folded across his broad chest. André scowled as his father lifted Mannie from the horse. 'I hope Pa-you-all had a nice ride?'

Etienne didn't look up. 'No. We've lost a gemsbok ewe — in calf.'

'How'd it happen?'

'Long story. Your cousin'll tell you.' Etienne threw the reins at André. 'Take Bliksem to his stall. Make sure it's Twi who rubs him down.' Then Etienne was up the stairs two at a time, Deon trailing behind him.

Feeling André's cruel grip on its mouth, the horse plunged and tried to shake free. André smiled and held on. 'Help me unsaddle him, Pip-squeak,' he ordered as Mannie tried to slip away. Mannie hesitated.

'Whazzamatter, hey? You scared of the big horsie?'

'I'm not scared.'

'Come on then, or do you expect me to be your kaffir boy and do all the dirty work?'

The stallion reared up and André dragged him down with strength beyond his sixteen years. 'Don't think I haven't noticed you boetie-boetie my Pa. Now he'll let you ride on his mad, blerry horse, but I can't.' He punched the stallion savagely in the chest.

50

Bliksem shied, wild-eyed. Again André held him and now he pinched the horse's upper lip between his thumb and forefinger, twisting it sharply. Bliksem's eyes rolled but he stood still.

'Come on, arse-kisser, now's your chance. I've got him.'

Gingerly, Mannie approached the horse. It stood still, trembling violently. Gently he lifted the saddle flap. The girth buckle was higher than his head. He daren't ask for help. He stood on tiptoe, legs shaking.

Stretching, struggling, he didn't notice André lean against the horse's chest, forcing it to step backwards. It planted its huge hoof square on Mannie's toes.

'Ow, ow. André, he's on my foot. Eina, man.'

'Ag, isn't he a clumsy oaf?' André grinned.

The horse felt the child struggling and made to move. André yanked up another hoof. More pressure on Mannie's toes.

'Eina, eina!'

Bent low so he could see between the stallion's legs André smirked at the boy's white face. Mannie tried wriggling his foot free. He felt the burn of broken flesh. He closed his eyes against the tears but they slid treacherously out.

Just across the yard the verandah door swung open again. 'What the blerry hell are you doing, André?' Etienne roared. André instantly dropped Bliksem's hoof and jerked the horse forward off Mannie's foot.

'Nothing, Pa.'

Etienne narrowed his eyes and addressed Mannie, 'You alright, son?'

'Ja, um-jaaa . . . ' Mannie swallowed, 'I'm er, f-fine, Uncle Etienne.' He felt André's eyes boring into his back as he stepped away. He dared not limp.

'Okay then. André, didn't I tell you to put that horse away?' Etienne snapped.

Mannie kept his head down. He heard clip-clopping across the yard, loud footsteps, the screen door bang. Safe now to hobble away and have that cry. He sat on the bench against the verandah wall, partly hidden by the golden shower creeper that fell over it. He whimpered, softly.

One day, one day soon, I'll be big enough to bugger up that André, effing bully, he thought. Then he'd hit him so hard he wouldn't walk for a week!

Mannie sniffed and wiped his nose on his scrawny forearm. His toes were beginning to swell but at least they didn't hurt as much. They'd gone numb. He decided to sit there for a bit, eyes closed.

★ ★ ★

52

'Ag, Liebschen, was the ride so tiring?' Marta bent to kiss her sleeping son; her plait, still long but less gold now, fell across her shoulder and the tip tickled his face. His eyes flew open. 'Only me,' she said as she straightened, hands in the small of her back to counter-balance her heavy belly. 'Have you been crying?'

'Nooo . . . ja. Well, just a bit. I hurt my foot.'

'What happened? Let me see.'

'It's nothing.'

'Let me see anyway.' She patted her thigh where she wanted him to place his foot.

'Ag, Ma, don't make a fuss.'

She rolled her eyes, 'Alright, little man,' and sat down next to him. 'So, did you have a nice ride? Did your Uncle show you anything interesting?'

Instinct told him he shouldn't tell his mother about the afternoon's gruesome discovery. Not all of it, anyway.

'We saw a gemsbok. And Uncle Etienne let me ride up front on Bliksem.'

'That's nice.'

He found a loose thread at his buttonhole and began to pluck at it with filthy fingers. 'Ma? Ma, can Bushmen be cattle-rustlers?'

She flicked her plait back over her shoulder. 'It's rude to call them 'Bushmen', son. Remember it's Khoisan now. Steal cattle, hey? Why do you ask?'

'Just because.'

'Has that uncle of yours been filling your head with prejudice?'

'No.' The white thread was now grub-grey. He began to twist it. 'Yes. I mean, what's prejudice?'

'Prejudice is disliking a group of people for no other reason than they're different from you.'

'Ja, well, but do they kill, I mean steal, people's animals, the Bush . . . Khoi . . . ?'

'Well,' she put her freckled arm around his shoulders, 'the Khoisan don't call it stealing. They think God made all animals for all people. They don't understand about private property. In their community everything is shared.'

He yanked at the thread and it began to unravel. Ma was alright but when she started on the stupid native thing, Bushmen . . . Khoikhoi . . . hoi polloi . . . whatever they were called!

The button flew off. He dived onto the ground after it. 'But why,' he said over his shoulder, 'would they kill a beautiful wild animal?'

'What beautiful wild animal?'

Mannie could have kicked himself. 'I dunno. Any one. Just, what if they did? Supposing they did?' He peeped up at his mother from under his fringe. His hair had the red gold sheen of hers in her youth but he was freckled only across his sunburned nose and cheeks. 'I mean, why would they, Ma, if they like animals so much?'

She tilted her head, studying him, her frown forming freckles into an arrow shape on her forehead. 'If they did,' she said slowly, 'it would be for food, I suppose. Meat to survive on. They haven't got cattle and sheep like Uncle Etienne. They can't grow crops in the desert areas.' She waggled her long finger emphatically. 'But the Khoisan never kill unnecessarily.'

★   ★   ★

Etienne sat at his dining table that night with the Bible open in front of him. A few years before, in preparation for his bid for office, he'd plugged the holes in his Afrikaner pedigree by acquiring some of the accoutrements of a passionate Boer republican — an ox-wagon, reputed to have been used in the Great Trek (the restoration of which earned him valuable column inches in the local paper), and the Old Testament that he was now thumbing through. Of course the family tree on the title page was not his but Maritz was close enough.

Attending the Bible-reading before supper was now obligatory for family and servants at Sukses. That night they heard Etienne read from Exodus 21, verses 12 to 24, ' . . . he that smiteth a man, so that he die, shall be surely put to death,' without irony and in high Dutch. This was the only time they heard anything but Afrikaans from their master, whose linguistic dexterity meant he was fluent in English, Ovambo, Himba and several Nguni languages too, but whose new-found Afrikaner nationalism forbade them on his farm.

After the black staff filed out to their meal in the compound, Etienne made an announcement, 'We men are going on a hunting trip tomorrow. We'll take the old wagon out, head towards the Mother Hills. Can you pack some padkos for us, Mother?'

Lettie Marais flustered prettily. She was the only child of the largest landowner in the area, a prize, not just because of her looks, but because locals thought she had style. She'd been to beauty school in the city. She knew how to dress, do a manicure and set hair. And her milk tart won first prize at the country show every Easter.

She'd been wooed and won by Etienne shortly after his arrival in the Onderwater area and in due course he took over the running of her father's farm too.

Now she patted her perm. 'Liewe Magies, Daddy, there's only the Christmas things in the pantry and we can't eat those. Tomorrow I could bake. But what about meat? If you waited a bit . . .'

'We don't need meat. We'll get a kudu. Weather's right for making biltong.'

Mannie noticed the inquisitive lift of his mother's eyebrows. 'One of your precious Sukses buck? Well-I-never!'

Uncle Etienne ignored her and nodded towards Mannie instead. 'You coming tomorrow, little man?'

'Can I, Ma? Can I, Pa?' but he knew the decision was his uncle's. He'd be going.

Mannie puzzled over Ma's attitude to his uncle. She was always arguing with him, getting annoyed over things he said about kaffirs — mustn't say kaffirs — natives, things about natives. And about the government. Instead of staying in bed like she was supposed to do with her pains she seemed to seek Uncle Etienne out. 'To needle him,' Pa had said with a laugh.

Uncle Etienne's funny too, Mannie thought. Most of the time he ignores Ma but sometimes, when he thinks no one's looking, he stares at her. Deon noticed as well. It made his top lip twist as tightly as barbed wire.

Chapter 3

'Okay, I think we've got everything, let's go,' Etienne said.

It was still dark as the party pulled out of the farmyard. A drover walked beside the oxen, holding a lamp. Mannie stood in the back of the wagon, among the spares and supplies: ammunition boxes, hunting knives, a fifty-gallon water drum, paraffin and more lamps, shovels and rope, tarpaulin, stools, bed rolls, cooking pots, tins and baskets of food, tied-up twice in muslin cloths to keep the dust off.

Mannie was in a sulk. He'd hoped they'd be going in the big wagon, the proper Voortreker cart with a tent, pulled by ten oxen controlled by a whip as long as a rugby pitch, but his uncle said there wasn't time for that — they had to get out on the trail fast.

Why such a big rush, Mannie thought, and why did he have to ride in the wagon like a baby?

André trotted past on a high-stepping boereperd. 'Hey, Pipsqueak, missing your Ma already?'

Mannie shoved his fists into the pockets of his shorts trying to drag them down over his knees. It was colder than he'd realised but he couldn't wrap his legs in the extra blanket Ma had given him. André would laugh. Mannie slumped down on the hard wooden seat next to Twi, shivering.

'Sun soon,' the driver said.

'Can I take the reins?' Mannie asked.

'No, Basie. We must fast-fast.'

'I can make the bullocks go fast. I can, let me show you.' But Twi just cracked the short hide whip and laughed, his yellow face folding into even more wrinkles.

Dried up old velskoen, Mannie thought crossly. But he forgave his companion when Twi handed him a spotlight and suggested he look for animal eyes.

There weren't many to be seen. The squeak and grind of the metal-rimmed wagon wheels frightened most wildlife off. But he did pick up a small group of kudu, a bachelor herd said Twi, judging by the ground height of their shining eyes. And closer to dawn, they startled a big-eared steenbok that zig-zagged away, rump swaying. 'Marilyn Monroe arse,' Etienne said as he passed on Bliksem.

59

Eventually Mannie nodded off. He woke to hear Twi call, 'Hokaai, hokaai,' to the oxen, putting a strange click into the sound. Etienne trotted over. 'We'll have coffee and watch the sun rise,' he said.

Mannie began to salivate — one of Auntie Lettie's rusks dipped into condensed milk coffee. Mmmm. But first he needed to pee. He sprang down from the wagon and hurried to a bush.

'So, little man.' André loomed out of the dark. 'Your first hunting trip, hey?' Mannie, midstream, ignored him. He felt André was staring at his penis. Then he heard the older boy free his own.

'Excited?' he asked him.

Mannie sensed André's nakedness but he couldn't hear his cousin peeing. He tried to concentrate on restoring his trickle to a spurt. A big gush would be manly.

'I said,' André stepped so close Mannie could feel him through his arm, 'are you excited?' Mannie didn't move. André's penis was long and thick and very nearby. He heard André laugh. '*This* is what excited looks like.' He waggled his erection at the boy. 'See? See?' André reached for something behind him. 'Yours is just ... fish bait.' André stepped back and Mannie heard a swishing sound. Too late he recoiled. The thorny branch caught him, a long, white thorn ripping across his foreskin. He opened his mouth to scream but noticed André's gleaming eyes and closed it again. Tears spilled down his cheeks and over his lips, tasting of dust. He fled, tucking himself in as he ran. André's laughter hyenaed through the dark after him.

★ ★ ★

Day came instantly as they sipped their coffee. One minute the veld flirted subtly with light, concealing its contours in discreet grey and mauve; the next, it lay brazen and exposed, bold gold as the fireball sun claimed the eastern horizon. The servants stowed the canvas stools, flasks and mugs — enamel for them, china for the whites — back in the wagon and the hunting party trundled onwards.

They were heading for the Mother Hills, Mannie knew — a spooky place, his cousin had said. The hills were on the horizon somewhere but something, smoke or a mist maybe, was making them difficult to see. It wouldn't be ghosts — that was just André chaffing him — but could it be the sea air all the way from the Skeleton Coast? He asked Twi.

'No, Basie, veld fire. No rain, since two summers.'

'Have you ever seen the sea, Outa?'

'No, Basie.'

Mannie looked disappointed. He'd never seen the sea either but then he lived much further inland than the Sukses folks did. Ma said they'd stop at the coast on their way back to Windhoek. A Christmas present for him. It was a long detour down a branch line but Walvis Bay had a nice beach, she'd said, and she was sure his grandmother, Ingrid, would have wanted him to see the sea. He'd never met Grossemutter Ingrid and knew nothing about her except she'd had some ugly jewellery and came from a seaside place in Germany. Ma didn't remember much about her either. She'd only been three when her mother died.

Pa worried about the expense of a seaside hotel in the Christmas season but Ma had said it was a treat they deserved, something the three of them could do together before the new baby arrived. Mannie was excited about the baby but he was more excited about seeing the sea.

They'd left the dirt road now and as the wagon bumped along they saw a Pale Chanting Goshawk swoop low, red talons outstretched after a fleeing mouse. The distraction made him miss his prey and he swooped back up to alight on a camel-thorn and glare down at the intruders with a fierce eye.

Mannie was excited to see a herd of springbok running from them. There weren't any at Impalala and he'd always wanted to see one pronk. Now several obliged, one after the other, leaping high into the air, legs straight, backs arched, heads down. Twi pointed out the fan of brilliant white hair that flared on every buck's back as it leapt. 'Smells,' he said, touching his wide, flat nose. Mannie sniffed. There was an odour in the air that could have been a secretion; it smelled rich, sweet and waxy. Soon the springbok were out of range.

Funny how none of the men seemed interested in shooting them, Mannie thought. Springbok was supposed to make the best biltong. But the riders kept their guns slung across their chests and their horses' heads towards the Mother Hills. Mannie picked at a scab on his knee, yawning.

It got hotter and the going even slower as the high orange grass hid dongas and antbear holes. When they weren't lurching into these, they were digging the wagon wheels out of soft, sucking sand.

Mannie flapped irritably at a fly trying to settle on his bleeding scab. He wished he'd stayed at the farmhouse. His penis smarted but he couldn't look to see. André kept wheeling back on his horse to wink and joke and jeer.

Eventually, Etienne reined in next to the wagon. 'Smoke's closer,' he said as he climbed aboard from his horse's back. He tethered the animal behind the wagon and then returned to the chest that served as a seat. He stood on it, planting his big boots between Twi and Mannie. They were the same height so he held comfortably onto each head for balance, scanning the veld like a captain on his bridge. 'Fire's moved east,' he announced.

Mannie noticed the khaki cloud where his uncle was pointing. The sun looked greasy through it, like a butter stain.

Etienne sat down between them. The old wagon chest sagged. 'Head for the black,' he ordered Twi, pointing to a section of burnt veld. And to André, 'Send the tracker ahead. If anything's been this way since the fire, we'll soon know about it.'

Mannie cheered up. The hunt would begin shortly.

Oxen and horses moved reluctantly over the charred veld. Tussocks still glowed from the fire while the remains of camel-thorn trees showered sparks. Mannie began to cough. They were stirring up soot. It was getting into his nose. He spat, trying to get rid of the acrid taste in his mouth.

They saw no game, other than a tortoise upturned and feebly flailing its legs to right itself. Using the butt of his rifle as a polo mallet, André whacked it into the air. Mannie was relieved to see it land upright and lumber off. To the left, an emerald-spotted wood-dove pecked through the charred debris of a tree. Then it lifted its grey throat and ululated its lament.

They saw a tracker jogging towards them, soot all the way up to his knees, like long socks. 'MaSarwa, MaSarwa!' he panted.

Etienne jumped up. 'Where?' he demanded. The tracker gestured to the east of the now visible hills. Etienne sprang down, untethered Bliksem and mounted. 'Whip these bloody oxen up,' he shouted to Twi before galloping off.

★   ★   ★

To Mannie it seemed ages before the wagon reached the huddle of men. He jumped down, shoved his head through the palisade of legs, but could see no animal tracks. Only footprints. One was perfect — five small toe-pads and the curve of a heel, like a signature stamped in the soot. 'MaSarwa — Yellow Ones,' the tracker was saying, holding up three fingers.

Mannie couldn't see. 'What is it, what is it?' he asked, but all the men were staring in the direction that the tracker was pointing.

'Opsaal!' The circle broke up on Etienne's command. Men sprinted for their horses. Mannie felt himself scooped up like a toddler. His uncle dumped him back in the wagon. 'Come on,' he said, 'or we'll never catch them.'

Catch *them*? How many leopards were there? 'Do you think it's a mother with cubs, Twi?' Mannie asked. 'Do you think she's the one that killed the gemsbok? Uncle Etienne wouldn't kill her if she's still feeding the cubs, would he? Hey Twi, hey?'

Twi stared straight ahead, the expression on his San features neutral.

★   ★   ★

The veld fire had forced Koba's family to detour. They were making slow progress through the blackened stubble as Tami insisted they step only on tussocks to avoid leaving footprints.

Koba's soles, not as hardened as her parents', burned as she leapt from clump to

66

clump. It was like jumping on red-hot hedgehog. Occasionally she cheated and cooled her feet in sooty sand, leaving a print as obvious as an advertisement.

Her chest was pounding — from the exertion or from what her grandmother had called her signal, she couldn't tell. And the soot made it difficult to breathe. Black, throat-tickling clouds puffed up every time she landed. To add to her misery, a wind spiralled about her, winnowing sparks from ash, fanning smoulders into spiteful little flames. Eventually she stopped, gasping.

Then she heard it, in the distance — a creak. Voices? Real ones, she asked herself? But her parents had heard them too. Tami was on all fours, his cheek pressed to the ground. Now Koba could feel the rumble of hooves through her seared soles. Animals, galloping their way, and a chasing cart with men.

The family ran. The water shell in Koba's sling thumped painfully against her leg. She stopped to rearrange it. Tami sped back to her, grabbed the shell and threw it onto the sand. It cracked. Koba froze, staring. Abandoning water?

Her father grabbed her hand. 'Run, or you'll never need water again.' He pulled, so fast she didn't have time to tussock-hop.

'Faster,' Tami urged.

They ran without stop until Tami held up his hand. Mixed with the thump of their hearts, the sound of hooves. Closer.

'We must hide,' Tami said.

N#aisa's words came in squeaks as her rib cage accordioned with the effort of breathing, 'You do not know that . . . the people with hooves . . . mean to harm us. Let's go forward . . . greet them in friendship. Perhaps . . . tobacco.'

'NO!' Koba shrieked. Now her fear had a name and pair of blue eyes. '/Ton . . . I hear, feel, lions' paws. We must get away!' She set off like a hunted buck. Now she was pulling her parents along in her wake.

★ ★ ★

'It's Bushmen, definitely Bushmen. Once you've seen those little footprints you never forget them.' Etienne spurred his horse.

Deon, astride a thick-necked mare, bounced next to him. The chase was sobering him up. He'd need another drink soon. 'Still find them this far west, hey?'

'Not often, man, not unless they've come to raid.'

They didn't gallop for long. The tracker had lost the spoor. They reined in, watching him zigzag across the ground like a jackal seeking a scent. He cowered when André berated him for his carelessness. Far behind, the wagon lumbered along.

'Do they give you trouble, these Bushmen?' Deon asked, unscrewing the top of his hip flask.

Etienne frowned. 'Plenty. Stole a prize heifer from Wiengaard's place last month, and yesterday, well, you saw the pregnant gemsbok ewe.'

'Marta says it's not stealing,' Deon took a swig, 'Bushmen don't understand about private land or animals.'

Etienne's look hardened. 'I suppose she thinks we should just let them help themselves, hey?'

Deon took another swig. 'Ag, you know her. She believes farmers should allow the Bushmen into the livestock in a drought.' He offered the flask to his brother. 'They only kill what they need to eat.'

'Bullshit!' Etienne wheeled his horse around, turning it in tighter and tighter circles in the blackened sand until it churned up a storm and he looked like he was astride a dust devil, not a horse.

That woman, he thought. He'd never met anyone who infuriated him as much as Marta. He remembered first meeting her, her chest heaving inside a man's shirt as she asked for money for her father's missionary work. Old man Hoffman had been one of those foreign busybodies, Etienne recalled, stirring up the natives with talk of their rights. Still, Etienne found himself handing over money to the man's statuesque daughter, even though he disagreed with her views and disapproved of the way she banged her fist on his table to get them across. But he'd come to respect that courage and passion. Hell, a person couldn't resist it. She burned red hot, did Marta.

Slackening his pull on the reins, he used his forearm to wipe his brow. Ja-well, Marta was off-limits — his brother's wife and all that. It was a shock to see her big-bellied. Who'd have thought old Deon still had it in him after all the boozing?

'Listen,' he said, letting the horse relax, 'Marta wasn't here fifty years ago . . . '

'Nor were you, Boet,' Deon said slyly. Etienne ignored him and said in stentorian tones, 'She wasn't here when Piet Schoeman's father found his entire herd with severed hamstrings — alive but crippled. In agony, hey! The old people still talk about it. I ask you, is that the behaviour of people who respect animals and only kill what they need? No, Siree.' He banged a fist on the pommel, causing his mount to shy. 'That's brutality!' Etiene battled to control the stallion, shouting over his shoulder as it wheeled about again, 'The Bushman's a savage!' He sawed at the bit, forcing the horse's head down. 'No better than a wild animal!'

Deon sat easy in the saddle, smiling. When the prancing stallion was close enough, he said, 'So you want revenge on the Bushman, hey? This is punitive, a hunting expedition, just like the old days? And . . . ' he tapped the side of his nose.

'Listen, man, there was nothing illegal or even secret about those expeditions. The government even ordered a few. Hell, around then you could even buy a licence to shoot a Bushman.'

* * *

Nowhere to hide in the singed savannah, no grass, no rocks, even the tree crowns were as scant as x-rays. The family's tracks showed across the sooty sand in stark saffron relief.

Tami steered them to an abandoned termite mound. It stood on slightly elevated ground, tall and as pointed as a wizard's hat. At its base was an antbear hole. 'In there.' He shoved Koba towards it.

She resisted. 'Something may be inside

— warthog, hyena, snake!'

Tami grabbed a branch and scraped inside the hole, tearing the silken lid off a small, deep burrow. A baboon spider scuttled out, hairs bristling 'Only a spider. Gone now. Get in, get in!'

'There might be babies. The mother might come back.'

He gripped her shoulders, his knuckles shining white through yellow-brown skin. 'And you might get bitten. It will hurt, but not kill you, Koba.' She'd never seen her father look so desperate — sweat streamed down his forehead, his eyes were wild. 'There is nowhere else. You must hide.'

He then pushed on her shoulders, forcing her down. 'You are more than water. You are our future. Now hide!'

Koba backed gingerly into the hole. 'Where will you be?'

'Leading the strangers from here. I'll run — down there. Over the burnt ground so they can see my tracks.'

'But they'll catch you!'

'Yau, not on these cheetah-legs!' He almost grinned. 'Your mother will run the other way . . . which to chase first?' He saw his daughter's face crumple. 'Don't worry, that will give us time to find a hold like this. But promise me you will not show yourself.' He looked hard into her eyes. They were huge with fear. He steadied his own gaze to reassure her. 'We'll come back for you when the strangers have given up the search.'

Koba started to cry. 'What if you don't?'

He put his hands on her heaving shoulders and spoke rapidly. 'If we don't return for you by dark, follow the fat hunting star towards the dawn, every night, till three sunrises have passed. Keep the salt pan on your left. You will come to our village. Do you understand?'

Koba nodded.

'Good. You will find the way, I know . . . ' He hugged her quickly. 'Crouch-quick so we can cover you.'

'Wait,' N#aisa ran up. 'Take this, my Koba, to cover your head.' She handed Koba her skin cloak then blew tenderly into her daughter's frightened face. Koba gulped at a sob that threatened to choke her, then retreated further into the hole as Tami dragged thorny branches across the opening and N#aisa swept up a storm of sand, eradicating their footprints.

Take me with you — run is better than hide, Koba wanted to scream. But she forced herself to lie still and quiet. Was it power, her grandmother had said, that lay in endurance? It felt like foolishness. Had Grandmother foreseen this? If she had, surely she would have warned them? Too late now; the earth drummed with hooves.

'Go with the wind,' she called to her parent's fleeing footsteps.

★ ★ ★

Back in the wagon Mannie held on with both hands. The four oxen trotted at full tilt, the wagon jouncing behind. André rode alongside, grinning at Mannie's discomfort. Nevertheless, Mannie wanted to talk to him. 'Hey André,' he shouted above the clanging and thumping, 'your Pa's not going to kill the leopard and her cubs, is he?'

'What leopard?' André looked surprised.

'The one we're chasing, with cubs. The boy said there were three.' Mannie held his fingers up in imitation of the tracker's signal. André still looked puzzled. 'The Yellow Ones, man. The boy found their spoor and . . . '

Laughter exploded from André like a shot. 'The Yellow Ones are Bushmen, fool. We're tracking Bushmen.' He came closer and dropping his voice said, 'And when we find them you'll need your knife to get a souvenir for your Ma — something small, like an ear!'

Mannie recoiled, turning quickly to Twi. The driver didn't seem to have heard. With a sick feeling Mannie realised André was telling the truth. They were tracking people, probably the people his uncle was so cross with for killing the gemsbok. He picked nervously at his scab, ignoring his cousin as André cantered off, still laughing.

Okay, thought Mannie, if we find the Littlefoots and they are the poachers, what's the worse Uncle can do? Give them a hiding, he supposed. André once said his Pa smacked naughty native boys. He wondered if Twi had ever had a hiding from Etienne. André said Twi was very sly. Mannie glanced at him out of the corner of his eye. What does sly look like exactly, he wondered?

Ahead, his saw his father sitting slack-backed on his ambling horse, his brandy flask in his hand. Ag no, Pa wasn't going to drink till he fell off, was he? 'Pa. Hey, Pa!' Deon turned and waved amiably but he didn't come towards the wagon. 'Can you come here? I want to ask you a question,' he called. But the horse ambled on. 'PA!' Mannie then shouted at the top of his lungs, 'B-U-S-H-M-A-N?' Deon turned, waved the flask, and let the horse lead him on.

Mannie sat down, shoved his hands into his pockets, grabbed a fistful of fabric and twisted. It'd be alright, he told himself. He didn't have to worry. Uncle Etienne would see to Pa. And the Bushmen. They'd chase them off the farm. That was all.

He unclenched his fists.

Come to think of it, seeing wild Bushmen would be bakgat! Maybe they'd have poison arrows with them and they'd give him one.

★ ★ ★

From within her lair, Koba felt the ground vibrate to the rhythm of racing hooves. She held her breath, closed her eyes. A rider passed so close she could smell him — sour sweat with pretend-fresh over. '/Ton keep their smell in a bottle,' Grandmother had once said. Koba wrinkled her nose and squeezed her eyes shut even tighter. The smell faded, the vibrations receded.

Slowly, Koba lifted a corner of the cloak and peered through the branches. From her vantage point she could see a black man, scampering in front of some pale riders, eyes sweeping along the ground as though he'd lost something. Probably their spoor but luckily Mother was a thorough sweeper. But now the black man was chattering, pointing. Had he spotted Mother and Father? She eased further out of her hole. There, in the distance, was her father, running deliberately slowly to draw the hunters away from her mother.

'Yau,' she held her hand to her heart, 'the /Ton have seen him! They've turned their tame animals. Even if Father flies he won't escape them now.'

Tami stopped running. He turned and faced the riders, an arrow in his hand but not in his bow. He raised his other hand in the traditional Ju/'hoan greeting.

★ ★ ★

Etienne slowed the stallion to a walk some distance away from the Bushman. Turning to Deon, he said, 'Bet that old blunderbuss can't hit him from here!'

'That tiny little man? What you want to shoot him for?'

'Not shoot him dead. Just give the bugger a fright. He'll be one of the poachers. Come on, see if you can put a bullet near his thieving feet.'

Deon fingered the 6.5 Schonhauer Mannlicher protruding from his saddlebag. He was a good shot, but he'd been drinking. He might hit the Bushman.

'Bet you can't do it,' Etienne goaded.

'I'm not a betting man, Ouboet. Nor are you!'

Etienne eyed him slyly. 'Some things are worth gambling on, hey?'

Deon nodded slowly, 'Some things are.'

Etienne threw back his head with laughter. 'Now you're talking, man. OK, I bet you a case of brandy you can't hit that Bushman from here.' Deon shook his head. 'Two cases?' Deon ignored him. 'Ten? And I'll make it cognac.'

Suddenly Deon felt disgusted. With himself, mostly. 'You know what? After this I'm going on one of those.' He jerked his thumb towards the wagon. Etienne snorted. 'That I'd like to see. And so, I bet, would your lovely wife.'

Deon's eyes narrowed. Etienne spurred the stallion forward until it was prancing round his brother's mare. 'Tell you what, Kleinboet, hit the kaffir from here, give up the booze and I'll give you Sukses as well as Impalala.'

Deon looked hard at him. 'You're going to give me Impalala? To do what I like with?'

'Ja. And Sukses.'

'Ag, kak,' Deon laughed.

'I swear it,' Etienne said, 'on the head of my son! But the way you've been knocking back the brandy I reckon both farms are safe.'

Deon shrugged. He hated farming, but if Impalala could be his own, if he didn't have to be Etienne's gamekeeper and could sell the farm, well hell, he'd move his family to the city, to Pretoria probably, and start a hotel. Just a small place.

He shook his head, trying to clear it. Dreams. His brother was bluffing. Bastard. Though he'd like to see Etienne squirm.

Deon dismounted and pulled his rifle free from the bag. 'Let's play, Ouboet.' Slowly, he inserted a cartridge, his eyes on Etienne. Etienne smiled down at him from the high stallion. Deon put his rifle to his shoulder and took aim. He could see the Bushman in his sights. The man looked unreal, stick arms and legs, like a child's drawing of a person. He looked across the barrel towards Etienne, waiting for him to retract his offer. He heard the wagon pull up, oxen blowing hard.

'PA!' Mannie screamed. 'Don't . . . '

Deon lowered the rifle. 'Just testing Uncle Etienne's nerve.'

A shot rang out. The Bushman dropped. Deon let his rifle fall, staring at it in disbelief. 'But I never even . . . '

'Uncle Etienne!' Mannie howled.

Etienne lowered his smoking gun. 'The bloody little bugger! Did you see that? He was stringing his bow.'

Deon stumbled across. 'Are you fucking mad?' He grabbed Etienne's gun. 'What the hell did you shoot him for?'

Etienne snatched the rifle back. 'Listen, Boet. All it takes is a graze from the bugger's poison arrowhead and it's tickets.' He buffed

79

the barrel of his rifle with his shirtsleeve. 'The stuff gallops straight to your bloodstream. There's stories of men trying to hack off their arms or legs to get away from the pain. And there's no cure for it.'

'Pa? Uncle Etienne?' Mannie called from the wagon, his voice frightened.

Etienne trotted his horse over. 'Now don't you worry, little man. Keep your head down while I go . . . '

'Mannie,' Deon arrived ashen-faced at the wagon. 'I was never going to shoot him, I swear. I was just calling your uncle's bluff. I . . . '

'The Bushman didn't know that,' Etienne said impatiently, 'That's why he began to arm. Lucky I had him in my sights.'

Mannie was crying. 'Is he dead?'

'No boy, I just winged him. Twi, keep the Basie in the wagon with you. I'll go see.'

★ ★ ★

Loud-bang. Thundersticks? I must look, thought Koba.

She pushed the twigs off the lair's opening and saw her father kneeling on the ground. He was hurt, but the /Ton seemed in no hurry to get to him. She wanted to call out but didn't dare. She noticed her father using

80

his knee to string his bow. His arm must be injured. She trembled, wondering if the /Ton had seen? Now a black man was running towards her father.

Tami let an arrow fly. It landed in the chest of the tracker. He fell, rolled in the sand, and plucked at the shaft, gibbering with fright. Stupid man — harder to remove the arrow tip now. Koba watched a big man canter over to him, lean down from the horse and shout. The other /Ton raised his gun and pointed it at Tami. Again she saw her father struggling to string his bow. She couldn't watch. Koba stuffed the corner of the kaross into her mouth and sank back into her hole.

She heard the rifle crack but didn't listen for a cry from her father. There would be none. A Ju/'hoan did not let his enemy hear his suffering.

★ ★ ★

Mannie was shaking as Etienne galloped back to the wagon.

'I can't shoot straight from that bloody horse the way it's cavorting today. Here, hold this,' he thrust the smoking Mauser at Mannie. 'Twi, there's two more out here. Let's find them before this turns into a bloody war!'

81

Twi gathered up the reins, very, very slowly.

'What have you done? What? Why?' Mannie shrilled.

'Hey?' Etienne looked puzzled.

'You shot a man, dead!' the boy shrieked.

'It was self-defence, son. That man was a poacher — a scavenger who rips babies out their mother's bodies. That's not human.' He wiped a fleck of spittle from the corner of his mouth. 'Anyway, I didn't plan to kill him. He was going for your father.' He made to put his arm around Mannie's shoulders but the child shrank back. 'I'm sorry you had to see, little man. It was an accident, though, believe me.'

Neither Mannie nor Twi would look at him. Etienne sighed. 'Okay, get this wagon moving, Outa.' He turned back to the child hunched in misery beside him. 'I understand how you feel. I saw my father beat a black man to death when I was a sprog. He didn't mean to. He was drunk.'

'*You beat natives!*' Mannie shouted.

'I've never beaten a kaffir in my life. It wouldn't be a fair fight.'

'You do, you do,' Mannie sobbed. 'André said.'

'Ag, André! That boy's got some blerry funny ideas. Needs a good clip around the ears. But first I must sort this mess out.' He

82

started to clamber down.

'I hate you,' Mannie said.

Etienne sighed impatiently. 'Look son, I didn't start this thing, hey?' He held the boy's eyes with his own and gave his words time to sink in. Mannie stared at him. Pa! It was Pa who'd aimed at the Bushman. Blerrydronkie-boozingbastard. What would Ma say? She'd never forgive him. She'd make him leave.

Etienne was still talking, softly now, 'You saw how the little blighter aimed at us. And how he got the tracker. Hey? Did you see that?' Mannie shook his head. 'Got him with his poison arrow. Poor Philemon. Part-Bushman himself. He'll vrek, and a bloody painful death it'll be too. Ja-no, a wild Bushman's a different kind of animal altogether, no matter what romantic stories your Ma's been telling you.'

★ ★ ★

Koba heard the wagon rumble away. She stuck her head out. She could see her mother in the distance, but so could the /Ton. A man on horseback sped towards N#aisa, whipping up dust. N#aisa wheeled and ran the opposite way.

Koba realised he was herding her towards the wagon.

83

* ★ ★

With the wagon blocking off one escape route and André another, Etienne knew he could grab N#aisa as she tried to run past him. Effortlessly he flung her over one shoulder and dumped her into the wagon.

★ ★ ★

Deon offered the tracker some water and then he and Twi helped the man over to the shade under the wagon. The arrow out, the wound looked small and innocuous. But the man would not accept Deon's assurances that he would be ok.

'MaSarwa poison no good. Black Mamba better! Two steps . . . dead! MaSarwa? Two hours — makulu pain. Give gun, Baas. Better to shoot.' Deon quickly walked away, leaving Twi to tend to the man.

★ ★ ★

In the back of the wagon, Etienne towered over the small, half-naked woman. André had her arms pinned behind her back. 'Here's a pretty little thing for you,' he shouted to Deon. 'Smells a bit — they rub animal fat on their skin — but you can always give her a bath.'

'Give me a bloody drink,' Deon said, climbing into the front.

'So this is you 'on the wagon', hey?' Etienne laughed as he produced a bottle of brandy. Deon ripped the lid off and sucked at it, hollow-cheeked.

'What you going to do with her?' he said, pointing the bottle unsteadily at N#aisa.

'Take her home. They make damn fine servants. Not afraid of hard work . . . see,' he turned her round, 'Small, but strong. Feel the muscles in that back.'

N#aisa shrank from his finger. Her skin shone with sweat. Her sides heaved.

Mannie looked nervously at her and saw a pulse fluttering in her neck.

'And have you seen this?' Etienne lifted her skin cloak.

Mannie saw a pair of coffee-coloured buttocks, out of all proportion to the woman's slim legs.

'Now you see where a Bushman stores his water,' Etienne said. André laughed.

Deon looked away. 'It's called steatopygia,' he said.

'OK, Mr Big Words, here's something you've never seen before. Bend her over, André.' Despite N#aisa's struggles the boy succeeded.

Mannie turned away, facing forwards.

85

'Open your legs,' Etienne shouted and tried to force them apart with his rifle. N#aisa lashed out at him, connecting with his chin. 'Shit! Fucking kaffir!' He rubbed his jaw.

Mannie saw him visibly control his anger.

'I'm not gonna hurt you, woman — just a biology lesson. André,' he barked, 'get the woman on her back!' With practiced ease, André kicked her legs from under her.

Mannie heard the thud of her fall and closed his eyes.

'Now, hold that knee. I'll do this one. That's right. Pull them apart . . . we want a good view. But keep her down, dammit — she's thrashing like a bloody crocodile!'

André gasped, then giggled at the exposed vagina. His small eyes glittered with excitement and bright spots appeared on his cheeks.

Deon looked up and was surprised to see two long skin flaps protruding from the woman's genitals. He'd never seen that kind of thing on a woman before. The flaps were hairless and darker than the skin around her pubic area.

With his splayed thumbs Etienne pinned back the labia, exposing more of N#aisa's vagina. 'Pink inside, just like any other, hey?'

Deon stared. The strange flaps fascinated him. They were like dewlaps hiding a soft, moist mouth. He felt his penis harden and quickly looked away.

The sound of squeaking sand made Mannie open his eyes. Wriggling towards the wagon, on his belly, was the Bushman — the one Uncle Etienne had shot! His left arm dragged at his side and behind him, a trail of dark-stained sand. The man grimaced with the effort, but slowly and surely he was inching forward — to within shooting range.

Mannie glanced about. Had the grown-ups not seen? Nor André? He dared not tell them. Heaven knew what they'd do to the man. But what about Twi around the other side? Mannie leaned over the brake to look for him.

The movement caught Tami's eye and he reared up on his good arm, like a cobra.

The gazes of Bushman and boy met in surprise. Mannie lowered his eyes.

Tami struggled to the lead ox and pulled himself upright. Using his teeth, he strung his bow, ignoring the spurt of blood that every movement caused.

Mannie felt nausea storm up from his stomach. He dared not move. Silently his breakfast gushed out of his mouth, until only bile dribbled down his chin. However, the Bushman was not looking at him but down the shaft of his arrow. Mannie heard a whistle of pierced air, then, 'Arghhhh! What the hell? Jesus Christ, I've been hit!'

Mannie turned to see Etienne with the Bushman's arrow sticking out of his stomach. His eyes were goggled like a cartoon character's. He collapsed into the food baskets in surprise.

Mannie threw himself out of the wagon, hit the sand howling and ran.

Meanwhile André grabbed a rifle from the box of spares. He loaded coolly. At twenty yards he couldn't fail to hit the Bushman. But Tami saw him and began to scramble away between the legs of the oxen.

'You little yellow bastard!' André screamed, firing wildly into the team. A shot thudded into an ox's flank. It bellowed and surged forward, throwing the team into chaos. Stamping, lowing, four oxen pulling in different directions, the brake screeched its protest. Tami crouched amid the bovine riot and André fired again. The lead beast fell, his dead weight splintering the yoke. His teammate then broke free but at the cost of a severed hamstring. Its bellows were pitiful and, almost automatically, Deon lifted his rifle and put it out of its misery.

Etienne roared from the back of the wagon. 'Will you two swines stop shooting? How the blerryhell do you think you're going to get me back without a team to pull this focken cart?'

'But Pa, he's getting away,' André shouted as Tami broke for cover. He fired, hitting Tami directly in the head, blowing the front of his face off.

N#aisa screamed, jumped out of the wagon and ran towards her husband. André shot her in the back. She buckled and then pitched face-first into the red sand. There she lay, one arm flung up in the traditional greeting.

*　*　*

Mannie was leaning against a termite mound. His stomach heaved violently, but nothing came out. Suddenly, the base of the mound exploded, spewing twigs, earth and a very determined assailant.

Mannie felt his face being clawed as he was pushed over. A weight was on his chest and something was pressing on his windpipe. He fought for his life, trying to heave the hissing, scratching, pressing leopard off him. Then he saw an eye — wild, but human — a child, no bigger than him. Maybe even a girl. Jissus, she could fight!

Koba scratched and bit while they rolled in the dirt. She was going to kill this /Ton cub with her bare hands if she had to. As they tussled she spat out every curse and obscenity she knew: The /Ton boy was a dry season child and his seed would never populate the earth; his penis was a worm that even carrion flies wouldn't piss on; his father was man who couldn't eat meat, who had n#ah seeds coming out of his arse; his mother's womb was a withered winter melon. She hated, hated, hated him and his kind, and she would never, ever forgive them.

By now the fight had gone out of the children. Mannie bit his lip and let the girl pummel his chest with her small fists. When she sprang up and ran away, he followed her.

He'd never seen anyone move like that. Her two slender legs were like four, so balanced was she as she tore down the rocky incline, leaping bushes that were in her path. When she got to the scene of the carnage, she tore across to a body lying dead-still in the sand.

Koba threw herself onto N#aisa and laid her head on the blood-spattered chamois of her mother's chest.

★ ★ ★

Mannie stood dazed. Around him, dead and injured oxen, André and Twi trying to catch the scattered horses, Etienne flinging the

90

contents of the cart out onto the sand and three lifeless bodies — the tracker and two wild Bushmen. The girl was lying across the breast of one, her shoulders shaking, but he could hear no sound from her.

And where was his father?

★ ★ ★

'Snakebite serum. Find it. Somewhere here.'

André began ripping through the baskets and boxes lying on the sand. 'Where, Pa, where?'

'Somewhere. Keep looking, damn you!' Etienne sat against a wagon wheel, his face grey, his shirt faintly pink from the arrow puncture. The mid-afternoon sun was searing but there was no time to rig up the tarpaulin to provide some shade. The serum was his only chance and even then it wasn't a proven antidote to the Bushman poison. Twi had said the toxin came from the pupae of a special beetle. The little bastards rubbed their arrow tips in it. He'd heard it took antelope a long time to die once the stuff got into their bloodstream. About men he didn't know. Perhaps if he stayed still, didn't shake the stuff up too much and they got him to a doctor in time? Ja, surely. He was big and strong and he'd cut the wound open immediately and poured water and brandy into it.

91

Bliksemse thing was stinging now though.

A shame about Philemon. A good boy. But maybe a wagon wheel going over your neck was easier than dying from the focken Bushman poison? Ja-well, he didn't intend to find out.

'Did you check the tin with the bandages? I usually put some of the serum in there.'

'I checked, Pa. Twice, Pa.'

'We left in such a focken hurry this morning I didn't have time to double-check. Hey, have you looked in the saddle bags?'

'All except Bliksem's, Pa. He's gone.'

'Lucky swine. Probably back at Sukses now. Where's your uncle, and Twi?'

'Uncle Deon's just sitting out there, near the bodies, watching Twi dig a hole.'

'Bastard's probably still drunk. Jissus, how did I get so unlucky? The one time, the only time I need to depend on my family, they let me down. I can't believe you focken shot the oxen, and all for a thieving little kaffir!' André started to snivel. 'Don't you focken cry. You get that uncle of yours and make a blerry plan to get me to a doctor fast.'

★ ★ ★

André plucked at Deon's sleeve. 'Jissus, Uncle Deon, help me, man,' he begged.

92

Deon struggled up as if from a deep, dark well. His shirt clung to him, uniformly wet, as though he'd been immersed in water. Yet it was hot, stiflingly hot, and dry. Was it blood? He glanced down. No . . . sweat. He didn't remember sweating like that. He shivered and listlessly followed André back to the cart.

Again they turned the entire contents of the wagon upside down, emptied all the saddlebags onto the sand, but no sign of the serum. 'Twi, you bastard,' André shouted, 'stop digging fucking graves and come help us. Can't you see your Baas is dying, man?'

Now they went faster, scrabbling through toolboxes, ammunition, under tarpaulin. They even upturned the milk tart Lettie had stayed up half the night to bake. They checked tins, baskets, pockets in trousers and jackets. Finally all had been triple-searched. There was nowhere else to look.

André stood in front of his father, biting his lip. 'It's not here, Pa.' He swallowed. 'I don't think you packed it in.'

André and Deon couldn't bear to watch as Etienne started to laugh. His belly wobbled and the pink patches on his shirt began to seep red. 'Me, the big provider . . . forgot to provide the one thing that could save my life! Ha, ha. You've got to find it funny, hey?'

'Don't worry, Boet, I'll make a plan,' Deon said.

'Ja-ja, you make your plans while you sit dopping on my stoep there at Impalala. Do you know,' he pointed a shaking finger at Deon, 'I was going to fire you, you drunken bastard, and now,' he laughed harder, 'now you get your very own farm to run into the ground. Good job it's only Impalala, hey? Ja, dankie tog, you were too chicken to shoot that Bushman otherwise all this would be yours to booze away too.' He sank back, sweating profusely. André fanned him with his hat.

'Come, we must build a litter,' Deon said quietly to Twi.

* * *

An hour later he and Twi had Etienne on a makeshift litter that could be pulled by the remaining ox. By now, Etienne was in pain. He clenched his teeth but didn't writhe. Deon passed him the brandy bottle and opened another for himself.

Chapter 4

Koba wasn't sure how many sunrises she'd slept through. She hadn't expected to wake up.

She had confused memories of a journey with /Ton who smelled of drink and fear and death, and a boy's body, the /Ton cub, tied to hers to keep her on the tame animal that walked so slowly in the dark, away from the Mother Hills, away from the hunting star her father had told her to follow.

She had kicked the tame animal as she'd seen the /Ton do, to try and make it run with her, but the limping /Ton shook his head sadly at her, and tied her ankles to the cub's and her hands to the seat. He made the cub hold her so she wouldn't slip off.

Koba had the sense that the sorrow of these two — were they father and son? — rose to meet her own pain when their eyes met. They said words she could not understand but whose meaning she sensed:

95

shock, sorrow, pain, guilt. When the /Ton boy saw that she couldn't bear his skin to touch hers, he tried to lean as far from her as the tame animal seat would allow.

She must have fallen asleep on the long, dark death journey. She woke to find herself leaning against the boy as a light shone on her. This was a world of evil spirits for sure. Strange faces in flickering light, shouting, crying, dangerous animal sounds, smells, lots of unnatural smells, and eyes staring at her with hate. Then a pair of kind hands, untying her. She was pulled from the tame animal and carried away in the dark. From the light of a burning torch she saw the /Ton boy stare after her, his eyes as big as a frog's. And wet.

She was thrown into this place that smelled of animals, and ugly faces loomed above her, jeering and spitting. But perhaps that was just a dream? Was the other place a dream, too? The place where her father had half a face and her mother lay on the sand waving?

She pulled N#aisa's kaross more tightly around her. She was alive and this was no dream. She was alone in this dangerous place and she had to get away and back to the Mother Hills to find Zuma before it was too late. Together they could set off back to their n/ore.

She tried to straighten up but her wrists and ankles were hobbled together and tied to a sturdy post. Koba struggled against her bonds. She froze as she heard footsteps approach. A stranger, dressed in black. Koba relaxed a little when she discerned a woman — very big but as clumsy as a cow in calf.

At the sight of the hobbled child, Marta broke into a run, one hand holding her belly and the other jamming her funeral hat onto her dishevelled hair. 'Who did this to you? Who?' She flung open the gate of the pen and immediately began to attack Koba's bonds with furious fingers. 'I'm sorry, ag, I'm so sorry.' She touched the small arm.

Koba recognised the kind hand, but this was a chance. She sank her teeth into the spotted flesh and tried to run. Her ankle bonds held. Quickly she worked the knots.

Marta was staring at her scalloped wound. 'I'm sorry.' She rubbed her hand. 'You must be frightened and I . . . '

But Koba was free. She vaulted the gate and ran for the high green growth she could see some distance off.

* * *

Marta disliked having to disturb her sister-in-law in the middle of the funeral reception but she didn't feel she could organise a search party without Lettie's permission to approach the servants who stood gathered outside the back door in their Sunday best.

Inside, the front rooms had been stripped of Christmas decoration and the mantelpieces were draped in black crêpe. Both rooms were packed with dignitaries — some local, some parliamentarians Etienne had worked with. Lettie was holding court in front of a huge flower arrangement, smiling bravely at sympathisers and dabbing her swollen eyes with a pretty handkerchief.

Marta thought Lettie was going to run her through with a cake fork when she explained what she needed. She felt someone take her elbow and steer her firmly away. It was Deon, pale and shaky, but sober. Marta shook his hand off. She wanted nothing to do with him after the way he'd behaved out at the Mother Hills, his excuses about bluffing notwithstanding. Yes, he had an inferiority complex about his brother — what man wouldn't have? — but she'd married him because she sensed a basic decency about him. His drinking seemed to have washed all that out of his character.

Chagrined, Deon went outside. A quiet word, some shillings passed around, and the men kicked off uncomfortable shoes, handed their hats to their wives and set off to find the child.

It didn't take them long. Koba had left a trail of trampled cornstalks. Grinning, they dumped the struggling girl into a storeroom Marta had prepared.

Koba scurried to a corner of her new jail and huddled there, her back to her captors. The men laughed. 'Out,' Marta said, shutting the door firmly on the interested faces.

She approached the girl cautiously, a bowl of warm Dettol-water in her hands. Gently she placed it on the stone floor. The child winced at the clunk. 'I only want to clean you up, little one, come on, I won't hurt you.' Gingerly she touched the tiny shoulder.

This time the child did not bite but she was trembling so violently Marta decided it was kinder to leave her filthy. 'I'll fetch someone who can talk to you,' she said. Taking the blanket from the camp bed she placed it around the child's shoulders and left, locking the door behind her.

★   ★   ★

She found Twi sitting alone outside his hut in the servants' compound. He was wearing a suit that had belonged to Etienne in his slimmer days. Nevertheless, it looked six sizes too big on this tiny man. Twi's wrinkled head poked out from the jacket like a tortoise's

99

from its shell. He had the trouser legs rolled up into thick cuffs and he was, as ever, barefoot. Marta smiled. She'd seen the minister frown at this when he spied Twi among the black mourners at the back of the big white church.

'Sorry to disturb you,' Marta said, 'but that Khoisan — MaSarwa — child you brought back, I need some help with her.' Twi remained seated and stared down at his feet. 'I want you to tell the child we mean her no harm,' Marta explained.

Twi's snort astounded her. This was rudeness like she'd never experienced from a servant before. But he wasn't her servant, Marta thought, and he had been through a lot out at the Mother Hills. That much was obvious from his haggard look.

'Please,' she said, stepping forward. The man looked up and then through her. Twi was staring at the chicken coop some distance from the compound. He was thinking about Etienne.

Twi had come to Etienne's newly-acquired farm one August night to steal chickens. Hearing the squawking commotion Etienne had stormed out with a shotgun. He saw he wouldn't need it for the inebriated little man who cowered before him in the coop. Instead he grabbed him by the scruff of his tattered shirt and thrashed him, using the butt of the gun like a paddle across his back and bottom. Afterwards, while the man crouched in a corner, sobering up fast and blubbering what sounded like abject apologies, Etienne felt he owed it to the fool to at least listen to him. It wasn't dignified, spanking a grown man, but what else could he do to teach the bastard a lesson? The big Boer leaned against the wire gate and gave the man a hearing.

'That I, a man who could trap any bird in the bush, should find myself so small as to steal one from another man's cage . . . huw-ah!' Twi lamented.

'So why did you do it then, man?'

'Big-big hunger, Baas.'

Etienne stamped one of his brown-booted feet. 'So come and knock on my door, for fock's sake. It would save me having to come out here in the middle of the bloody night. Jissus, kaffir.' He banged his fist on the chicken wire causing renewed panic among the hens. 'I've never turned a hungry man away. We'll make a plan. If I feed you and you do some small job for me then neither one of us can feel bigger or smaller than he should.'

It was too dark for Etienne to see the shrewd interest in Twi's eyes. The Ju/'hoan studied the big blond man, his brain clearing with every throb of humiliation. Twi tried to set aside his natural prejudice about whites. True, this one was a real animal, but not that dangerous. He'd chosen not use his gun. Not to shoot with, anyway.

The big-genital had arrogance though, treating a grown man like a naughty child. His back hurt. And his buttocks — stinging like he'd sat on a swarm of bees. Huw, if he'd had a poison arrow to hand he would have stabbed the bastard, no matter what the consequences.

But it was a long time since he'd had anything to do with bows and arrows. Hunting was a hard-hard way to fill one's belly and there was no beer in the bush to slake a thirst like he had. Maybe the lion on the other side of the cage could be de-clawed and persuaded to share his plenty with little Twi?

When the Ju'/hoan saw Etienne lean forward to better study him, he decided to gamble on honesty. With a touch of theatrics, Twi rubbed his sore buttocks then dropped his chin to his chest. 'My hunger is not for food, Baas,' he mumbled, 'it's for the beer. Since I left my n/ore for the town, the beer-hunger has clawed at me. See my hands.' He held out a genuinely shaking brown pair, as small-boned as a child's. 'These hands could string a bow, or skin a giraffe. Now they shake-shake-shake and can't even hold a spade.' He shook his head and tried to see from under lowered lids what effect he was having. 'I am sick.'

Etienne snorted, so powerfully Twi was convinced the dust rose obediently, summoned by the massive nostrils. His giant gaoler straightened up but had to remain stooped to stop his head touching the roof.

'Ja-ja-ja, I've heard it all before,' Etienne said. 'Too sick to work but not to steal, hey? Now listen, I'm giving you one chance and one chance only. Here's your chicken.' He reached for one of the hens still fluttering frantically. Wringing its neck without taking his eyes off the black man he handed the limp fowl over. 'If you're still here in the morning, with all the birds alive except this one, you can work for me.'

Twi eased his aching shoulders as his eyes swept up the length of the man bent over him. No doubt the lion had counted his fowl and would keep watch from his house, gun at the ready. But, true to his word, he was giving food. Twi began to pluck the chicken.

Etienne laughed. 'Ja-jong, Kaffir, don't you worry. Stay and work by me and I'll keep you so busy you won't have time for the beer hunger to ever catch you again. And we'll see

103

if we can put a bit of meat on those bones of yours, hey? Jissus man, you're as thin as a bloody mielie stalk.' With that Etienne smacked him playfully on his burning back and left.

Twi became Etienne's best worker and an accomplished pilferer. Tools, clothing, tobacco, seed, fencing, fertiliser. As the labour force grew at Sukses, newcomers learnt they could buy or barter whatever they needed in Twi's hut. But not alcohol. The blind eye Etienne turned regained sight when Twi used alcohol on the farm.

'I have enough grief from my brother. I'm not putting up with a drunk boss boy as well,' he had said.

So Twi's thirst drove him to a shebeen in town. Occasionally he was too drunk to return in time for work. Then Etienne asked friends in the police force to locate him. Twi understood the trade-off — he was never to let slip that the Baas called on a certain Mrs van Tonder whenever her salesman husband was off on a trip

And now the big-genital was gone. Killed by an arrow from Twi's own Harmless People. Twi shook his head. Who'd have thought he'd miss the bastard /Ton? But he would, he would. Etienne had been his father — father to all the other workers on the farm too. A harsh father, but a fair one. He looked after his people. Gave them food, medicine when they were sick, helped them bury their dead. Twi's face puckered like a sultana as tears slid down his yellow cheeks.

★ ★ ★

In the storeroom, Twi stepped softly towards Koba. She shrank from him, retreating again into the corner of the room. He touched her and spoke quietly. To Marta his talk sounded like the rapid clicking of a touch typist. Koba kept her back to them.

Twi shrugged. 'Her throat is closed. Must be she fears things.'

'What things?'

'/Ton — white peoples,' he spat out, 'dangerous things.'

'But I'm not dangerous.'

Twi's look was implacable.

Marta bowed her head. 'I'll wait outside.' She turned back at the door. 'Please — make sure she understands she's not being imprisoned. I'll lock her in, but just for the time being, for her own safety.'

Twi looked at her with interest. Marta brushed hair that wasn't there from her eyes. 'Oh, I don't know, it's just a feeling I have.' She shrugged. 'Anyway, I'll get her back home, I promise. You tell her.' She left the room.

Twi squatted down in front of Koba and slowly gave her Marta's message.

Koba found it impossible to stop the shivering down her back, the shaking in her legs. The muti that Leopard-woman had left in the room smelt strong — like poison. Would it kill her slowly, or just take the run from her legs? She wanted to ask the uncle, but her voice would not come. More /Ton magic? What were they doing to her?

Tears slid down her cheeks, snaking silver through the grime. She felt herself sobbing, heard it in her head, but knew no sound was coming out of her mouth.

The man was talking. Talk-talk, talking, but she found him difficult to understand. He has my face, but only half my tongue, she thought. And I have no tongue at all. The /Ton have taken it. She gesticulated at her throat, shaking her head, crying harder and faster.

Twi stared helplessly at her. Eventually, 'Yau, perhaps you are speechless.'

He squatted back on his heels, studying her. Perhaps this child was deaf too. That was why she didn't respond to his questions. Better if she'd been blind, he thought. Him too. He wished he hadn't seen that mess out at the Mother Hills. But it was not of his making and it was none of his business, especially if he wanted to keep his position under his new, murdering boss. He could advise this kin-child, that was all.

He tried to speak clearly, keeping every word distinct, 'The woman who was here, she with the spots, will not harm you. She bids me tell you this is not a prison. She locks you in to keep you safe. She says she'll send you home.'

Koba looked baffled. Twi shrugged and stood up. 'My heart is sore for you, little closed-throat, but what can I do? I can't help you here. The new Baas doesn't like us. But you go with the big spotted woman. My Baas used to like her — very, very much. She is soft. She will help you. Stop your shake-shaking now. Drink some water. The woman will help you. You are not in prison.'

* * *

Koba had understood just one word that the man said: 'prison'. It was the new word Grandmother had used at the Mother Hills, the one that put such fear into her. Now Zuma's explanation came back, 'Sometimes, /Ton do not kill fence-crossers. Sometimes they bury them alive. /Ton tie a person's hands and trap the person behind high walls. You cannot escape. Men guard you with thundersticks. You are caught, tighter than a sandgrouse in a snare. Worse-worse is,' Koba could picture her grandmother's bony finger wagging, 'they do not kill you. You cannot join your ancestors. No,' she had shuddered, 'they feed your body but inside your spirit shrivels from the hunger. Uh-uh-uhnn. That is what I know. That is what I have heard. Prison, they call it.'

Koba pushed the water bowl away, spilling the solution. She fell back on the bed, rigid with fear. A tiny window was set high in the wall, but barred. As she gazed, the walls shifted and seemed to draw closer together. The ceiling sank. The sky through the window was far, far away. Koba felt a tightness in her chest. Breathing became difficult. She began to gasp. The room was shrinking; soon there would be no air for her. Panting, she felt her head spin. She mustn't faint. She had to get to Zuma.

Chapter 5

The day after the funeral, Mannie heard his mother step into his room.

'You awake, Liebschen?'

He lay tense, eyes shut. Were the police here? Had she come to call him for questioning? If he pretended to be sick would they all go away and leave him alone? He didn't want to have to talk about the shootings, to say he saw the Bushman crawling towards the wagon. He didn't want to have to say what the grown-ups were doing to the Bushwoman in the back of the cart. Even now his cheeks burned at the thought and he felt sick.

The funeral had been terrible, but not as bad as before when Uncle Etienne had lain in an open coffin and he had to stand there with Ma and Pa and Auntie Lettie, pretending it had all been a tragic accident.

He'd never explained to Ma what he'd said the night they came back from the hunting trip, when she'd been fussing with him instead of helping Uncle Etienne. Ma seemed to have forgotten how he'd sobbed that it was his fault Etienne was dead. But it was his fault really, Mannie knew, and he'd have to keep the terrible secret to himself forever.

So he couldn't go out, couldn't get up and had hardly managed to hand koeksisters round at the funeral. Every time André came into the same room as him, he'd had to leave, the cake plate shaking so violently the koeksisters nearly landed on the floor.

Now he pulled the blanket over his head, even though it was sweltering in the room. He heard his mother walk over to the window. There was a scratchy, sliding sound as she drew open the curtains. He was aware of the intense brightness of the day, even through his covers. Ma was coming towards him. He squeezed his eyes shut. She flicked back the blanket and rested her hand on his cheek.

'Magies, but you are hot. Have you got a temperature? Mannie,' she shook him. 'Mannie, wake up.'

'Ag, leave me, Ma,' he grunted.

'I'm going to get a thermometer. If you've got a temperature I'll have to brew up some leaves.' Marta was mentally running through the dispensary available to her out in the veld. She knew a lot about the healing properties of plants, knowledge acquired on Impalala from the Tsonga women. They, like her, wouldn't dream of going to the trading store for pills and potions. But would she find something for fever here, amid vegetation that had become alien to her? She felt her son again. His forehead felt a bit cooler. Perhaps if he got out from under the bedclothes? 'C'mon, c'mon. It's too hot for lying in bed. Sit up so I can pull your 'jama top off. You're sweating in it. C'mon.'

Mannie sat up, scowling. His mother was wearing a black dress he hadn't seen before. She looked too pale in it. Even her freckles looked as light as sesame seeds.

'You've missed breakfast, but it's nearly time for lunch. Get washed and dressed and come.'

'Don't want any lunch.'

'Mannie,' she reached for his hand. 'You must eat.'

He shook her off. 'Not hungry.'

She leaned towards him. 'This has got to stop. You can't keep hiding in this room, Mannie. What are you so afraid of?'

She hadn't forgotten!

He sat trying to control the trembling in his hands by plucking at the crumpled sheet, balling it up in each fist. Marta watched him and let the silence grow. They heard the rattle

111

of crockery as the maid carried a lunch tray down the passage to her mistress's room. Lettie had rallied for the funeral, but show over, she was inconsolable and was being kept sedated. Marta said they should extend their stay to keep an eye on her. It meant having a very quiet Christmas, no celebrating, and they wouldn't be able to go the seaside. Mannie found that he didn't care.

Once the footsteps had passed, the loudest sound became the ticking of Etienne's grandfather clock out in the passage. Ticking, tocking steadily, like a heart, thought Mannie. Wasn't there a song about a clock that stopped when the master died?

He longed for things to be as they were: tractors coming in from the fields; workers splashing at the water pump; the cook banging a spoon on the huge, blackened pot to call them for their midday meal of pap and boiled meat. And Uncle Etienne, banging one boot against the other to get the dust off before he stepped onto Auntie Lettie's polished floors.

Now it was so quiet he could hear the wind wafting the curtains. And still Ma said nothing.

'Have the police been yet?' he asked in a small voice.

'Yes.'

'And they didn't want to talk to me?' He unclenched his fists slightly. His mother looked grave as she sat down heavily beside him.

'No, my boy. Nor to me. They were only interested in the death of the MP for Onderwater. Snakebite is what's been put on the certificate as the cause of death.'

'But Ma . . . ' He knew his voice sounded young, like it did last week, before all of this. 'Mama, what about the dead Bushmen? Do they know about those?'

'I told them, but I doubt they'll even drive out to get the bodies.' Marta's head was bowed. He could see red blotches on her neck. She always got them when she was upset. 'The thing is, the Bushmen — Khoisan — aren't white. Or even black. And they were trespassing and André is the son of the MP, so . . . ' She swallowed hard and when she lifted her eyes they were filled with tears. 'I argued, said I'd write to the Minister, said I was prepared to put you on the witness stand to say what happened, but . . . '

Mannie gasped then started to sob with fear. 'I can't, I can't. Mama, don't make me.'

'Ag, baby.' She gathered him into her arms and held his trembling body. 'There, there. Toemaar now. There won't be a court case. It's over now. But son,' she held him away

113

from her, 'I need to know you understand that what happened was wrong, very wrong. Mannie?' He nodded vigorously. 'Good.' Then Marta began to cry, tears coursing unchecked down her cheeks.

Mannie put his arms around her and rocked her as best he could. He patted his mother's back. Somehow it made him feel better that someone else felt as sad and helpless as he did. After a while he felt her give a shuddering sigh and pull gently away. 'Ag, I'm sorry. Don't know what's the matter with me, crying every five minutes. And I haven't even been to Oupa Manfred's grave yet. Don't know how I'm going to fit that in now.' She wiped her cheeks with the hem of her dress and her reddened eyes held Mannie's. 'Now, I'm sure you'll be very kind to the little girl when we take her home with us.'

He sat back in surprise. To feel sorry about the way bad grown-ups carried on was one thing, but to have to face that girl every day, knowing what his family had done to hers, was another. 'I don't want her back on Impalala,' he said.

'Manfred, I'm surprised at you. This family is now responsible for the girl. We orphaned her, remember? It's a guilt we'll bear for the rest of our lives.'

114

'But it wasn't Pa who shot anyone. It was Uncle Etienne and André!'

'I know, I know. But all André will promise is that Twi can take her back to where you found her.' She twisted a strand of escaped hair round and round in frustration. 'That's not going to help her find the rest of her tribe, is it? She's obviously from the Kalahari — that's many, many days walk away. She might not survive out there on her own while she wanders around trying to find people who have probably moved on by now.'

'Why can't Twi take her in a truck?'

Marta tucked the strand behind her freckled ear. 'Ja-well, that would be the best thing — if Twi or someone else set out on a proper expedition, carrying enough supplies with them. If that had been done in the first place instead of setting out like some boy scouts on a Great Trek, Etienne might still be with us. Anyway, whatever kind of expedition, it takes time, money and men.' Marta frowned. Keeping her tone as neutral as possible she said, 'André doesn't want to commit to that now when there's so much he has to see to around the farm.'

'Can't we take her then?'

Marta stroked his cheek with the back of her hand. 'Ag Liebschen, I wish we could, but Pa . . . ' She trailed off and looked out of the window at the horizon beyond the cornfields. Ludicrous to think of Deon coping alone out there. He had no bush sense at all. He got lost on their own farm. And out in the Kalahari Desert there were no signs for those who couldn't read the searing sand. There was just heat and thirst and shimmering mirages that lured unwary vehicles to rusty graves in the vast salt pans.

'But when this baby is big enough,' Marta touched her bulge, 'and I've saved enough money, I promise I'll take the girl back to the Kalahari myself. You and me, we'll take her. Won't that be an adventure, hey?'

Mannie would not be drawn. It could be months, years even, before Ma gathered enough in the jam jar — even if they found a hiding place for it that Pa wouldn't find. 'But you're always saying how sad it is to see Bushmen losing their bush ways. That will happen to her when she becomes a maid at Impalala.'

'Khoisan, Mannie. You must start using the proper term. And don't you worry. I've got a plan for the girl that will keep her pure Bushman. Er, Khoisan.' She gave a light laugh. 'Now come on. Get dressed. And I'd like you to come and say hello to the girl. She's scared, just like you. Everything's so strange to her. But at least you'd be a face she recognises.'

116

Mannie kept his head down. The silence began to build again. Marta stood up with some effort.

'Well, my boy, I won't force you. But you know going to see her would be the kind thing to do.'

Oh-ja, he thought after the door had closed, imagine what the Bushgirl'll think when she sees me! What she'll remember.

Chapter 6

With Lettie in her room and Mannie and Deon avoiding her, Marta spent more and more time in the storeroom. The child fascinated her. She was so delicate with her tiny features and graceful limbs. Marta would have liked to draw her to try to capture her extraordinary bone structure — the acute angle between cheekbone and jaw, the high, smooth forehead — but the quiet dignity of this small person seemed to forbid it.

She hasn't reached puberty, Marta decided. She could be Mannie's age or a few years older, at most. Maybe a young twelve?

Koba, meanwhile, was assessing the person she'd come to think of as Leopard-woman. If she understood the skinless Ju/'hoan man, this /Ton was her way out of prison, her route to survival. And Koba meant to live. Every atom in her was adapted to survival under the harshest physical conditions. But to live without people, without someone to press against in the night, or to call to as she gathered food in the veld, without someone to tell her stories of the Early Race, or to braid ornaments into her hair, without someone to tell her she was more precious to them than water? The emptiness filled her with fear, a fear that made her insides ache, like winter-morning fingers gripping them and numbing her. It made her struggle for breath as she had that first night in the room.

Grandmother had said it was best to make a friend of what one feared. She would learn to like her aloneness. She would tell herself stories, about all the things she remembered from her n/ore. She would say the names of her playmates, remember who was good at catch-clap, who made the best bird sounds, who could climb to the top of a baobab the fastest. She would list all the things about her mother, her father, Grandmother and all their kin so that when she got back, she would know them all and they would know her as one of their own.

She wouldn't fear the tappings in her chest. She would listen and learn to understand them; use them as antennae, like grasshoppers did to keep themselves out of harm's way.

Koba sighed. It was strange how a person's life could change between one sunrise and the next. At the Mother Hills she had felt like a child and now, in this new place, only part of a moon later, she was older and needed to consider things for herself. Like this /Ton woman.

Koba steeled herself not to shiver when the woman touched her with her pale, spotted claws. She tried to eat the unpleasant food Leopard-woman put out for her — thick white paste, too hot to keep in her mouth if she ate it immediately, too stiff to swallow without gagging if she let it get cold.

Misunderstanding her dislike of the porridge, Marta brought some honey and drizzled it onto the child's breakfast. She rubbed her stomach and licked her lips, pushing the bowl towards the girl.

Koba tasted it tentatively and immediately gagged. How could she tell this /Ton on whom she must depend that she hated honey? What she longed for was salt. It made most things palatable.

Christmas came and went and Marta became increasingly concerned about keeping the girl cooped up. But she couldn't risk the child making another bid for freedom that would most likely result in her death. She reckoned on having to stay another week at Sukses to help Lettie and then she could take the child back to Impalala where she could put her plan into action.

In the meantime she began to bring bits of the bush into the storeroom, ostensibly to draw them while she sat and talked at the girl. But she left them behind afterwards and noted how eagerly the child grabbed a croton tree branch and crushed the silvery leaves under her nose, breathing in the lavender smell. She'd heard that Khoisan women dried and powdered the leaves to make a perfume.

Koba watched Marta carefully as she drew. She saw how the woman was in pain from her pregnancy, how an arrow formed between her brows when the pain attacked. She noted Marta's straight hair, even admired its colour — like red grass. She wondered what it would feel like to touch.

Leopard-woman's sketchings intrigued her. She craned her neck, trying to see into the lap across the room. Was Leopard-woman making a leaf? Could she make people, animals? Figures like those in the great painting?

One day Marta brought an empty tortoise shell, set it down and began to draw. Koba could resist no longer. She stood up, walked over to Marta's chair and gazed at the sketch. She saw a flat tortoise, without movement.

'Tortoise,' Marta said, pointing to the reptile. Instinctively Koba tried to copy the sound. Nothing came. Quickly she turned her face to the wall.

Marta kept talking. She placed her hand on her breast and said her name. She pointed to the plate of food, 'porridge,' and to the sickly sweet substance, 'honey'.

Koba pouted. She didn't want these strange words, this horrible food. She wanted to be back with her people, eating mongongo nuts, monkey oranges and meat. She didn't want to be older. She wanted her father and her mother and the time before the Mother Hills. She pulled her mother's kaross over her head and sat tented inside it. She heard Leopard-woman packing up her things. Koba noticed a sliver of light shining through a tear in the kaross. She stuck her finger through and waggled it about. Then she thought better of it. She mustn't tear it further; she had no way of fixing it. She heard Leopard-woman leave the room.

Ten minutes later, Marta returned with a needle and thread. She showed them to Koba and saw something like comprehension cross the little girl's face as she seized the needle and jabbed at the skin cloak. The child pricked her finger but didn't flinch. Gently, Marta indicated that she would sew it for her. Koba hesitated and then handed over the kaross.

Marta was surprised at how soft the hide cloak was. It smelled of plants. She supposed it had carried a lot of veld food — berries, tubers, bark. Khoisan women used their karosses as slings for their children too. Had the Bushgirl been carried in it by her mother? Was this her equivalent of a treasured cot blanket?

Marta spread the cloak nervously over her knees and plunged in. The needle broke. She rethreaded another and broke that too. This was a job for an expert sewer, like Lettie, but she couldn't ask her for help, not now. Marta felt the solemn gaze of the child beside her. She tried harder.

Her first repair was clumsy, the stitches too far apart. She pulled them out, aware of the intense concentration of the girl.

Half-an-hour and another needle later, Marta had done it. The tear was mended with neat, even stitches. She handed the cloak back.

Koba took it without a word but, for the first time, she met Marta's eyes.

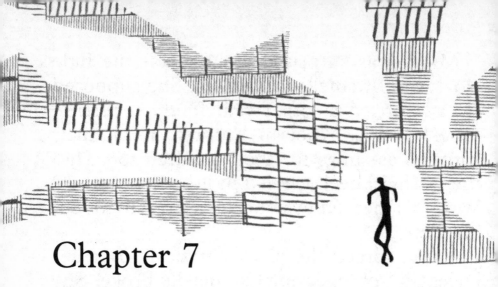

Chapter 7

The long journey from South-West Africa to
Nelspruit, in the north of neighbouring South
Africa, was a nightmare for Marta. Not
because of the length of the trip as the train
went south then east across the breadth of the
African subcontinent and then north again.
Nor had there been any trouble getting the
awestruck Bushgirl onto the train. The
problem was the conductor, a little man with
brilliantined hair who checked their tickets in
Windhoek and refused to allow the girl to
stay in their reserved compartment.

'Third-class,' he'd said, pointing to the
carriages closest to the smoke stack. Marta
had anticipated the problem. She put on her
haughtiest, most educated accent.

'I think you'll find we all have tickets for
this compartment, my good man.'

'Ja-but, this . . . ' the man floundered, unable
to categorise Koba. 'They must go third-class.'

'This Khoisan child — Bushman — from the bush, has never been on a train before so I'd be most grateful if you'd oblige me by letting her remain in the compartment with us. Otherwise she may feel frightened.'

'Sorry lady. We can't make no exceptions or we'll have kaffirs sitting everywhere. They're getting very white these days, wanting places up front on the buses and things.'

Marta stopped the aristocratic pretence. The man would obviously not be bullied. 'Look, if we're prepared to pay the price for a first-class ticket . . . '

'Listen lady, I don't make the rules. I's only doing my job.' But noticing how Marta pressed her hand to ease the pains in her lower back, he softened. 'Tell you what, you put her where she belongs and I'll give you a refund. I'm authorised.'

'I am not leaving this child on her own, not on a three-day journey.'

'Ag, don't worry. I'll tell one of the kaffir-girls to keep an eye on her. They can be very motherly, you know.'

'God!' Marta turned to Deon. 'Can you believe this man?' she asked in English.

Deon lifted his head from his paper and winked at his wife. 'Don't make a fuss, Martjie; this Boer will make a plan.'

'What plan?'

'When the train gets going, I'll find him, slip him ten bob and . . . Bob's your uncle!'

'You mean you'll bribe this odious little servant of the Apartheid system? You'll collude with him so he benefits from this immoral law in every respect? Not on my account you won't! And certainly not with my money, thank you very much.' She sat back in her seat, her neck aflame, and glared at the clearly fascinated conductor. She couldn't leave it there. She leaned towards Deon again and hissed, 'By virtue of his colour, Mr Unskilled White over there probably has the job that some better qualified black man used to have before Job Reservations, and now you . . . '

Deon glanced quickly at the conductor. Judging from his blank look the English had been too fast for the man to follow. Nevertheless, Deon felt himself redden. 'Must it be now that you get on your soapbox, Marta? You knew the law when you insisted on buying the ticket for her. If you carry on like this, I won't be able to help you and he won't agree to it — not even for twenty bob.'

Marta began to gather up her belongings. 'Good,' she said, 'because I want nothing more to do with men who don't seem to know what's right anymore.' She stood up

126

and addressed the conductor in Afrikaans. 'This child is my responsibility, so if she can't stay here with me,' she heaved herself off the seat, 'I'll go to third-class with her.'

The conductor looked appalled. 'You can't!'

'Why not?' she demanded. 'Is there some rule about that too?'

'Ag-no. It's just that . . . well, you'll be uncomfortable, lady. The seats are wooden and it's crowded, hey. Place stinks of them!'

Marta stepped towards the man, so close he was obliged to look up at her. 'I don't suppose it ever occurred to you that *they* might think *you* stink.'

The conductor spluttered, patted the ticket dispenser on his belt, removed his pencil stub from behind his ear and tugged his jacket straight. He addressed himself to Deon, 'Mister, you better keep this wife of yours in check, man. Railways reserve the right to put trouble-makers off the train.'

Deon laughed, 'Good luck, man.'

Ignoring him, the conductor glowered at Koba. 'Pasopjong, don't let me catch you here when I come back, hey?' and he banged out of the compartment.

Taking the girl's hand, Marta turned to Mannie. 'Coming?'

Mannie squirmed on the green leather seat.

He should go with Ma, he knew, but blerry-bugger, no! He didn't think the Bushgirl should be here with them either — not in this compartment, not on the train, not in their lives. Just looking at her standing with her hand in Ma's made him want to hit her.

He knew that was unfair. She didn't want to be here anymore than he wanted her to be — if Ma hadn't kept such a tight hold on her at the station she probably would have run away.

But no way did he feel like sitting in a dirty carriage; he wanted to be here, with room to spread out, his own hand basin in the corner with its golden plughole. Tonight the steward would come and let down the bunks and make up beds for them with starched white sheets. Pa said they'd go to the dining car, now that they'd saved the money they would have spent on a hotel in Walvis Bay.

So Mannie said nothing. He simply shook his head at his mother's enquiry without meeting her eyes. Then he turned towards the window. The world outside was still dark, so his mother and the Bushgirl were clearly reflected in the glass. They stood together, bodies almost touching, then slipped from view, just like the dark shapes flashing past the train window as it gathered speed.

★ ★ ★

Marta felt ill as she and the girl lurched down the swaying corridor. The baby inside seemed to somersault. Marta clutched her stomach as a band of pain tightened around it. I must stay calm, she thought. She knew she'd brought the situation on herself.

By the time she reached the dimly-lit passage approaching third-class, Marta could hear the din. She leaned against the inter-leading door, clutching her bag to her, her eyes wide and showing white in a face already sooty.

'I must sit down a minute,' she said to Koba as she sank to the filthy floor.

Why, oh why did she get herself into these situations? Of course it would have been better for her and for Koba to stay in whites-only. The last thing she wanted to do was spend three days in a filthy, overcrowded carriage if it was as bad as that horrible little conductor had said. And now she'd made it impossible for Deon to come and rescue her. She dropped her head into her hands.

Standing in the inter-carriage space, Koba wanted to scream her panic. She was in the carapace of a metal monster and she was not safe. There were gaps in the body of the giant creature and through them she could see ground, dark and rushing, as the monster raced over it. It puffed bad smoke up through the holes and ate the flowing metal with clacking teeth. She wanted to get out, go back to the room they'd just left, even if Hyena/Ton and his cub were there. Leopard-woman had to take her. She must make the woman move.

Koba tugged at Marta's hand.

Marta looked up with a tear-stained face. 'Okay. I've made my bed, now let's go lie in it.' She struggled up, wiped her face, took a deep breath and depressed the greasy handle of the third-class carriage.

The noise was stupendous as the compartment door swung open — several languages all spoken at once, all at open-market volume. Babies cried, card-players whooped, transistor radios blared Kwela music.

To the left, a housewife was haggling with a hawker over the price of the live chicken he dangled before her. She prodded it, seemed satisfied and dipping into her bra, produced several coins. As he took them, the hawker made a lewd remark about their warmth.

'It's because they have lain with me,' the housewife said coyly.

'I'd like to be in their place,' he leered.

She sized him up. 'Cocky fellow, counting chickens. But you aren't royal enough for this.' She tapped her ample bosom.

'Royal?' He pushed his dusty fedora back on his head and scratched his temple. 'What d'you mean, Mama?'

The women around her cackled. One of them undid her blouse, offering him her overflowing cleavage. He stared at the coin-studded flesh. She pulled a penny off her flesh and showed him the imprint — a perfect bust of Queen Elizabeth II. He retreated amid their jeers.

The laughter stopped suddenly. Haggling halted, babies were shushed and blank stares from dozens of dark eyes met Marta's nervous smile.

She stilled her panic and tried to catch an eye, any eye. All looked away.

Near the door, a group of men, miners probably, coughed obliviously over a game of dice. No good approaching them for a seat. Towards the back she spied two young men with slick hair and switchblade-sharp side-burns, jiving on an empty carriage seat. Two-toned shoes flashed beneath their baggy trousers. A Herero matron in full Victorian dress was bearing down on them, demanding sitting space. Beckoning to Koba, Marta followed, clambering over the bundles and cardboard suitcases that blocked the aisle. She narrowly avoided a backhand from an

131

onyx-cheeked mother who flung her arms wide to untie the blanket that kept her wailing baby strapped to her back. With practised ease she swung the child round to her front and slipped her dark nipple into its mouth.

Marta walked in the matron's wake, watching as the woman's wide hooped skirt brushed hats and even a transistor radio from the carriage bench. Finally, the woman plumped down and, spreading her skirt, nodded apologies to her neighbours. Her turban looked like a vibrantly upholstered anvil.

Marta stopped next to her, greeted her formally and then whispered, 'If you could move up, just a little, we could squeeze in.' The woman, together with every other person there, looked at her in frank astonishment.

'The Madam wants to sit here?' Marta nodded. Resentment replaced wonder on the woman's face. 'Why don't sit you with the white peoples?' she asked in a loud voice. Marta shrugged. The woman made a great show of peering around her at Koba. She snorted. Her disapproval rippled out across the rows of benches. 'MaSarwa, MaSarwa,' echoed all around.

Marta turned to go. Wouldn't Deon laugh to see her now, she thought. Then she felt a tap on her shoulder. An elderly man, one of the passengers who'd had his hat knocked off by the Herero woman, stood up.

'Sit here,' he said, speaking English with a rural black accent.

'Oh, I couldn't take your seat,' Marta replied.

'I've been watching for you,' he said. 'I heard your words with the conductor. Me also.' He pulled a first-class ticket from his waistcoat pocket.

'I don't suppose you were offered a refund before you were chased in here?'

The man's laugh was terse. 'I know better. I do it only as matter of principle . . . ' Marta nodded vigorously. 'I am a lawyer, but to them,' he jerked his thumb in the direction of the conductor, 'I'm a baboon in a suit.' Marta made to protest but the man dismissed the gesture and indicated impatiently that she should sit down.

'Thank you. Thank you very, very much. I can't tell you how grateful I am to you for speaking to me.'

Touching his hat, the man bowed. 'Have a good journey.'

Pulling Koba down beside her, Marta sank against the hard backrest.

★ ★ ★

Koba's knuckles shone like the undersides of cowries as she gripped the edge of the bench. Now she'd seen the joints of this metal monster, she did not want to be inside it. Not even in a big room like this. People hated her here. And the /Ton woman too. What would happen to her? Was she going to be stuck in a hate place? Hate stuck, like honey. She disliked honey.

This had puzzled her father, who climbed baobabs and risked the fury of bees to rob a hive. Koba preferred the savoury sting of salt. She used to stop next to rocks after the rain had evaporated to check hollows for salty deposits.

'Salt tells no lies,' she'd explained to her grandmother. 'Its taste hides nothing, only makes sour sharper and meat stronger.' Zuma hadn't laughed and a few days later she presented Koba with a beaded case for her little salt gourd.

Koba felt the pain of her loss begin to engulf her. She was too tired to worry about what would become of her and if she'd ever see her tree-water again. She let her grip loosen, her spine relax. Her body swayed with the movement of the train. As her head emptied she tuned into the rhythm of the wheels and the puff of the pistons, finding music there — sa-ka-pa-ka, sa-ka-pa-ka, clack, clack, clack. Sa-ka-pa-ka-sa-ka-pa-ka, clack, clack, clack. It reminded her of the beat of a trance dance. When there was trouble in the camp, people would build a large fire and gather around it. Zuma would often start the clapping. Other women would join in and begin to chant. Some would stand up, shuffle around the circle, skin-skirts flapping. Men would wind dance rattles around their ankles and begin to stamp, round and round, wearing a path in the sand, churning up dust that shone like copper gauze in the firelight. And she'd be there, lolling against her mother, or an aunt, or laying her head on Zuma's bony breast to better feel the old woman's conviction that healing was on the way.

She felt that peaceful anticipation now, knew she could abdicate responsibility for her survival for a time. Leopard-woman's smell was beginning to sit comfortably in her nose — it was salty. She allowed her heavy lids to close. Soon she was asleep against Marta's shoulder.

Chapter 8

Bushveld, South Africa.

Impalala wasn't a big farm by South African standards and it lacked an accessible underground water supply like Sukses. What it did have was a boundary with the Kruger National Park, largest game reserve in southern Africa. Smaller game, like warthog, steenbuck and duikers, passed freely between the farm and the reserve while inquisitive giraffe peeked over the high fence as they grazed in the tree canopy along the boundary. Breakouts of the bigger wildlife such elephant, lion, buffalo and rhino were rare, but not unheard of. A bush walk had to be taken with caution. Mostly, the farm was stocked with impala buck, dainty tan-coloured antelope with elegantly curved horns. The resident population of leopard, and occasionally in the past Etienne and his guests, kept the numbers down.

Now, thanks to Etienne's surprise bequest, Deon planned to turn Impalala into a guest farm for the growing number of Kruger Park tourists — people who wanted to shoot animals only with cameras. Over the next few weeks, Deon busied himself designing a complex of rondavels with accommodation, laundry and braai facilities, a dining room and a small supply store.

Marta sat in silence in the Impalala kitchen watching him bubble with enthusiasm. The kitchen was small and dingy with corrugated iron walls and a cooking range so old it could have had pride of place in a museum. Deon had always promised her a better house with a modern kitchen but he'd never done anything about building one. Marta didn't mind about the kitchen; she disliked cooking and the housemaid, Selina, did it all. But a house with proper brick walls would have been nice. These tin ones contracted in the cold, the metal shrieking in disbelief at the temperature differential between night and day so near to the Tropic of Capricorn. Marta, never a sound sleeper, found it disturbing.

Now she raised an eyebrow as Deon mentioned building an outdoor cinema for what he was already calling 'the game lodge guests'. She was sceptical about Deon's ability to follow through on a project and with reason, she thought, remembering the sieves and sorters stacked in one of the derelict outbuildings. Those were the legacy of her husband's interest in alluvial gold. He spent weeks up at Pilgrim's Rest, panning in the river, but he lost interest when all he found was fool's gold. Next he decided they could supplement their income with biltong. He built huge drying boxes and butchered a few impala, seasoning the meat deliciously, she thought. But every farmer in the area made biltong, so there was no market for it. He tried keeping bees and the hives now stood like an apian ghost town in a camel-thorn copse near the koppie. Then he had thought about hand-making velskoens.

Marta sighed. There was a half-built reservoir at the back of the house where Deon had started a swimming pool for Mannie, but she decided not to mention it. She was too tired for an argument and maybe, just maybe, this project would amount to something. Deon had been a very good hotel manager — when sober.

★ ★ ★

To Koba, the bushveld looked astonishingly lush. So many big-canopied, broadleaved trees — some with long, soft branches that swept to the ground, others with striking, fever-yellow trunks, one festooned with bright-red flowers, and several with fearsome-looking knobs on their grey trunks. And the grass was so high, birds were so plentiful and there was a smell of wet in the air. Here, food would hang from the trees, not hide itself underground. A shame she would not be staying.

The hill she was being taken to now looked strange, protruding up on an otherwise flat landscape. Later she would learn it was called Pasopkop — Beware Hill — and also that it reminded /Ton who lived across the sea of something called a castle. They said its summit looked like battlements. In due course she would also learn that the local Tsonga people shuddered to hear the name 'Pasopkop'. They swore the hill hid a monstrous mouth, fangs bared to the sky, and was capable of eating people.

On Koba's first sight of it, she simply thought 'Egg'. Where shell-smooth curves should have met to form an apex, she saw gnawed edges. A snout or beak had feasted on the life inside. Nothing could live up there. Certainly she couldn't. She would run away just as soon as she could.

Next to her, Marta was struggling up the

139

steep slope. 'Home,' she panted, waving her arm to indicate a view clear across the bushveld. The land was covered in bleached-blond grass high enough to hide elephants. Thorn trees poked through, opened against the sun like dark umbrellas.

'Now, I want you to understand that I'm putting you up here for your own good. It's not that you're not welcome down at the house — you are, any time — but I don't want you to lose your Bushman ways before I can take you back to your people,' she said.

'Ag, Ma, save your breath. She doesn't understand.' Mannie was worried by the exhaustion on his mother's face. 'You stop here, Ma. I'll take her.'

Marta nodded her gratitude. Her womb felt like dead-weight dragging on the muscles of her lower back. She handed Mannie a torch and a box of matches and indicated to the girl that she should follow him.

Koba pouted. She did not want anything to do with this /Ton boy. She turned her back on him and continued to mentally log her strange surroundings. The boy capered around her, gesticulating comically, rolling his eyes. He seemed to be able to make them protrude, like a frog's. She almost laughed. She watched him explain in sign language that up on the hill was a place for her to sleep. Would there be food there, she wondered? She was very hungry.

As they climbed she noted several plants that looked promising, but first she'd better find a safe place to lie. There were leopard prints here.

★　★　★

It took longer to reach the summit of the hill than it should have. Koba kept leaving the path to investigate plants, snapping leaves between her thumb and forefinger to sniff or taste them. She picked up dried buck droppings, investigated wallows and even followed a lizard hot-footing it across a sun-baked rock. Mannie began to droop in the boiling heat.

Finally they reached the top and he indicated that Koba should slip into a rocky gully, one of several that made the summit look crenellated. Koba obliged reluctantly and was surprised to see a shallow bowl of lush vegetation spread out before her — bushes of all shapes and sizes, and a wildly-contorted fig tree that had forced its way between the rocks. And there was fruit on these trees. She hurried over and plucked a wizened-looking fig. It bled a white milk onto her fingers, bitter to the tongue, but its heart was sweet when she tore into it with her teeth — too sweet for her. She threw the fruit down and looked around. Which direction did the Mother Hills lie in? She scampered along a rocky ledge that she thought might serve as a lookout.

'Girl,' Mannie shouted impatiently, 'come to the cave.'

Koba turned towards the sound. No Frog-boy. She blinked. He'd been there, just behind her, but where was he now? Intrigued, she approached the ragged line of bushes where he'd been standing. Yau, a chasm in the rock floor.

From below, Mannie saw her peer into the fissure, her body partially blocking out the sun. 'Come on. What my mother wants you to see is in here.'

Koba dropped into the cave like a cat. Mannie swept the beam around the room and then held it steady on the far wall. He heard the girl gasp and clap her hands as she caught sight of the painting. Then she was beside him, clicking ninety to the dozen and running her hands over the stick animals and people. He wasn't pleased when she snatched the torch from him, but when he realised she had tears streaming down her face, he let her keep it. He wondered if she knew why the men in the drawing had buck ears and hooves? And what did she make of the snot streaming from their noses and the sticks through the end of their willies?

Mannie pulled a box of matches out of his pocket and struck one so he could see the girl better. She was kneeling in front of the painting that his mother said was Bushman rock art. He supposed it was, seeing the excitement of the Bushgirl, her tongue click-clacking like knitting needles. But he had the feeling she wasn't talking to him but to the painting.

Mad. She kept touching her throat and blowing at the rock art like someone in church. He lit another match and three more after that so he could keep an eye on her. Ma would want a full report.

Eventually the girl sat silent in front of the painting.

'Ja-well, I should go now — Ma'll be waiting.' Mannie took the torch from her. 'Sorry, but Ma said to leave you with these.' He put the matchbox on the cave floor. 'A torch is too Western, or something.'

★ ★ ★

When he'd left, Koba pressed her forehead against the mural. As she'd expected, it didn't feel hard or rough, like rock. It was soft and slack, like the skin on her grandmother's cheek. Zuma was here, somewhere. She couldn't leave now.

Chapter 9

This land is dangerous, Koba thought to herself the next morning, as she stood on the edge of the summit warming herself in the sun. A person could sense danger in the grass that covered this land. It was the same colour as lion's fur.

Was she right not to run away, she wondered? She could leave tonight, take her chance with lions and follow the hunting star. How long would it take to get back? The metal journey had disorientated her. She'd tried to keep track of the number of sunrises-and the direction they were travelling, but the stifling air, the swaying seat and the music of the wheels had made her too sleepy for much of the time.

Now she narrowed her eyes and tried to see beyond the scrub-studded horizon. No sign of anything resembling the Mother Hills out there. She could walk and walk and walk, but if she didn't die from hunger or thirst would Zuma still be alive when she reached the ledge?

She knew the answer. Zuma was dead. How else could she have felt her in the rock last night? She must wait until her grandmother's spirit sent her a message.

In the meantime, she must eat. The flat white food Leopard-woman had given her was all gone.

Below the hill, she could see a circle of huts with thatched, conical roofs. A cooking fire burned outside some of them and black figures moved around inside a reed fence. There was no path tramped through the bush between the compound and the hill so she assumed the locals avoided the place. Would they avoid her too? Judging by the hostility of the black people on the journey, she assumed they would.

She spied a grey path leading from the huts to a /Ton house in the distance. From the hilltop it looked like a long scar in the lion's pelt. Better not walk that way either. She must find her own path while she waited for Grandmother na!'an.

★ ★ ★

Little by little Koba arranged her new home. For sleeping she cleared a flattened section of

146

cave floor, sweeping the bat droppings into a far corner with her grass bushel broom. Here she spread her mother's kaross as a sleeping mat. Next to her mat she placed two empty tortoise shells for use as food bowls. She was proud of them. Prising the shells off their live owners had been no mean feat. The big leopard tortoise had to be drowned as the horny armour of his legs proved impervious to her stabbing stick. Once it was dead, it had been a battle removing its body without damaging its shell. The little tortoise she had simply asphyxiated in her fire. It'd tried to walk away until she smothered it in hot ash and coals. It was soon baked deliciously.

Only water proved a problem. When it rained she could collect the water from various rocky hollows on the hill, but in dry spells she had to fetch her supply from the river. It was a long walk.

Koba's two most prized possessions had appeared mysteriously at the entrance to her cave one morning. One was a battered zinc bucket, which reduced the frequency of her walks to the river. The other was a pocket-knife. Koba marvelled at its folding blade and the efficacy of the small hook for opening nuts. If only Father could have seen these tools, she thought.

While she polished the blade on her pubic

apron, she considered the gift. It couldn't be hxaro or the giver would have identified themself so she could return the favour. A gift without obligation then. Must be from a person with many riches. Must be from a /Ton. Which one?

Not Leopard-woman; she gave nothing but words when they met in the veld — strange words that she repeated at Koba so often they began to crop up in her dreams. Maybe Frog-boy? He avoided her — they'd had no contact since the first day but she was aware he watched her from a distance, believing himself unseen. Ha, the /Ton. As noisy in the bush as raindrops on dried leaves. That left only the quiet /Ton as her benefactor — the one with the dragging leg. Hyena /Ton. If he'd been up here, he'd been careful not to step on the sand; she had looked for his footprints.

Koba's days were busy. She had to familiarise herself with new plants and animals, birds and insects, noting their behaviour and habitat with the eye of a born naturalist. The ones around the river were the most interesting to her. She'd heard of crocodile, from Ju/'hoan who had travelled north to the great Okavango, but she had never seen them. Now she sat for hours waiting for them to leave the water where they drifted like logs, just eyes and snouts showing. Their short, bandy legs made them so clumsy on land, but the lightning snap of their jaws made her believe quite readily that they were more dangerous even than lion. Hippo amused her with their ridiculously small ears and fat, tame animal bodies. She imagined they'd be very tasty, but how to get past their big snapping jaws? Easier by far to get the flapping silver food she secretly observed young Tsonga boys pulling from the brown water. But she would need tools like they had.

One dawn she boldly ventured to the edge of the compound where the Tsonga lived. Their refuse heap was a treasure-trove — twine and a scrap of fishing net; enough for her to learn to weave from. Now she too could pull the shining food from the river and throw it onto a fire until it turned black and smelled mouth-wateringly good.

Koba never allowed herself to be seen by the Tsonga. She was afraid of these people with their black-black skin, their loud voices and their powerful magicians.

There was a story, told around Ju/'hoansi campfires, about her father's uncle's cousin, who was cheated by a black witchdoctor. Koba's kinsman had demanded the witch-doctor pay him fairly for the cobra skin he'd brought him, but the man refused. Eventually the witchdoctor's Headman was approached and reluctantly the witchdoctor paid up. But he'd cursed the coins and from the moment the kinsman touched the money, his hand began to burn. Hot-hot pain. His hand became paralysed and though trance dances were done for him, his whole body was soon poisoned and he died. No, she did not want to be near the Tsonga. She was safer up on her hill.

Nights were the worst for Koba. She would watch her fire cast long, threatening shadows on the cave walls and she felt her unprotected back prickle. She daren't allow herself to sleep soundly. She might not hear Pawed Things coming.

On nights when she did hear the low cough of a prowling leopard, she threw logs onto her fire until the flames leapt all the way up to the roof entrance. It made the chamber very smoky but it was better than being a Pawed Thing's prey.

On very bad nights she would hide under N#aisa's kaross and smell her mother there. But she wouldn't let herself cry. Tear-time was over.

Now I must just live and live, she told herself.

One night in a dream, Koba sensed a bony

back against hers. She saw her dreaming self leap out of the cave and tear down the hillside, shouting. 'I must run-run-run til I find the metal track, then follow it back to the Mother Hills.'

'Easier to find a tear in a pool,' said a stiller Koba, floating above. Dreaming Koba ignored her and flew across moon-silvered sand until she saw the forbidden pool. Above, on the ledge, she saw bones, a neat pile; the spine intact and curved like that of a very old woman.

Koba howled then, waking herself up with cries that scared off the prowling leopard and woke tiny Tsongas tucked up in their huts. The terrified children knew then that the tales of the Tokoloshe were true. 'He lives on Pasopkop, Mamma, with the Yellow One. Maaaaa, he comes.'

Up in her cave and now fully awake, Koba felt certain that her grandmother was dead. But Zuma was not absent. Koba could feel her as certainly as if she lay cradling her bony back. Death had given her grandmother back to her. Her heart lifted and she sat up.

'Greetings, spirit of Grandmother na'an,' she said into the less-lonely darkness.

Chapter 10

'Koba, Koba!' Mannie heard his mother call. He was helping her gather a selection of spring flowers for a drawing she'd planned when they spotted Koba some distance off.

'What's 'Koba'?' he asked.

'Her name,' Marta said. 'At least, I think it is. She taps her chest and makes this 'Koba' sound every time I say 'I'm Marta'.' She strode ahead swinging her basket. ' 'Mata', she calls me — can't manage 'r', though Heaven knows why. It must be easier than those complicated clicks of hers.'

Mannie ran to catch up with his mother. 'Has she said anything else?'

Marta stopped and turned a sad face to him. 'Yes. She wants to go home. She's indicated 'home'.'

Mannie almost whooped his relief. 'So when's she going, Ma?'

'As soon as we've got money to spare, son.'

'I thought we had. From Uncle Etienne?'

'He left Pa the farm, but no money. Pa's

having to borrow from the bank to build the guest facilities. Even if he sticks with this project, it could be years before we've paid the loan back and have anything to spare.' She sighed. 'No. We're no better off than we were, I'm afraid.'

Koba reached them. She seemed to be wearing a grey, feathered scarf dotted with blue. As they got closer, they realised she had a pair of dead guinea fowl slung over her shoulders.

'I see you've already got tonight's supper. Well done, Koba.' The girl just looked at Marta solemnly. 'Er . . . I'm collecting these, see . . . ' She showed the contents of her basket. 'This red one we call 'Barbeton daisy'; the wild pear blossom you may have seen before . . . '

Koba nodded, understanding from Marta's manner that Leopard-woman was relaxed today, without the pain that put an arrow between her brows. A good time to strengthen their alliance then. She looked around for an offering for the basket. She pulled a small branch off a thorn tree, pointing to the pink and yellow catkins dangling from it.

Marta beamed at her. 'Yes! Yes, sickle bush, dichrostachys cinerea — dichrostachys because of its two colours.' She saw but ignored her son's grimace — she'd have a word later. 'The Tsonga people call this plant 'tassles for the chief's hat' . . . '

'Muti,' Koba said and made her forearm rear up with her hand cupped like a spitting cobra.

'Oh, for snakebites. Yes, yes, I understand.' To her son, Marta said, 'She'll know all sorts of plant remedies. And I bet she could teach you to snare guinea fowl too.'

Like I need some blerry girl to teach me, Mannie thought. Marta noted his scowl. 'Ag, these feet of mine. I must sit down. Let's find a pretty place next to the river.'

They didn't have far to walk. Once Marta had scanned the mahogany tree canopy to ensure it was leopard-free, they settled in its shade. Mannie fiddled sulkily with a thick, woody pod he'd found. He split it in two, exposing pithy compartments for the eight scarlet, black-tipped seeds.

His mother prodded him gently with her toe. 'Show her,' she said.

Reluctantly he handed a seed to Koba. Marta prodded him again. 'Lucky bean,' he muttered.

Koba turned the seed over in her yellow palm. It was a pretty thing and would look good on a necklace. She ignored the surly boy and began collecting pods for herself.

Marta let them get on with ignoring each other. They'd be friends in time. There were green shoots piercing through the earth, flame creeper cascading down the riverbank and pink in her son's cheeks. First time he's looked well since that hunting trip, she thought. And Koba too — skin glowing, clear eyes, no bald patches in her cap of woolly hair. Her diet must be good, thank God. It was hard resisting the urge to feed her from their table, especially when Deon kept questioning her decision.

★ ★ ★

They'd been sitting around the kitchen table, the atmosphere between them still tense. Selina, their maid, was clearing up. She'd remarked that the Tsonga on the farm weren't happy about having the 'Yellow One' around but Marta said nothing.

'It's true,' Deon said. 'Having a wild child dressed in skins, hunting for food in this day and age is damn funny. What were you thinking of, bringing her here? I mean, she could end up being a tourist attraction.'

Marta flushed with fury. 'Do you seriously think I would allow that? Can't you see I'm simply trying to do the right thing for the little girl? Have you forgotten how much this

155

family owes her?' She looked at Deon, green eyes glittering like emeralds in the shaft of a drawn dagger. Selina scuttled from the room as fast as her enormous bulk would allow and Deon stared down at the table-top, his thin face pale. Marta tried to keep her anger in check; agitation might be bad for the baby. 'I think the right thing for Koba is for us to ensure she doesn't lose her Khoisan ways before we can take her home.'

Deon pushed his chair back. 'Take her home, hey? And what are we going to use for the train fare? The building's taking every penny we've got . . . and plenty that we haven't.'

Her lips taut with the effort of speaking calmly, Marta replied, 'But eventually . . . '

'Eventually she'll become a miserable, tame Bushman just like the ones on Sukses.' Deon stood up. 'Face it, Marta. You may as well put her in a doek and let her start living with the Tsonga. At least she could do some work around here.'

Marta faced him across the table. 'No! She is not a servant. It won't cost us a penny to keep her; she'll be totally self-sufficient, you'll see. Her people have been living off land a lot less abundant in food and water than we've got here. And they've survived. For thousands of years. She'll adapt. She's a Bushman.'

156

'She's a child.'

Marta's resolve had wavered then. But she had to be strong, for the girl's sake. 'You leave her welfare to me. I'll make a plan just as soon as the baby's born.'

That afternoon she sat down and wrote to a publisher of books on wild South African flowers. She sent them some of her drawings and asked about the possibility of a commission. If she got work, the money could go towards Koba's train fare. She knew Deon would contribute what he could when things calmed down. His bark was far worse than his bite. And even the bark was easier to bear, she admitted to herself, now that he was so involved with the building project.

★　★　★

Back on the riverbank, Marta thought idly about writing to the publisher again. It was two weeks since she'd sent off her samples. Perhaps they'd got lost in the post? Ja, she must see to it before the baby came.

She pulled two oranges from her pockets and peeled them. She handed one to each child in turn.

Koba sniffed hers. Yau, delicious-smelling! Without bothering to break it into segments, she bit into the orange ball. Yau-yau-yau! This was like monkey orange but much, much better. Juicy, tart and meaty, all at the same time. She let the juice run down her chin, over her hands and along her forearms as she pushed the fruit into her mouth with both hands. Her cheeks bulged and her eyes watered with the effort of chewing and swallowing such a mouthful.

Mannie began to laugh.

'Manfred,' Marta growled, then sweetly to Koba, 'Have another orange.'

Koba peeled it, seething. Frog-boy had laughed at her. How dare he, he who had plenty-plenty and family. Taking a careful aim, she bent a segment between her thumb and forefinger and pressed. As she'd antici-pated, this /Ton orange worked even better than monkey orange. Frog-boy winced and began rubbing his eye. Good, Koba thought. That would make it sting more.

'Koba,' Marta gasped, 'you did that on purpose!' Koba laughed, exposing unchewed orange chunks in her mouth.

In response, Mannie leant over and with both hands shoved the annoying Bushgirl in the chest.

Koba hadn't spent years wrestling other boys and girls in camp without learning something. She grabbed his hands and rolled backwards, pulling him off balance.

'Stop it, stop it, you two!' But the fight was

on as the children locked together, Mannie grunting, Koba hissing, as they tussled in the dirt, rolling down the riverbank and landing in a pool with a double splash.

'Crocodiles!' Marta shrieked, scrambling down after them. But she could see the water was too shallow to hide a large reptile.

The children looked sheepish as she scolded them. Then, stealing a sidelong look at each other, they grinned.

Marta couldn't help noticing how they sat, arms almost touching — brown indistinguishable from white because of the mud.

* * *

Marta winced. A strong contraction, if that's what it was. She still had weeks to carry this baby, surely? She fiddled with the blank paper in front of her and decided she should draw. The flowers were wilting. But her hands were swollen — she'd be unwieldy with a pencil or paintbrush. Her stomach felt hollow as though she was famished but she couldn't face the thought of food. She was too nauseous. She stood up, bent forward to relieve the discomfort in her back and sat down again but couldn't settle.

I'm like a pregnant bitch trying to find a place to pup, she thought. Maybe I've got my date wrong?

She then became conscious of a wetness between her thighs. Waters breaking? She grabbed a tea-towel, shoved it up her skirt and dabbed. A rosy-coloured stain. Here it goes, she thought, with rising excitement. Not long now and she'd meet her; it is a her, she just knew it.

★ ★ ★

Hours and the agony of numerous contractions later, Marta was alarmed to see the sheet she'd put down was stained with a greeny-black mucus. Myconium? Her contractions were still more than ten minutes apart. The baby was in distress.

She lurched to the bedroom door and shouted to Mannie, who was playing marbles in the passage, 'Please, please, fetch Pa. Quickly, son.'

★ ★ ★

A week later, Koba saw Mannie standing next to a small, newly-dug grave. He was quivering like a sapling in a stiff breeze. So, Leopard-woman's baby, Koba thought. She crept away. It was bad where he was standing, downwind from the graves. The death spirit would blow onto him and make him sick.

160

Perhaps Frog-boy was already sick? He looked thin, with frightened eyes.

But where was Leopard-woman? Koba hadn't seen her about. Only Hyena/Ton and he no longer whistled as he worked with the men building huts. Koba began to worry that 'Mata' might be sick somewhere and soon another, bigger grave would appear. How then would she ever get back home?

The girl climbed the jackalberry tree. It gave her a view of the small cemetery. She watched the boy. His skin was paler as if he hadn't been outside in the sun as much. Was he tending his sick mother? Koba felt a stab of guilt. She'd known the Leopard-woman would do badly with the baby. She'd even told Zuma of her fears. Her grandmother had pointed out that there was nothing she could do about it. The girl-baby was too weak for the world.

Seeing the boy looking so forlorn, Koba decided being /Ton must be lonely. They lived in such small groups and kept too much to themselves. From what she saw, a /Ton child had only one mother and father. Ju/'hoansi children had a whole tribe full. When the women and children had gone out foraging, she, as a toddler, had been as comfortable in the sling of an aunt or a cousin as in that of her own mother. If she was tired or hurt or just sad, she could turn to any adult or older child in her n/ore for comfort — even when she was far too big to be carried. And with Grandmother never far away, she almost didn't need N#aisa.

An emerald-spotted wood-dove called across the veld, a mournful arpeggio of notes that Koba remembered her grandmother saying was a lament for dead children. The girl shook herself out of her reverie. It was the /Ton's fault that she had no mother and was even lonelier than they were in this ugly place. Why was she wasting pity on them?

She climbed down from the tree so fast she took some skin off her shin. As she set off across the veld she heard the wood-dove call again. This time she was sure the bird sang that it wasn't Frog-boy's fault her parents were dead.

Koba shrugged. She still didn't like him but it would do no harm to keep him near her eye.

★　★　★

It wasn't difficult. The next morning, Mannie began following her as she foraged. She paused, idly kneeling to lick a rock as she allowed him to catch up. His shadow fell across her.

'What you doing?' he asked.

She thought she understood. She tried a Mata-word, 'Taste.' She indicated the white deposit on the grey stone.

'What is it?'

She scraped a bit off with her nail. 'Ihn,' she said, offering salt to him. He dabbed some onto the tip of his tongue, then spat. Koba laughed. Mannie scowled.

'You don't need to lick it off rocks, you know. There's an earthworks for salt nearby. The Tsonga have been working it since the olden days.' He stopped. The girl had understood little of what he said. 'Listen,' he tried again, 'you like?' He indicated the deposit. Koba nodded vigorously. 'If I bring you salt, will you give me honey?'

Koba understood the /Ton word 'honey'. Getting it was no problem on Impalala, unlike in the Kalahari. There, unraided hives were scarce. Here, a honeyguide would often land on a branch in front of her, making its rattling 'Quick-quick, honey-quick' call. It would flutter, agitating for her attention, then fly off low, trying to lead her in the direction of a hive. Sometimes she'd follow and smoke the bees out, just to please the bird. It was a long task, best done in the early morning when the bees were immobile due to the cold, but even so, a few stings were inevitable.

Though she didn't like honey, she'd chew on a lump of beeswax, remembering how fond her father had been of it. Tami would be proud to see how well she'd managed to clear a hive, how she remembered to reward the bird. It liked the bee larvae in the wax so she always tossed the lumps towards the honeyguide afterwards.

Tami had told the story of old Dàbè, a greedy man, who ate all the beeswax, leaving the bird only liquid. On his way home Dàbè had stepped on a puff-adder. That was the last time he was able to climb a tree to steal honey.

Koba cocked her head, considering Mannie's proposition. Plentiful salt was worth a few bites from the buzzings.

★ ★ ★

A few days later she handed over a large shellful of honey. She watched Mannie plunge two fingers into the shell, snatching at the dripping liquid with his mouth, then closing his eyes as he sucked his fingers clean. Quickly he opened them again. 'Sorry.' He held out the shell. 'Did you want some?'

She shook her head.

★ ★ ★

164

Soon the children were bartering not just salt and honey, but anything Mannie could spirit away from the farmhouse — a blanket for some crocodile eggs, the tiny reptiles living and squeaking inside them, a matchbox for a puff-adder skin, a tin mug for an evening around Koba's fire. They gave each other things of little value to themselves, never guessing how much the other prized the gift.

* ⋆ *

'Ma's back from the hospital. She won't come out of her room, though. Will you come see her? Pa says you might cheer her up.'

Koba understood the gist of Mannie's request, but more interesting to her was the cost to him of making it. He could not meet her eyes and his fingers twisted the corner of his sand-coloured shirt. She knew he'd resented any time his mother spent with her. Often he'd hovered between her and Mata, twittering like a honeyguide, trying to distract when she spoke to the /Ton woman. Now he was begging her to see the woman.

'If you come I'll give you watermelon — that pink food.' Koba pulled a face. She'd tried it — much too sweet for her.

'I know,' Mannie's face lit up, 'I'll give you an avocado pear. We've got a tree at the back

165

of the house. I'll find a ripe one. Avos are delicious with salt. You'll love it. But you must come to the house.'

★ ★ ★

Koba hesitated on the threshold leading to the farmhouse door. Was it safe to go into this /Ton place? It was as dark as a cave but it stank. A pungent, waxy smell but not from real bees. And there was the big black woman who always glared at her, on her hands and knees rubbing the floor. Yau, it was her making the horrible smell with that paste from her pot. Was that avocado? She wasn't going to eat that.

'Come on,' Frog-boy called from the gloom.

Koba stepped inside, not looking at the big, black woman.

Selina stopped polishing and sat back on her wide haunches, staring at the Bushgirl. Perhaps the Yellow One was as mad as was whispered in the kraal? Ancestors-only-knew what her husband, Gideon, would say when he got back from the mines. He always had a fund of MaSarwa stories, telling tales of the old days when MaSarwa's poison arrows killed Tsonga. Huw, the white people were mad to invite this dangerous person into their

166

home. She shook her head and went back to her buffing.

Deon appeared from the bedroom door. 'It's all right. Don't be afraid,' he said, taking Koba's hand and leading her into Marta's room.

Koba was surprised by the sight of the /Ton woman, thick-necked, puffy-faced, as though stung by a swarm of bees. She had a tiny pink garment clutched to her chest.

She is so-so white, even her spots have paled away, Koba thought. And the bright has gone from her hair. This is not Leopard-woman.

Marta stared at Koba as though she couldn't remember who she was. Koba took the opportunity to look around the room; she saw zebra stripes where sunlight sneaked through the shutters, saw a roof sky-high above her head, saw a sleeping place with four clawed feet she knew would give her nightmares. The room smelled of sweet, sick and sadness. She winced as Deon crossed to the door, making the floorboards shout.

'Make yourself comfortable,' he said, pointing to a chair wearing the hide of a tame animal. Then he left the room.

Koba heard the bed groan as Marta turned in it.

'He blames me, you know. He hasn't said so, but I can tell from the way he looks at

167

me.' She struggled up onto one elbow and glared through a tangle of wilted-looking hair. 'I don't need him to make me feel guilty. I'm sick with it.' She flopped back and lay staring at the ceiling.

Koba wondered what she should do. Most of Mata's words were a mystery to her — too strange, too fast, as though the /Ton woman had bad spirits controlling her tongue. There should be a medicine dance for her. A n/omkxaosi should trance and drive out the pain.

'I was careless,' Marta's voice was low. 'There were signs — I ignored them.' She shifted her legs irritably under the covers. 'Well, I'm not a midwife and there was so much going on: Etienne's accident,' she sat up again and almost smiled, 'finding you and getting you settled here. What were a few headaches, some foot swelling? The doctor said it wasn't my fault. She'd have died anyway. But that doesn't help . . . ' Marta lay slowly back. After a silence in which the loudest sound was that of a bluebottle trapped between the insect netting and the window, she began to cry.

Koba settled herself down on the floor. Grief she knew about; it needed accompaniment. She began a mournful 'Ehay-oh,' like a descant to Marta's sobbing, but she did not look at the woman. Her role was not to see.

Now was the time to help the woman bear a burden.

Time passed. Koba rocked, crooned and kept up her hypnotic chorus, never varying the pace or the volume until Marta quietened.

Eventually, Marta sat up, smoothed her hair off her face and looked at Koba, lucidly. 'The baby, Ingrid, would have been good for Deon and me. Now, I don't know what will happen . . . ' A long, shuddering sigh. 'I wanted that baby so badly I even taught myself to knit!'

Marta reached for the pink matinee jacket, laughing unnaturally. 'I'm all thumbs when it comes to housewifely skills, you know. Selina does the cooking. The mending . . . ' She shrugged, smiling ruefully, 'Well, you saw how I struggled with your kaross. I grew up without a mother to show me these things, you see. But I knew the baby was a girl so I bought a pattern and some pink wool . . . ' She held the miniature jacket up, 'Too ambitious for a beginner, this cable, but I thought I'd be able to work it out. Selina taught me the basics, knit one, purl one, but she was baffled by a pattern.

'I should have gone to the woman in the wool shop, asked for her help. But I was shy. She's a real 'Women's Federation' type

169

— you know, very traditional. Well, I felt ashamed about admitting I couldn't knit. All the women around here can. They still sew shirts for their husbands and bake for the church fête.'

Koba shifted her weight from left haunch to right. Her eyes wandered across the flower-patterned wall behind Marta's head.

'I'm sorry,' Marta slapped her fingers over her bloodless mouth. She was talking too much and to a person who couldn't be expected to understand her.

Of course she'd thought of talking to Deon but had found it impossible, despite his solicitude — all that plumping up of her pillows, spooning broth between her lips, fresh flowers on the dressing table — and all the time his heart was breaking. She just wasn't strong enough to support his grief too. She felt her lip tremble and knew she was going to cry from self-pity.

Koba came over to the bed and picked up the matinee jacket. 'Good,' she said solemnly.

Marta blinked. A word, an Afrikaans word. She swallowed, blew her nose and dried her eyes. Automatically, she began to braid her dishevelled hair, thinking of all the things she could teach Koba now.

The girl watched, fascinated. Hesitantly, she put out her hand to touch the plait.

Marta held it out to her. Koba fingered the silky tip. It was softer than she'd expected. Not like grass at all. And she could see strands of silver where there had been gold. She dropped the braid and stepped back, smiling sadly at Marta.

On her way out of the house, Mannie thrust an avocado pear into her hand and some salt in a twist of paper.

★ ★ ★

After that day Koba often went to the house and sat with Marta. She wandered around the room as Marta spoke, looking at things, touching them as she became bolder — the soft mattress she longed to lie on, the bed linen whose fineness she liked to feel. Marta's tortoise-shell hairbrush amused her but most marvellous of all was the mirror on the dressing table. She stared into it for hours, pulling faces, checking views of herself in the left and right wing mirrors.

Marta didn't mind talking to the back of her head. There was freedom in being heard by someone who didn't understand and who wasn't sufficiently interested to try to. So she relaxed and made Koba privy to her most contradictory, illogical and even ungenerous thoughts. It made her feel better. Slowly, mad grief ebbed away. She became less self-absorbed, began to ask questions Koba could understand — about veld food, weather and animals. A stilted dialogue began.

Later, when Marta was well enough to receive Koba in the kitchen, the girl's greatest delight was turning the tap on and off. Yau, to have the power to summon water with the twist of a wrist, she thought. She shoved her whole head under the gushing stream, slurping ecstatically at the cool water and emerging with a tiara of liquid diamonds.

Marta touched the 'tiara's' springiness and laughed, surprised there were still things that gave her pleasure.

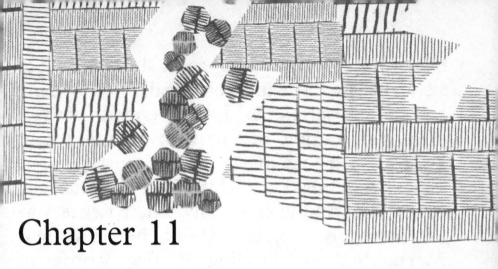

Chapter 11

Summer was almost over by the time Marta felt well enough to sit outside. Deon placed a wicker chair in the deep shade cast by the old avocado tree and helped her to it. She leaned comfortably against him. Strange how her weakness had seemed to give him strength, she thought. It was as though Ingrid's death had sobered him up, permanently.

He settled her in the chair and left. As she watched him move from the shade into the bright sunshine she realised that the change had probably begun with Etienne's death; she'd just been too distracted to notice.

She gazed into the canopy of the old avocado tree nearby. It was older than the house, grew higher than the wind pump and was home to a colony of weaver birds. Hundreds of them. Every branch was festooned with their pear-shaped nests.

Marta had planned to write to Lettie that afternoon. She'd received a rare letter from her sister-in-law — was she still her sister-in-law, Marta wondered? — offering her commiserations. Lettie ended with a postscript urging her to bear in mind that grief was very ageing.

Marta chuckled. But how could she respond tactfully, especially when Lettie was so obviously worried about her son and Marta had the feeling a few words of reassurance would be very welcome. The trouble was, she didn't think André would grow out of what his mother called his 'wildness'. The boy was a brute and it could only get worse now that he had power.

She sighed. She didn't feel up to being diplomatic yet. She preferred to just sit and think, about Koba mostly.

Perhaps Deon was right? Perhaps she shouldn't keep Koba separate from everyone? But her wildness was special. Marta felt it gave the child an insight into nature that others had long lost.

She flapped irritably at a fly circling her head. Deon had accused her of treating Koba like something from a 'Tarzan' film — a noble savage. That was nonsense of course. If anything, she was probably treating Koba more like one of them, like a daughter perhaps.

Was that why Mannie had seemed so

resentful when she'd mentioned at supper last night that she'd started teaching Koba to read?

'I thought you didn't want to spoil her,' Mannie had snapped.

Feeling too fragile for confrontation she let his impudence go. 'Well, I've been thinking that perhaps Koba was sent to us for a reason; perhaps I'm meant to educate her, get her used to Western ways. Then send her back to her people equipped to help them.' She smiled cajolingly at the two men. 'You see, I'm beginning to agree with Pa that the Khoisan can't stay untouched by civilisation for ever, even out in the desert. Soooo,' she wound a strand of hair around her finger 'wouldn't it be better if one of their own becomes familiar with Western ways and then goes back to help them . . . '

Marta had caught Deon and Mannie rolling their eyes at each other.

She found she was envious of the new closeness between them. She'd seen how Mannie sought Deon out first when he got back from school. She watched them walk around the building site together, talking and laughing. Mannie never said what they discussed. For her, Mannie kept the stories of his school day: what book they were reading, what the little vixen, Katrina Botha, from the farm next-door had got up to on the school bus.

Marta found her most relaxing times were with Koba, reading stories to the girl from one of Mannie's fairytale books or hearing Ju/'hoansi myths told in Koba's soft vernacular. The extraordinary range of click sounds she used were almost as fascinating to Marta as the girl's skilful imitation of the animals who peopled her stories.

Deon came into view. He had instructions for the labourers. They gathered around, cheerful and willing. Even they seemed to respect this new Deon, Marta noted. He was friendly but authoritative. Despite his crippled leg, she'd watched him match them brick for brick as they laid the foundations of the guest lodge. Three rondavels were roof height already. Soon the Tsonga women would cut the grass and begin thatching them.

Marta felt something fall lightly onto her shoulder — a long strand of straw. No doubt dropped by one of the feathered maintenance men working nearby. She watched a handsome male bird, vibrantly yellow but for its black mask, making exacting adjustments to the weave of his nest.

Just like Deon. She smiled.

Then she had an idea. What if she offered

to weave Koba's hair into one of those elaborate styles she'd glimpsed on the heads of the Tsonga women when their doeks slipped?

Now she thought about it, she realised Koba might well have a problem with her hair. The child had taken to wearing an old woolly cap she could only have found in a rubbish heap somewhere. It was full of holes and hardly yellow anymore. She had longed to snatch it off her pretty head. It made Koba look so poor and — Marta cast around for the word — neglected.

Yes, that was it! Ever since the child had taken to wearing the hat and a pair of Mannie's old shorts — where had she got *them*? — she'd started looking scruffy. And like a boy, despite the breast buds.

She shifted uncomfortably in her chair. The thing was though, would Koba want to have her hair braided?

Marta couldn't remember ever seeing a Khoisan woman with an elaborately woven hairstyle but she did recall that they didn't tend to cover their heads like other African women; their hair was always close-cropped, showing off their beautifully shaped heads. Was Koba covering hers because her hair had grown too long and she had no way of cutting it?

Oh God. Marta dropped her head into her hands. She'd been so stupid. So blind. Yes, the child was Khoisan — Ju/'hoansi was her tribe, Marta had now learned — but first she was a girl, a young teenage girl, who cared about the way she looked and would want to fit in. She needed scissors, a mirror and a bath!

How could I have been so toe, Marta thought? And what could she do to make it up to Koba? She stood up and began to pace. She could buy Kobatjie some clothes. A skirt and a few blouses. Ja, but was that practical for bundu-bashing? Wait. Why did Koba have to live in the bush? Why couldn't she move into the spare bedroom?

Marta hurried inside as fast as she was able to start preparing the room.

★ ★ ★

As she worked she remembered a bitter exchange with Deon on Koba's first day at the farm. 'I thought Pasopkop would be the place for her,' she'd said as Deon and Mannie unloaded their travel bags.

'You mean make her live in a cave?'

'It's got the painting!'

'Well, that's alright then. Rock art should keep her nice and cosy.'

178

'Well, what do you suggest then?' Marta asked through clenched teeth.

'Put her in the kraal with Selina-and-them.'

'You know, you Boere amaze me. You live in a land you think you belong to, but you don't even know the first thing about it. Let me put it in words you'll understand: Kaffirs don't like Boesmanne; Boesmanne are frightened of Kaffirs. Boesmanne and kaffirs don't like Boers . . . '

Deon threw a suitcase violently out of the back of the truck. It landed on the drive with a thud of red dust. 'Put her in the blerry kitchen then,' he shouted.

'Like a dog, to sleep in front of the stove?' Marta retorted.

He jumped down clumsily from the truck bed. 'Not like a dog,' he snarled. Taking Marta's arm, he steered her away from the onlookers who had gathered outside the servants' compound. 'I thought we brought her here so we could improve her situation. She needs food, clothes, education — a name, just for starters.'

'Something nice and Christian, I suppose?'

'Jissus, woman! I don't care what you call her. Anything man, just something to make her seem more human, more normal — so she can fit in.'

Marta yanked her arm from his grip. 'Did

it ever occur to you that she might have a name — a perfectly good Khoisan one?'

'I'm sure she has, but how the blerry-hell are you going to find out what it is?'

* * *

Room ready, Marta set off to find Koba. The girl was up the jackalberry tree, balanced on a branch metres above the ground. She was wearing Mannie's cast-offs and her woolly hat. 'Be careful, child,' Marta said as she watched Koba clamber carelessly down. The girl had a handful of yellow-purplish fruits in her hand. 'Those any good for eating?'

Koba shrugged and dropped them into her kaross, tied like a sling over one shoulder. It was lumpy with bits of bark and roots she had gathered earlier. She also had a chipped enamel mug Marta recognised as one she'd thrown out. She looked away, embarrassed.

Koba waited. Something was in Mata's heart, she could tell. She hoped the listening wouldn't take long. She wanted to collect some jacket plums before nightfall. She fidgeted with her sling, waited a few more moments, then said, 'I go.'

'Wait,' Marta knelt down with a suddenness that startled Koba. 'Would you like to move in with us? I mean, into the house? We

180

could get some nice clothes and I could do your hair.' She pulled the cap off Koba's head. A bush of hair sprang free, dusty and matted. Tenderly she touched it.

Koba immediately grabbed for the cap and pulled it back onto her head. What did Mata think she was doing?

'Koba, I think I was wrong before, trying to make you live like a Ju/'hoansi. Come and live in our n/ore.'

Understanding then dawned on Koba. Mata wanted her to leave the cave and she wanted to do something to her hair. She touched it self-consciously. It needed shaving but without a blade and someone to help her . . . she didn't like to ask Frog-boy for these things; she wasn't sure why.

But suddenly she knew she didn't want this woman's help. The cave was hers, a place she'd made her own — with difficulty. Her hair was her own. Something she would rather have had help with, but not from /Ton. They had taken her mother, her father, her n/ore, and now Mata wanted her Ju/'hoan skin too. Leopard-woman wanted to eat her up, in her own lair.

NO! No-and-No! They'd taken enough from her. She hated them. How could she have forgotten? Now she must show them, once and for all, how she despised them. She turned her back on Marta, pulled her shorts down and thrust her naked bottom in Marta's face. Then she pulled them up and, grabbing her sling, stormed off across the veld.

Chapter 12

A year later, when Koba tried to recall landscape details from her home in the desert, she felt it was like peering through the silver shimmer of a heatwave. Even massive baobab trees she'd sat under for hours listening to Zuma's stories seemed spectral now. All she remembered was searing, paler sky and the sun's yellow whited-out as the desert baked and burned. Her memories of the Kalahari were becoming dimmer every day but she could still picture small black figures undulating across the sand dunes.

The trouble was, the longer she looked, the quicker they seemed to evaporate. How much longer would they be with her, she wondered?

Somewhere, far off across the veld, an emerald-spotted wood dove mourned.

Don't cry; you can fly away, Koba thought. She watched a drongo land on a nearby sweet thorn, its two-pronged tail bobbing for balance as it avoided impaling itself on the long white thorns. That, she knew, was the thing to do.

'I must just live and live among dangerous things until it becomes easy,' she said to Zuma that night in the cave. She stared at the mural. Soon the figures would dance with life borrowed from the fire. In the flickerings, giraffe would lope across the wall, dancers would disappear into the obscurity of the shadows, only to be licked into life again by the fire's tongues. This was a beautiful painting — even better than the one at the Forbidden Pool. She loved the patterns scratched into the rock — lines crossing as in a fishing net or hexagoned like honeycomb. They reminded her of the pictures she'd seen behind her eyelids when Grandmother gave her gwa.

It was bitter and made her retch but her grandmother said she must eat the root. It would help her to trance. She hadn't gone into a proper trance — for that she would need training and a drum-dance — but she had trembled and sweated and seen the patterns. It comforted her to think people had seen the same patterns in trance since the time of the Early Race. If only there had been time for Zuma to continue with her trance training. Who would teach her now?

She dropped a piece of animal fat onto the smooth stone in the middle of the fire. It sizzled before she smothered it with the clammy cold of the fish she had caught. She smelt the fish beginning to cook. For once, the aroma did not please her. She was hungry for real meat. All she ate on the farm was white meat: hare, tortoise and fish. Her stomach craved the satisfaction of gorging on the red meat of something with hooves. Like the swift buck she'd sometimes glimpsed, mostly beyond the high fence at the edge of the farm. She had seen one like it in the Kalahari, but not the same. The one from her n/ore had a black face. People said its meat was good. She'd like to catch this buck — impala, Mannie called it — but how? The little snares she could set wouldn't trap it.

No, she thought, the impala must be shot with a poison arrow and tracked until it drops. She had no arrows and, anyway, it was forbidden for females and children to touch hunting tools.

As Koba picked the fish from the bones, she thought about metal. It could be fashioned into arrowheads. She tossed the fish skeleton into the flames and wiped her fingers on her bare thighs. Koba began to plan her weapon-making. If she could cut off a piece of metal from a fence, if she could find a cutting tool strong enough, she could melt and shape it into arrowheads. She'd seen her father do it. And what was so difficult about making a bow? She already knew where a tree with just the right switches grew. She'd cut one, carve and smooth it, then heat it in hot sand so it would curve more easily across her knees. She'd decorate her bow. It must be beautiful.

She grabbed her knife and began sharpening its blade against the hard heel of her foot. The only problem, she reflected, was the taboo. Would pains pierce her if she made an arrowhead? Would she fall down dead? Women could make arrows, Zuma had been skilled at it, but they and children should not touch arrowheads. There was magic in them only for men, her father had said.

Then she remembered her mother talking with awe about a woman who hunted. This woman lived near the Makgadikgadi pans, according to N#aisa. She had a lazy husband and her craving for meat was strong so she taught herself to hunt.

'She grew fat and sleek,' N#aisa had said. 'Her husband too!'

Koba remembered her mother laughing at that and saying nothing bad happened to the hunting woman.

Was it perhaps because the woman didn't

believe the taboo magic, Koba wondered?

'Neither do I!' she suddenly shouted out loud.

She then found herself with a clear memory, of the delirious excitement that had greeted anyone who walked into the camp with a buck slung around their shoulders. Along with the other children she had scampered before the hero, whooping with excitement, jumping up to sniff the carcass, yapping and scrapping with playmates like a hungry puppy. The old people hobbled from their huts, querulous voices raised to remind the hunter of a favour owed. People stood about, salivating, while they speculated about the division of the dripping, red meat. And after bellies were full, people with faces greasy from the feast sat at the hunter's fire and begged him to tell of the chase.

It would be a fine thing to be so admired, she thought, but who will I tell hunting stories to?

★ ★ ★

Winter left the veld bleached, but not bald, thanks to Deon's veld fire vigilance. There was little water in the river now and even the thorn trees looked bare except for the odd, tenacious corkscrew pod.

187

The holidays came and Mannie had whole days to spend with Koba. She was glad — it was company. She chattered like a vervet, giving him instructions in his own language as he helped her hammer out arrowheads from bits of metal that she'd cut from the fence with a borrowed wire-cutter. She spoke of a Kalahari beetle whose pupae contained the poison needed for the arrow tip.

'Ja, but where will we find one?'

'None here, arrow must kill alone,' she said, noting with satisfaction his intense interest.

They spent many hours practicing their stalking and shooting skills, with Mannie eager for instruction.

Zuma, garrulous in the cave that night, was the only obstacle. 'You must keep the Ju/'hoan traditions,' Koba heard her urge.

'But if women can make arrows, why not hunt Grandmother na/'an?'

'They do not make arrow-tips, as you do. It is forbidden for women or children to go near a meat-bringer tipped with poison.'

'My meat-bringer has no poison!' Koba crowed.

'Then how will you ask the meat-animal to die for you?'

'Quickly. My sharp-sharp arrow will go straight into its heart.'

'Uhn-uhn. Still you run like an eland with its head down. You will fall, Koba. Listen to me: sure as no-rain, you will return to our n/ore. If you have forgotten your skin, people will refuse you.'

Koba returned to her sharpening. She didn't have to listen to whispered words.

★　★　★

One afternoon Koba decided that she and Frog-boy were ready to hunt a buck. They set off, Koba carrying a quiver full of arrows, Mannie with a long, sharpened stick. The pale soles of Koba's feet kicked up dust as she trotted in front of him. Mannie coughed.

'Quiet,' Koba hissed. 'Walk like a hunter or never have full stomach like one.'

'Kkek-kek-kek-krrr' suddenly sounded — the alarm call of guinea fowl. The birds fled in a flurry of blue-grey, announcing the presence of intruders.

After an hour without spotting any impala, Koba suggested they crawl through the fence and into Kruger Park.

'It's not right to hunt there. It's a Reserve. Anyway, it's against the law. If they catch us we'll go to prison for poaching,' Mannie responded.

'Prison! G//aoan gave animals to feed

people,' she replied.

'The ones in this Reserve are not for eating.'

'Hhn! Does the /Ton of this big fence think all animals there belong to him?'

'No, they belong to everyone. But they're only for looking at — so that people can appreciate them.'

Koba placed her hands on her slim hips. 'Don't I know their beauty?' She then thought about how the fluffy white undersides of impala tails reminded her of thorn tree blossom and how graceful the backward curve of the ram's horns were. Just because she couldn't express it in the /Ton language didn't mean she didn't appreciate these things. She swiped viciously at the tassled heads of the surrounding grass with an arrow. 'My people always-always love the animals we hunt,' she said mutinously.

'I know, I understand, okay?'

'What must I eat when my heart needs red meat?'

Mannie shrugged. 'Listen, we can hunt anything we find on this farm, but I can't go in there, okay? If you go, don't tell me about it.'

Koba shook her head. Truly /Ton were strange. Did they really believe that what their eyes did not see wouldn't hurt their hearts? Well, if the crazy Frog-boy wanted to hunt on the farm, she would take him on a trail he'd wish he'd never been on.

Koba set off at speed towards the densest thicket of thorn she could see. 'In there we will find a spoor,' she shouted. When they got there, she sat down with her back against an abandoned termite mound and directed him towards the thicket. 'Call when you find.'

★   ★   ★

To Koba's surprise he did find something in the thicket. Or it found him. A warthog sow disturbed by Mannie's crashing and cursing, stormed out.

'Quick, quick!' Koba scrambled up.

They couldn't keep pace with the sow as it bulldozed through bushes, but its tracks led them to a burrow in an earthbank.

'She got away,' Mannie moaned, flinging his stick down.

'Yau, you hunt like a man with a meat-tired stomach. This pig is full of fat. We can get her out. Be ready.' She handed him her quiver and took his spear. 'Warts-on-the-face, we come!'

She climbed the earthbank and began to plunge the spear into the sand. At first there was no sound apart from Koba's grunts as she struggled to withdraw the weapon from the earth. Then, after a particularly vicious jab, they heard a muffled squeal. 'She comes now,' she called down to Mannie. 'Be careful! Tusks like lion's teeth. Sharp on sides too.'

The warthog suddenly bulleted out of the burrow, mane bristling, tail aerial, its eyes murderous as they darted about looking for its tormentor.

Mannie had a clear view of the lethal tusks and the warty mound under the eye that focused on him. But he stood transfixed, bow drawn, his arrow immobilised in the grip of his petrified fingers.

'Shoot, shoot!' Koba shouted but all Mannie could do was jump to one side as the warthog slashed, ripping the hide of his boot but miraculously missing his skin. As the animal spun round in a fury, Koba let fly with her spear. It pierced the porcine flank and diverted the animal's attention. It squealed and then, with no change to its barrelling pace, swung in Koba's direction.

Mannie saw her look for a tree. The big marula was too far away. Almost in a dream Mannie went through the aiming ritual Koba had taught him. 'Look up — is the arrow's path clear?' He adjusted the trajectory to miss a branch. 'Stand still — the prey's ears must flap-flap in peace, not be raised because it hears you coming.' Too late! 'Look steady — hit heart or legs so the animal cannot run too far.' 'Arm soft, wrist soft, don't skew.' Mannie released the arrow. 'Watch where it hits.'

Mannie did not see his arrow fly through the air. Nor did he see it sink into the rugose brown chest. He was therefore surprised when the animal stumbled to its calloused knees a few feet short of Koba.

He ran forward and reaching the animal began hacking at its still-pulsating throat. Was that his guffaw that greeted the warthog's last grunt? Could that be him scampering around the body to hug Koba, giggling when he squelched in sand soggy with blood? Was the flushed, blood-spattered boy posing with his foot on his quarry really him?

'Now you can bring meat home, you can take a wife,' Koba teased as they dragged the hog to camp. Mannie bubbled with joy and jokes as they skinned and gutted it. While Koba roasted a portion of ribs, Mannie lazed bare-chested in the sun. When they ate he chattered with his mouth full, spattering gristle onto his sun-warmed skin. Afterwards he lolled like a full-bellied pup watching Koba mix charred plants with warthog fat.

'No way am I'm eating those vegetables,' he yawned.

'For cuts, not eating.'

'What cuts?'

'For first buck you must get cuts.'

Mannie sat up. 'What buck? I didn't shoot a buck?'

'Yes-yes, but ceremony the same for buck or for eye-lumps.'

'Eye lumps?'

'Eye-lumps is warthog, Frog-boy. Didn't you see?' He nodded, remembering the grotesque mounds beneath the piggy eyes. 'Your first meat-animal is female, so I must cut this side.' She approached him, pointing to his heart with the tip of her knife.

Mannie scrambled backwards. 'Hey, now wait a minute . . . ' Koba quickly flung a leg across him and sat astride his chest, knife in one hand, tattooing mixture in the other. She then pinned his arms to the ground with her knees.

He didn't struggle. He could easily heave her off his chest when he wanted to, he thought, he was bigger than her now, but she was giving one of her rare smiles and he liked the way her skin felt pressed against his.

'What you going to do?' he laughed up at her.

'Don't be feared. Behave with koaq.' She

pinched the taut skin above his left pectoral muscle and made short, parallel cuts through the pinch. Blood welled out of the cuts but quickly Koba rubbed the mixture into them. Only when she released the skin did Mannie feel the sting.

'Eina!' he roared. Raising his head to see where the pain was coming from he stared aghast at the smear of blood and blackened fat. 'What the fock have you done to me, you crazy kaffirgirl?'

'Medicine to lift your heart and make it long to seek meat.' She was still smiling but not as confidently. 'Now I must cut arm to make aim good and head to make eyes see well.'

'Not on your bloody life!' He remembered now that she'd pinned him down like that years before, out at Sukses near the Mother Hills. She'd tried to stop him breathing. Mannie quickly pushed her off his chest and stood up. 'I'm not walking around tattooed like a heathen.'

Sitting in the dust, recovering from the surprise manoeuvre, Koba hastily rearranged her pubic apron, but not before Mannie had noticed the pale honey thighs normally hidden from view by his old shorts. Such a different colour from the skin she exposed to the sun, he thought.

Seeing her so small, sprawled among the debris of her ceremony, he felt terrible. He knelt down in front of her. 'I'm sorry man, Koba. I got a fright. I, we, er, white people, we don't do that to each other.'

Her long eyes locked onto his, searching for insincerity.

'Look man, we're still friends, aren't we? D'you want me to give you some cuts for the warthog?'

Koba shook her head, sadly. 'For a woman to hunt is not Ju/'hoan way. Man must hunt, woman must gather. Man must have first buck cuts, woman must have first blood cuts.'

'First blood?'

'When girl sees moon for first time.'

'Huh?'

'The moon!' She clutched her stomach, miming menstrual cramps. Mannie stared at her blankly.

Koba sighed and began gathering up her things. Frog-boy was like Pishiboro, that stupid god who did not know what his wives were for until they climbed a tree above his head and called him to look upwards.

Chapter 13

Mannie watched the big car bounce up the track. Jissus, a Chevvy. Convertible! A real Yank tank. Who could be visiting them in this?

The driver revved the V8 engine before skidding to a halt in front of the farmhouse with a spurt of dust and grit. A young man jumped out from behind the steering wheel, clearing the two-tone door.

It was André — bearded with a mane like a lion.

Mannie unconsciously touched his own chin where down was just beginning to harden into bristle. Realising he was gaping, he quickly closed his mouth but not before André had noticed.

'Catching flies? You never seen a Chevy before? Bel Air, Limited Edition. Just fetched her off the boat at Durbs. Beauty, hey?' He patted the long, cream coloured front seat as he lounged against the door. 'Only six in the country.'

Mannie was torn between his desire to drool over the car and his wariness. He still had a scar across his toes from the long-ago incident with the horse. He narrowed his eyes and assessed his cousin's physique. Ja, the oke was big, but he himself was no pipsqueak now. He'd bet André was handy with those sledgehammer fists of his, but his beer boep would definitely cost him. Ja-no, if it came to it, he reckoned he could take the bastard.

Deon emerged from the shade of the verandah behind Mannie. He shook André's hand, 'This is a surprise.'

'Ja-well,' André stretched his arms out wide above his head and yawned, 'wanted to see what Uncle-and-them have done with the old place so thought I'd take her,' he patted the Bel Air's bonnet, 'for a nice long spin before I put her on the train for the trip back to South-West. Loading her in Jo'burg on Monday. 8am sharp.'

'Ja-well then, you must stay with us for the weekend. Marta will be pleased. How long's it been? Five, six years since we were with you at Sukses?'

Deon took André off on a tour. Prosperity was coming slowly but surely to Impalala. Where Etienne's business thrived on water,

Deon's had flourished when it was scarce. Drought brought holiday-makers to the Kruger Park in ghoulish droves. They came to see gaunt herds of zebra, wildebeest, giraffe and antelope scuffle for space around the shrinking water holes. Here predators lurked — lion, leopard and even crocodile were clearly visible as they went about their deadly business in the denuded veld and shrinking rivers. To the gasps of onlookers, irritable hippo, trying to submerge themselves in the diminishing mud, snapped their gargantuan jaws at any intruders, even elephant. The hippo knew better than most that soon the cooling slush would dry and set as hard as crazy-paving while the animals all around lay dying. Rest camps in the Park could not accommodate all the macabre tourists so private camps like Impalala benefited.

And even now, with the vegetation lush again after good rains and the savagery of nature less evident, the lodge was full. Deon was the sort of host who ensured return custom. In the evenings he was to be found mingling with guests in the communal barbeque area — huge Afrikaner men in khaki shorts with a beer in one hand and long braai fork in the other. Their wives made curried banana salad in bowls the size of washtubs and their sons, ears protruding from shorn scalps like unhinged doors, played rugby or climbed trees. In the play area Deon had built, little girls in shorty pyjamas squealed on swings or queued for the seesaw. The air here was blue with braai smoke and it smelled strongly of mosquito-deterrent. Deon listened patiently to stories of the most exciting lion kill ever seen and answered questions about the best place to glimpse rare roan antelope.

The effect of a full lodge on the farmhouse was noticeable too. The tin shack was now a gracious colonial-style bungalow. Marta slept soundly amid thick brick walls, plastered and painted bright white. The green wooden shutters matched the new tin roof, complete with expansion gaps to accommodate metal movement. It was a cool, welcoming house now with its deep verandah and cascading bauhinia. Most evenings a sprinkler chattered on the broad lawn, arcing borehole water into the sultry air. The men approached the house along a path lined with white washed stones. It was swept and watered daily by a uniformed gardener to keep the red dust down.

★　★　★

Mannie kept a close eye on André all the way through supper. Was he sneering at them, at their table that only seated four, at their cloth of cotton instead of lace like Auntie Lettie's? And why had Ma done the cooking? Had André noticed the gem squash was burned underneath and the stew was almost dry?

But soon he realised that André was too full of himself to register his surroundings, bragging non-stop about the things he'd bought — the latest rifle, the latest motorbike, some flying lessons. And he drank brandy almost as fast as Pa used to.

André said nothing about farming until Marta specifically asked him.

'Ja-no, things carry on. Place runs itself really. Twi knows what to do. Bushmen are bakgat once you've knocked the bush out of them.' He threw his big head back and laughed at Marta's expression. 'I can see Auntie's still a kaffirboetie. Ma says that wild Bushgirl's still here and you treat her like a daughter.' He turned and winked at Deon. 'Thought she might be sitting next to me at the table tonight.' Again he roared with laughter. Deon smiled thin-lipped while Mannie prayed his mother wouldn't start a political argument with André.

Marta looked at her plate — Koba should be at the table, she thought. The girl did feel like family, despite her refusal to move in. She spoke Afrikaans fluently now and often appeared at the house in the skirt and blouse Marta had left outside the cave. She still wore her beaded pubic apron over her skirt or shorts and always had her kaross draped over one shoulder but the yellow hat had gone. Instead, Koba wore a variety of headscarves, the source of which remained a mystery to Marta. What the girl's hair looked like underneath the scarf, Marta had no idea. She'd sent scissors and a mirror up to Pasopkop but didn't know if they'd been used.

Ever since the shorts-dropping incident, Marta had been wary of making assumptions about Koba. They were cordial on the rare occasions they met in the bush but the reading lessons had stopped for over a year. Eventually Koba asked to resume them.

The teenager was bright and soon Marta was covering a full curriculum of school subjects with her as best she could. She tried to keep her relationship with the girl professional — teacher to pupil — but it was difficult.

Marta felt her compensation was seeing a young person forging her own identity. And what an individual one it was! Koba was neither black nor white, neither fully westernised nor tribalised in her attitudes or dress. To Marta, Koba was the future of South Africa.

Now at the dinner table, Marta began to

see it could be time for Koba to go back to her people, assuming of course she still wanted to. With a heavy sigh, she made a silent resolution to allow her to do what she wanted.

★　★　★

Mannie was disconcerted to find himself assigned to taking André out shooting the next morning.

'I'll bag a few guinea fowl for the pot, seeing like I dropped in unannounced on Auntie,' André had said. He borrowed a gun from Deon.

'Won't you blow a bird to smithereens with that?' Marta asked.

André grinned. 'Only if I want to.'

They skirted the guest rondavels where people were already loading up their cars for an early morning game drive in the Park. They could smell breakfast boerewors cooking. Soon they'd left humanity behind and smelled instead the territorial markings of hyena that'd passed in the night.

'So, Bumfluff, show me this cave where your Ma's precious savage lives,' André said, pushing through the long grass.

Mannie forced himself to keep walking casually but he felt every hair on his body rise.

'It's far. If we go there you'll miss the birds. They roost up when it gets hotter.'

'Don't you focking tell me about shooting birds, Pipsqueak. I've bagged more birds than you've had breakfasts.' He stopped, a look of lewd concentration on his face. Can't walk and think at the same time, Mannie thought. 'Birds, *birds!*' André shouted out. 'Get it?' He gyrated his pelvis. 'I've bagged a focking lot of birds, Ouseun.' He giggled like a hyena. 'When your worm's been in half the places my python has, then we can talk. Now, take me to Bushgirl's place. Maybe she'd like a bit of this.' He slapped his khaki-trousered crotch.

'I'm not your blerry tour guide,' Mannie shouted. 'You wanna go exploring, you find your own way.' He turned and ran from André.

Out of sight, he slowed to a jog. He wished he hadn't run, striding off would have been manlier, but Koba was in danger. It was a twenty-minute walk to the cave but if he ran she'd have time to leave before André found it. Mannie sped up.

⋆　⋆　⋆

Meanwhile, André veered off and followed the path to the servants' compound. Once

204

there, he banged on the reed fence to announce his presence and then strode into the kraal, scattering chickens, goats and mangy mongrels. 'Hey,' he shouted to Selina, who was pounding maize in an X-shaped mortar, 'come, help me.'

She ignored him. One of her daughters-in-law appeared, her hands still studded with the grains she'd been sifting for beer. A naked toddler trailed after her and hid behind her skirt, peeping out in wonder at the sight of a strange white man being so noisy in their world.

André demanded to know where the Bushgirl was. All the Tsonga stared at him, slack-mouthed. 'MaSarwa. Yellow One, like this.' He pushed his nose flat against his face and stuck out his bottom. The little ones laughed and one child pointed across the veld, towards the river. Selina swooped down on him, scolding in Tsonga, and pinning his chubby arms to his sides.

'Tell me what he's pointing at,' André ordered. Selina shook her head and with lowered eyes backed into a hut, taking the child with her. André stormed in after her. 'You tell me now,' he said, grabbing the child and squeezing its arm so the flesh rose like a brown balloon behind the tourniquet of his grip. The child began to cry. Selina snatched him from André and with a curse she picked up a three-legged pot with her other hand and she swung it at him. Andre backed away from her weapon, tripping over a clay pot that smashed. Swearing, he left the kraal.

Bloody kaffirs, they'd never get away with focking him around at Sukses. But he'd find the Bushgirl, even if it took him all day and all night; the Bushmen weren't the only ones who could track. He settled the rifle more comfortably across his shoulder.

Then a young woman with a bundle of kindling on her head called out that he would find what he was looking for in a cave on the hill. He threw her a couple of tickeys.

★ ★ ★

Koba wasn't in the cave, or anywhere on Pasopkop, as far as Mannie could see. He called as loudly as he dared, not wanting to risk alerting André who might already be in the vicinity. He crawled out along Koba's lookout ledge. Jissus, it was scary; how come she could run along it with no fear?

He scanned the land spread out before him. Koba wasn't checking snares in the guarri copse nor walking along one of the veld paths. But in the distance he could see a swaggering shape heading towards the hill.

André! Quickly he lay down and peering over the edge of the ledge he checked the ravines below — sometimes Koba went there for figs.

Nothing and André was getting closer. The only thing to do now was to find Koba before André did. He'd have to search the whole farm and on foot that could take a day. He decided to go back to the house to see if he could borrow the farm truck.

★ ★ ★

André dropped heavily into Koba's cave then lit a match to look around. Must be hers, he thought — some of that Bushman shit on the wall, like a kid's drawing. He'd seen one before, above the pool at the Mother Hills. He'd found a human skeleton there too — small with a really curved spine. An old woman, Twi had said, some kind of witchdoctor, 'cos the little bliksem picked up a muti stick or something from next to the bones. Another blerry Bushman trespasser probably. Good job for her that she vrekked before he found her.

André crossed to the fire and stuck the tip of his boot into the ashes. Cold — it hadn't been used since last night. He sat down near a pile of skins, letting his eyes adjust to the dark. With the nose of his rifle he lifted the skins. Duiker, mostly, and one kaross made from impala hide.

What was this? André held up Koba's pubic apron. He ran his finger over the fine beadwork. They wore nothing underneath this scrap, he thought. Mmm, would the little one have those long flaps like her mother had in her poes?

He placed the apron over his groin and began rubbing. Okes said there was nothing like a bit of brown meat. Brown meat, full of raw, red holes. He closed his eyes and could see small twitching bodies, like he saw sometimes at night. He whimpered and longed for his father's rough shake. 'Pull yourself together, man,' his Pa would have said.

He sprang up. Fock Pa. He couldn't remember the bastard saying even once that he loved him. No, it was always that he wasn't clever enough in the classroom or quick enough on the rugby field. The real problem was that he wasn't the son of the woman Pa really loved. O-ja, even at sixteen he'd been no fool, no matter what his father thought. Auntie Marta was the sort of woman his Pa had smaaked, even when she was pregnant — flashing those fierce eyes of hers at him. It was disgusting; all women were focking cunts and he was sick of waiting for the Bush one.

He'd go and do some shooting instead.

As Mannie rounded the corner of the farmhouse he saw the truck driving off, followed by a landrover with the Kruger Park insignia on the door. In the back he could see armed rangers. Marta stood on the verandah looking worried.

'What is it, Ma?'

'Oh, thank goodness you're back. The warden's just been. Says a bull elephant broke through our fence last night. They're going to find him and dart him. I must go warn the guests still in the camp to stay indoors for the time being. I need you to run to the compound and tell Selina-and-them to be careful if they go out for wood. You know how irritable an old jumbo can be.'

★ ★ ★

As he sprinted back from the compound Mannie passed André's car. The keys dangled from the ignition. A jumbo at large was not unheard of at the farm, but a Bel Air! And it happened to be the only vehicle available. Ha, wouldn't André have a blue fit if he knew he'd used it to find Koba!

Mannie vaulted over the door and landed grinning on the deeply padded seat. He placed his hands on the polished brown wheel and stretched his legs to the floor-board. Hell, this was lekker. He felt for the pedals. No clutch. Automatic. He'd never driven one before but he was sure he could manage. Mannie turned the key. A purr of power. Quickly he turned it off again. He shouldn't be doing this.

He sat still, eyes like ping-pong balls peering over the dashboard as he waited to be caught. Nothing. No one. Mannie turned the key again. He thrilled at the engine's throaty rumble. He looked around. Still no one.

It occurred to him that his mother probably wouldn't mind if she knew he was taking the car to rescue Koba. Anyway, he was only borrowing it; he'd have it back before André even knew it was missing.

He was certain now that he knew where Koba would be — down among the sweet thorn near the river. She'd mentioned she was out of salt and wanted to trade. Mannie said he'd bring her a bottle of 'see-how-it-runs' from the store; they bought it in bulk now. Honey too. But she'd looked fierce and said she didn't want something for nothing. She would get him the honey; if he didn't want to eat it — shrug-shrug with those small shoulders of hers.

He slipped the car into gear and took off

with just a slight jerk. Bakgat, he thought. This car was easier to drive than the truck. Mannie pressed his foot to the floorboards and it took off down the track, dust billowing out behind it like a battle banner.

* * *

In a clearing near the river, Koba stopped to listen. Was that the honey-guide chirping? Still far off. She sighed. She'd been searching since sunrise. All the familiar hives showed recent honey-badger damage. She could still smell the foul fart people said it used to stun the bees. But there had to be an undisturbed hive somewhere. She set off for the bushwillow thicket.

Had Koba been up on Pasopkop she would have seen the long veld grass parting, as it did when a lion padded through. Here, on the edge of the thicket, her view was obscured by the dense foliage. But then a honey-guide appeared, making its distinctive rattling call, a sound she'd come to think of as that of a box of matches being shaken lengthwise. The bird flew in a circle, undulating and swooping upwards with a spread tail. 'Chitik-chitik-chitik' it called, guiding her to the stump of an old ironwood tree.

'You're a clever little feather,' Koba said,

kneeling to examine the stump. Uhn-uhn, the hive was deep in the hollow, best to smoke the bees out. But it was hot and she was tired. She jabbed at the hive with her hare hook. It broke open. Quickly she clawed out a hunk of comb. Confused bees poured out of the breach. They massed in the air and turned on the marauder, dive-bombing her. Tossing down a piece of comb for the little bird, Koba ran, laughing.

★　★　★

André heard something coming through the undergrowth towards him. Koba, her ears full of buzzing, heard nothing. As she ran past, he tackled her and she fell, gasping, the comb rolling out of her hand. The swarm descended on it, crawling all over to check the larvae. Some flew up to attack the large man looming over their quarry.

'Jissus,' André panted, 'what are you doing? Taking your bees for a walk? Eina-dammit, that was a sting; we're getting out of here.' He tucked Koba under his arm and used her head to force a path through the undergrowth away from the angry swarm. Koba felt branches tearing at her face.

When he threw her down in the clearing she looked up at him through trickles of blood and saw a Lion, a pawed, clawed, dangerous thing. She kept her pain to herself as he dragged her across to a sapling and bound her to it, lying down, arms above her head. He ripped her shorts off and sat astride her, pulling his penis from his pants.

She was transfixed by the crumpled pinkness of it — and so ugly-hairy. She spat at it.

'You cheeky little cunt!' He punched her full in the face. Her head whipped backwards, striking the tree trunk with a thud, making her vision blur. She tried to focus but saw double-Lion leaning towards her. His weight crushed her into the ground. 'Not so brave now, hey?' He heaved himself off her and, reaching for his rifle, wedged her legs apart with it. 'Ok meidjie, let's look.' Koba felt metal pressed against the inside of her thigh. 'Make sure you lie nice and still, hey?'

Koba saw the pink worm swell to python size and remembered again her mother's humiliation in front of this animal. She felt rough thumbs part the lips of her vagina. She closed her eyes. Suddenly, water that was not her own was splashing onto her belly. She opened her eyes.

The Lion was sobbing. Crouched between her legs he was shaking, eye-water splashing down, some onto her skin, some into his nest of mouth hair. Glancing at his groin, she relaxed. The Lion would not be eating her with that softness.

She began to ease her leg away from the weapon.

André didn't notice. Images gushed into his consciousness: Pa grinning as he displayed the Bushwoman; Pa staring at the poisonous pink patch creeping across his shirt; the long, torturous journey back with the body and all the time his fear, making him sick to his stomach. What if, one day, someone did decide to prosecute? Everyone said the country was changing, that one day it would be run by kaffirs. If this girl spoke up he might have to go to jail. It would be her dirty word against his. Better to kill her now and throw the body into the river. The crocs would soon have it.

Koba felt something that made her stop her surreptitious manoeuvring — a gigantic mass was moving through the thicket without so much as snapping a twig. She could see nothing but beneath her she felt the ground give as though a colossal weight had been placed down nearby. André felt it too and stood up, frantically scanning the surrounding thicket. An elephant? Here? There couldn't be, but if there was, where? Spotting an elephant in undergrowth when it wasn't feeding was like looking for a needle in a haystack. And he wanted to be very sure of the direction this particular needle was pointing so he could stay downwind.

* * *

On the outskirts of the thicket Mannie had a better view of the elephant. It seemed to be dozing, resting the weight of its old head on one massive tusk. The tusk was so long it touched the ground in a graceful white curve. The other tusk was only a stump, lost in a fight many years ago. Mannie knew because he was sure this was the famous Mafuta. People had written books about him. No one knew for sure how old the bull was but his tusk was worth thousands of rand and poachers had tried many times to trap him.

No wonder half the Kruger rangers were out searching for him, Mannie thought. But the jumbo looked listless. He stood dead still in the mottled shade, his eyes closed and his ragged tail twitching feebly at flies. His skin was dull and even baggier than was usual for an elephant.

Just like an old man with no arse, Mannie thought. Funny that he wasn't feeding.

Perhaps the old bull had come here to die. He could still be dangerous though. And somehow he had to get past him to see if Koba was there.

He drove a little closer. The elephant didn't stir. He wasn't surprised. The Kruger animals were used to engine noise; they knew it wasn't threatening.

★ ★ ★

André heard the engine — the unmistakable vibrato of his beloved Bel Air. Here? What-the-hell! He began to run towards the sound.

André saw Mannie behind the wheel of his car. At the same time as the elephant saw him.

Mafuta lifted his trunk and sniffed the air. With amazing agility, he rotated himself, his immense tusk scything through the undergrowth. His huge ears began to flap.

Heedless, from fifty yards away, André screamed at Mannie, 'What the foek do you think you're doing with my car?'

Mannie saw blood on André's shirt and, as he got closer, his undone fly. He was too late! 'Where's Koba? What have you done to her?'

'Don't you focking talk to me about a kaffirgirl when you've stolen my focking car and driven it through the bushveld. So help me, I swear, if you've got so much as a scratch on her I'll focking kill you, you little . . . '

Mafuta seemed to have had enough of the commotion. Trunk aloft, he trumpeted, a sound that silenced André mid-rant. He spun around just in time to see the bull's mammoth ears begin to flap furiously. Then Mafuta began to charge.

The ground shook; pods, twigs and leaves showered down from the trees as he thundered past. There was dust, the squawking of a ground plover desperate to protect her nest, and more of the terrible trumpeting. André sprinted for the car as though his life depended on it.

Mannie knew it did. Dry-mouthed, shaking, he pushed the gearshift into drive and pressed his foot hard on the accelerator. The car shot forward with a spin of wheels, passing André and bouncing towards the bull. Mannie pressed his palm on the horn as hard as he could. André stopped, horror-struck. 'No, no, no,' he shouted, arms flailing hopelessly, 'mind the car!'

The distraction worked; Mafuta slowed his charge. He paused, one massive foot raised, and tossed his head from side to side. Irritably he then brought the foot down on a bushwillow. One of the tree-trunks split under his weight and half the canopy began to sheer off. The sound of cracking branches seemed to annoy the elephant. Wrapping his trunk around a massive branch he yanked and brought it down with a shriek of splitting wood.

The Bel Air was now close. Mannie sat white-faced behind the wheel, perspiration running down his forehead. His heart seemed to oscillate, not beat, and he felt ice-cold. How much further dared he drive?

Mannie waited until he judged himself to be almost within tusk-reach but for the buckled tree, then wrenched the steering wheel and skidded to a side-on halt behind its protection. The car stalled and Mannie scrambled along the front seat, kicked the passenger door open and rolled onto the ground. Then he was up and running, shouting for André to do the same.

But André stood transfixed, watching Mafuta consider this new impediment. With a swing of his shapeless foreleg and what seemed only slight pressure from his trunk, he elected to continue with his demolition work. A forty-foot fever tree was excavated, and it started to topple over towards the car. There was a huge explosion of glass and metal as the windscreen shattered and the car frame buckled down to bonnet level. The boom echoed across the bush and bounced off the distant rock-face of Pasopkop. Mafuta trumpeted in alarm and began to reverse as quickly as his tusk would allow, leaving André howling with anguish. 'Where's my gun, where's my focking gun?'

Mannie's last sight of him was as a dummy dancing with rage, undecided whether to pursue the elephant or inspect the wreck.

* * *

Mannie found Koba not too far off. 'Are you alright?' He undid the rope from her wrists. 'Your face — it's all scratched, and here,' he touched the jaw where a swelling had started. 'Did he hit you?'

Koba did not answer, nor did she meet his eyes.

'Wait, I'll go get some water for your face.'

'Yau! Leave.' Koba struggled unsteadily up. Mannie supported her.

* * *

At the river all was peaceful. If Mafuta had crossed here on his way back to the relative quiet of the Park, he'd left no sign. The brown water drifted downstream, like a lazy crocodile. Koba leaned against an overhanging trunk while Mannie took off his shirt and wet it. She closed her eyes and allowed him to wipe the blood from her face. When she opened her eyes he was staring intently at her. Awkwardly, they stepped away from each other.

Mannie wanted to ask what had happened to her, but he didn't dare. He wished she'd seen him skid-stop the Bel Air though, right in front of the elephant. Jis-man, he'd been bakgat; more daring even than James Bond. But it didn't seem right to brag about saving André, not in front of the girl he'd raped.

Looking at her he was sorry he'd saved the bastard — he didn't suppose he'd get any thanks for it. He decided he'd better go home and start explaining.

'Gotta go back and face the music,' he sighed.

Koba smiled, then, lips vibrating, she made a passable V8 engine sound. Mannie stared delightedly at her. She honked in perfect imitation of the Bel Air's horn and began tussling with an imaginary wheel, bouncing up and down on an imaginary seat.

Mannie laughed. 'You don't know the half of it . . . ' And he began to give her a detailed account.

Chapter 14

One afternoon, Mannie, who should have been revising for his exams, was trying to teach himself to jive using the diagram on the back of the record sleeve. When Koba tapped on the window, he was glad.

'Come in. You can help me learn this dance.'

Koba jumped lightly onto the window ledge. She used the door when Marta was around but Leopard-woman was clearly away, she thought, if her cub was making such a noise in the den.

Mannie took her hand and pulled her inside. She was under five foot to his almost six and her toes didn't reach the ground as he held her at chest-height for a moment.

She hadn't realised Frog-boy had become so tall and broad. It made her feel shy. He set her down and she stepped away from him.

'Hey, c'mon, Koba,' he offered her his hand again, but she stood stiffly, looking down at the carpet. He frowned. 'Okay then, I'll close the shutters.'

The gloom helped. She put her hand in his and made a fair mime of Mannie's movements. When he pushed her away from him, then pulled her back, Koba got the idea. She giggled, but kept time to the music. Mannie grinned, raising their linked arms and with a push on her waist, spun her. She chuckled. A few minutes later and she was able to turn in both directions without losing the beat.

Suddenly Mannie dropped Koba's hands as he became aware of the blonde-haired figure in the doorway — Katrina Botha, a neighbour, in shorts and a blouse tied high under her breasts. 'I knocked, but you were too busy to hear. All shut up, hey?' She raised an overplucked eyebrow.

'Ma-and-them are out. We, er, I . . . hold on, I'll just turn off the player.' Mannie scurried over to the gramophone, his cheeks and ears red.

'I just came to ask about the homework — biology, actually.' She smiled, her eyes glittering at the thought of the mileage she could make out of this scene. Mannie Marais, toast of the under-seventeens rugby squad, with his dark little secret.

'Dancing with a kaffir girl in his front

room, *with the shutters closed*,' she'd tell the girls. And while they were still gasping, she'd deliver the final blow to his reputation. 'And guess what they were dancing to? Bill Haley!'

Nevertheless, Katrina thought, Mannie Marais had potential. He was handsome, in a very young way. They'd played together as kids and now the little scrawn was filling out nicely.

But his Ma was a trouble-maker. Probably a 'Commie', her father said. Mrs Marais had been on that march-thing with all those kaffir women who were put in prison. And after Sharpeville she'd tried to get people to sign a petition protesting about it. She was lucky she wasn't arrested, Katrina's father had claimed.

Well, like mother, like son, the girl thought. Though why Mannie was interested in this filthy little scrap, Heavens only knew. She looked like a caveman with that animal skin over her skirt.

There had been talk about this kaffirgirl — Bushman or something. The Maraises kept her around the place like a pet, people said. But would you dance with your dog or your monkey?

Her mama had said Mrs Marais had educated the Bushgirl and wanted her to sit Matric next year, like her and Mannie. Apparently Mrs Marais felt the Bantu exams

223

were an insult for such a clever girl so she'd already applied to the education board for the ones the white children took. Cheeky, the women in Ma's sewing circle said. Katrina remembered her mother calming them down, saying the Minister would never allow it.

'Koba and I . . . ' Mannie was saying, 'have you met Koba?' As he turned his scarlet face from Katrina's cool gaze he heard the clap of shutters being thrown open and saw Koba jump out of the window. Katrina laughed lightly but her eyes were hard. How dare this boy think he could introduce her to a kaffir?

'She's a bit shy.' Mannie shrugged. He became aware of his hands hanging awkwardly off his wrists. He should do something with them. 'Can I . . . get you a drink? Coffee, or something?'

'No time. Pappie's taking us to the dam for the weekend. We're staying in a hotel.' She drummed her fingers on the doorframe. 'So, if I could borrow your biology homework book? Quickly.'

''Ja-ja, of course. I'll fetch it.'

She was looking over his record collection when he got back, buttocks flared towards him, waist tapering above. She straightened up and held her hand out for the book. Her nails were painted a shimmering pink, like the inside of shells. He couldn't take his eyes off them. How did she keep them so clean in all this dust? He watched, mesmerised, as she used one pristine talon to flick a long skein of hair back over her shoulder. Now he could see down the neck of her blouse, a bit of bra very white against her tanned skin.

'Thanks,' she said, mincing over to the door. He felt his groin go with her.

Over her shoulder, Katrina said, 'By the way, Mannie, the jive's out — it's the twist you should be learning, unless you want your Boswyfie to look out of place at the dance.'

Mannie cursed. She was going to crucify him at school on Monday; he just knew it. And it wasn't going to be easy with Koba either, he felt sure.

★ ★ ★

He found her up on Pasopkop, near her cave, leaning against the contorted trunk of the wild fig tree. She had a dog-eared book of fairytales in her lap. She didn't look up when Mannie flopped down beside her. 'Jis, it's baking.'

No reply.

'Too hot for hunting, hey?'

She turned a page.

'Want me to read it to you?'

Now she looked up, scornful. 'I can read myself.'

Mannie sighed. When they were younger he'd read her fairytales and been told Ju/'hoansi stories in exchange. The stories were funny, often rude, with small animals getting the better of big ones, or long-suffering wives playing tricks on their god husbands. In one, they gave the god shit to eat instead of sausage. He'd laughed at that.

Sometimes, Koba didn't bother with translation. She told the tales in her own language, as if he could understand her. Funny thing was, he sort of could. The clicks were all different; he could hear that. And many of them sounded just like the thing they were naming, like the galloping sound when she was telling about a herd in flight. Koba also made all the animal movements with her hands, fingers trotting rhythmically across the ground like the tireless jackal, or splayed like a heavy-pawed lion. Ja, it was surprisingly obvious. Pity there wouldn't be a story-session today.

'You in a mood, or what?'

Yes, what? Koba thought to herself. Why did she feel so dejected? She stared out over the distant veld; its blondeness reminded her of the /Ton girl's hair. The girl that Frog-boy had wanted to have food with. A fierce face

226

with sharp eyebrows and nostrils permanently flared, a serval cat about to pounce . . . but not on Frog-boy. He did not interest her enough. Yet.

I am alone, even with him here, even with Grandmother in the cave every night. There is no one to touch me, to hold me. My heart hungers for people with my skin, but my head whispers 'afraid' — afraid to go back to my n/ore.

Koba knew there was now money for her train ticket to Onderwater; Marta had said as much months ago. She'd even offered to accompany Koba on the journey home.

Koba hadn't responded because she didn't know what she should do.

'Grandmother n!a'an,' she'd said when the spirit came to her one night, 'why does my heart lean towards our n/ore *and* draw back from it?'

'Your heart knows a dream is better than eyes-open.'

Koba nodded. 'I will be disappointed.' She sat staring into the flames, imagining herself among her people. She could see faces just like her own, chattering, smiling, but not at her. To her they turned blank faces. Some even looked hostile.

'No different from here, then.' Zuma remarked.

Koba flapped irritably at the empty air. 'Stop that. Don't press your ear to my thoughts.'

'Yau, you Bone-and-Bloods are slow-slow-slow.'

'You Spent Breaths are . . . ' Koba bit her lip. She made a determined effort to empty her mind. Zuma would have to wait to hear her thoughts until she had them in some order.

'You wish to know if the Ju/'hoansi will reject you?'

'Yau. Go away!'

'Uhn-nh-nh. Must be that you are sitting on your manners.'

Koba pouted. It was infuriating the way Zuma took advantage, breaking rules that suited her, enforcing those that didn't. Spirits. Yau!

'The answer to the question you are too fat-lipped to ask is: the Ju/'hoansi will accept you if you wish to belong.'

'But they might find me ugly, my tongue clumsy in their talk. The woman for whom I am named may not be alive. There may not be one kinsperson of mine still living there. Who will know me? Who will take me to their fire?'

'Uhn, Koba. What I hear is what you have already decided — to stand still. You have time. But do not grow roots here, child. This /Ton n/ore cannot feed you. One day you will have to leave.'

★ ★ ★

Koba shook herself out of her reverie as she realised Mannie was staring. 'What's the matter?' he said.

'I am spoiled.'

'Spoiled? How?'

Impatiently, Koba twitched the apron that hung over her shorts 'By being here; not growing up among my people; not learning proper Ju/'hoan ways. Here I live like a man — I hunt; I wear boy-clothes; I like dry food. You've seen me with salt; I prefer it to honey. Could be because honey is wet, woman's food.' She sighed. 'I am not a proper Ju/'hoan woman.'

'Ag, man, kak!'

She ignored him. 'I am like Rose Red who spoke toads.' Mannie looked confused. She tapped the fairytale book.

'Oh.'

'Like Jackal in the Ju/'hoansi story. I am so unwoman, I will give birth to n#ah seeds. From my arse.'

Mannie winced, then said patiently: 'Look, man . . .'

'You see!'

'Ag, Koba-man, you know . . . '

'There, you said it again.'

'You're just being otherwise, woman. You know you are.' She half-smiled. 'Ja, so the way I see it, you don't eat honey because you don't like the taste — finished and klaar.' He tugged irritably at his shirt back. It was plastered to his skin with perspiration. Jis, it was too hot for all this nonsense.

'Listen m-er, Koba, you should cheer up, hey? I mean, you're lucky, you know.'

'Lucky?'

'You can make up your own mind about things. Decide for yourself what you will and won't do. I can't do that. Pa says I need haircut,' he ducked his prickly pate for her to see, 'and look what I got — blerry sandpaper. Only Jaaps still have hair like this.'

'You are a Jaap.'

'I am not! I've been to Jo'burg. Well, through it, anyway. So have you. Do you remember? When we brought you from South-West . . . ' He cut himself short. That was dangerous territory. A place they hadn't ventured to yet. Koba seemed not to have heard. She was staring at the patch of red earth between them. Then she lifted watery eyes to his.

'When a girl goes to the moon for the first time, the women dance for her. Rub her with eland fat, give cuts here,' she indicated her

230

cheekbone, 'so she looks as beautiful as zebra. Where are my marks, where is my beauty?' Two tiny tears slipped from beneath her long lids.

'Ag, Koba, you don't need stripes on your face. You're fine,' the tears were coming faster, 'Um, pretty even,' and faster, 'You're beautiful, man. You look like a little steenbok with your long, thin legs and soft eyes, and your face here . . . '

Gaats, he was getting carried away. He'd almost put his big, dirty finger on her face.

'You don't understand,' Koba said.

Mannie shrugged. He didn't. Girls were baffling to him and now Koba, his best friend, was blerry-well turning into one.

He stood up and offered her his hand to rise. 'I've got an idea — it's a long walk, but if we go along the riverbank . . . '

'You want to honk.'

It was a joke between them — whenever they were in the vicinity they stopped at what had become known on the farm as 'The Wreck of the Bel Air'. There they pretended to honk the horn of the car already removed by a team of amazed insurance assessors. A picture of the wreck now hung in the insurance company's boardroom, alongside one of Mafuta.

'So where you want to go?' Koba asked.

'To the Botha's.' Mannie's eyes jived. 'For a

231

goef. They're away for the weekend. They'll never know we've been in their swimming pool. And afterwards we'll pee in it. That'll teach Miss Eau de Cologne.'

★ ★ ★

The Botha's garden was like an oasis in the middle of the scorched brown bushveld. A revolving sprinkler pelted giant palm and paw paw trees. It made a loud, papery clatter before spinning on to douse the cascading creepers: golden shower, bauhinia and bougain-villea. The gleaming kikuyu lawn felt springy underfoot as they ran towards the kidney-shaped pool.

Koba gasped as she got closer — the colour was almost like that of the other water, from her worst nightmare, in the pool at the Mother Hills. Despite the heat the skin on her back began to goosebump.

Mannie was already dipping his foot into the water. 'Water's a bit green, but never mind; it's as warm as a bath. Come feel.' Koba shook her head and retreated to a spot some distance away, under the frangipani tree. It smelt wonderful there.

'C'mon man. You must swim.' He walked over and stood looking down at the top of her head. 'What's the matter, hey?' Her fingers twirled a frangipani flower. 'Ag man, there's nothing to be scared of. If you can't swim I can quickly teach you.'

'Not that,' Koba mumbled.

He flopped down in front of her. 'What then? Tell me.'

And because she had started, and because she really needed to talk, she found herself doing just that; telling him all about the pool at the Mother Hills, about leaving Zuma, about watching her father and mother being shot.

It took a long time and all the while she didn't cry and nor did Mannie. Quietly, while he too fiddled with fallen frangipani, he filled in his impressions of the day. Finally, without looking up, he admitted to her what he'd never told another soul — that he could have warned Etienne and saved his life.

She opened her arms to him and they held each other, sharing silent sorrow.

It seemed only natural to Mannie to kiss her face, along her cheekbone, down her slim neck. Her fingers explored his head, tracing along his nose and caressing his neck. Then she ran them down his shirt and up under it, discovering the hardness of his young body.

Mannie moaned. The sound acted like an alarm for Koba and she stopped instantly. She needed something from Frog-boy and it wasn't this. She pulled away. 'I want you to help me with something,' she whispered.

'Sure,' Mannie said, still trying to nuzzle her ear.

'It's not food,' she insisted, pushing him away.

Mannie sat back and drew his knees up to hide his erection. Koba was talking but he was buggered if he was going to pay any attention. She tapped impatiently on his arm. 'I had a message from the spirits,' she said. 'I must make a trance dance and become n/omkxaosi.'

Whatheblerryhell? 'Listen Koba, you gotta give me a minute here,' he said. 'I need to cool off.' And with that he jumped up, dived into the pool and swam five furious lengths. Afterwards he flipped onto his back and floated. Let her see that she didn't affect him.

He got out and lay on the concrete to dry off. Koba came and lay next to him. 'Sorry-sorry,' she whispered. He grunted and buried his face in his crossed arms. 'If we feast now, my muti won't be as strong,' she said.

He lifted his head, frowning. 'What muti?'

Koba began to explain the trance initiation ceremony. It was difficult and she didn't have a translation for many of the Ju/'hoan words. But finally he understood and sulkily said he'd help. 'So what must I do?'

'For the dance I must have the drum-medicine song to help my blood boil. When it boils my n/om will be strong.'

'N/om?'

'Healing power. It will make me sweat and tremble, maybe even jump in the fire or fall down like dead. Then you must care for me. You must stop me injuring my body, you must blow in my face, rub me.' He grinned. 'You must bring me back from the spirit world or I will die.' Now Mannie looked worried.

'Do you really want to risk this?'

'I must-must-must.' He could feel her body tense with determination.

'Okay. When do we do it?'

'Next time ringed moon.'

Chapter 15

In the days that followed, Koba made preparations for the dance. She collected a mopane stump for firewood — not easy to find but worth the long walk to fetch it; it would burn long and sweet. Next she needed ankle rattles — cocoons from the mopane worm would do and seeds for the rattles. Koba tested their clatter in her shaking fist, then inserted them into the cocoons and threaded the filled cocoons onto the sinew.

Hair decoration was next.

'Take,' she whispered to Mannie the next morning as they passed the wash line where curtains from the guest rondavels hung out to dry.

'What d'you want a curtain for?'

'No, that.' She pointed to a brass ring still in the curtain. He slipped it out. 'What's it for?'

'My hair. I will put in some beads, then,'

she dangled the ring over one eye, 'see.' Mannie wolf-whistled. She laughed. 'It's for Zuma n!a'an, not you.'

Mannie slowed his pace. 'Why do you want to be a nom, er . . . ?'

'N/omkxaosi,' Koba prompted him.

'Yes, a nomakasi thingey?'

'If I am an owner of medicine I will be respected. People will welcome me.'

'But you can already cure people with plants. Didn't you give Selina some stuff for that baby with dysentery?'

'Bah, many people know plant muti. Mata even. But if I could heal illness from the spirit world, that would be big.'

'But it can hurt, you said.'

'Yau, pain!' She flapped her slim wrist dismissively. 'Women,' she struck her chest, 'do not run from the pain of childbirth. Can trance pain be worse?'

Privately she was afraid, but not of pain or discomfort. What if her quest was successful, Koba thought, and she did reach the spirit world? Would she see her father there with half a face, her mother, eyes pecked out by vultures, Zuma's bones splintered by hyena? She shivered violently.

'What's the matter?'

'We call, a word like,' she cast about, 'um, Sunspooks. At sun's highest,' she pointed to the noonday sun, 'bad medicine men walk. These poisoners do not cast shadows.'

✳ ✳ ✳ ✳ ✳

'Spirits dance! Spirits dance!' Mannie woke to see Koba's face looming over his. How had she got into his room? The window, of course. He groaned and pulled the sheet over his head. Being woken up suddenly always gave him a headache. He felt a gentle prod. Grumbling, he sat up, rubbing his eyes. When they cleared he saw Koba dressed in skins with a hoop in her carefully braided hair. He hadn't seen her hair for years. It looked nice like that.

'Show time, huh?'

'Come-come-come.'

Mannie was still doing up the buttons of his shirt as he followed Koba's bangle jangle across the moonlit veld. It was a jewel of a night — stars studding a satin sky, a moon so bright even a dappled leopard would show up in it. The path up the hill was a silvery trail but the pace Koba was setting was doing his head no good at all. He felt a stab of pain in his temple with every footstep. At the top of Pasopkop she allowed him to stop as she pointed out the distinct ring around the moon. 'That's c-cloud,' he gasped, 'maybe it'll rain.'

238

'No, the Ju/'hoansi say it's spirits dancing. Quick-quick. Drum-medicine dance.' She handed him a halved calabash with a skin stretched taut across it. He tapped it once. A good resonance.

Koba brought two tortoise shells over to him. 'What are those?' he asked.

She pointed to the first. 'To make medicine smoke. It will help me trance. But it can sick me. Then you must use the other,' she lifted the smaller shell and held it out to him, 'to cool me.'

'What is it?'

'San powder.'

He sniffed the pungent green powder. 'Phew, smells like what Ma used to put on my bruises.'

But Koba had no time for reminiscence. 'Begin your drumming.'

Mannie sat down and gave the drum some tentative taps. Koba took a few short, shuffling steps. 'Are you afraid of the drum that you tap so shy-shy?'

'It's the dead of night, Koba. The Tsongas will think the Tokoloshe is coming.'

'I need the noise.'

'Okay-okay.' Mannie thumped the buck hide. An owl flew from its perch screeching with shock. He laughed. This could be fun and might even make him forget the throb in his temples. 'Hey,' he called to Koba, 'you call yourself the child of a Ju/'hoan and you don't even dance?'

Koba smiled. Frog-boy was joking like a Ju/'hoan! She began to stamp her feet in time to Mannie's improved tattoo. Her ankle rattles shook. She circled the fire, flicking her fly-whisk with a rhythmical swish. She sang a few notes, 'Ehay-o, ehay-o'. Perhaps it was time for the medicine smoke.

She lit the greyish powder in her tortoise shell and inhaled deeply from the aromatic fumes. The smoke made her eyes water and nose burn, but her head soon felt light. She began clapping in counterpoint to Mannie's beat. This was good. 'Now you sound like a real person! Now our rhythms are talking.'

Koba bent forward in her dance, breasts bare and hanging from her chest like golden pears. Mannie could see the curve of a buttock through the parting between kaross and pubic apron. The amber skin glimmered with perspiration. He felt his penis press against the leg of his shorts.

From a shell held high above her head Koba poured water into her open mouth. Her back was arched, her breasts proud as she stood in profile. Water splashed down her cleavage and she giggled, cupping her breasts and squeezing them together to trap the cool drops. Mannie's eyes stretched wide. She glanced in his direction and he looked away. Koba returned to her dance.

I mustn't cool. My n/om must boil. Warmth at the bottom of my spine. Soon it will rise up and power will flow through me. Ha. This is not painful — what was I afraid of? I do not need a healer to hang onto. I do not even need the voices of women singing. Now I am moving through water. My body is weightless. The drumbeat comes from a world above. I see the /Ton boy. Tiny — a frog on the side of my waterworld.

Yau! Yau! Something grabs my insides. What is pulling at the back of my stomach? It is climbing up inside my back! I'm being dragged down — I cannot breath, I cannot swim. A snake, from the Forbidden pool!

★　★　★

Koba was shaking, shouting, contorting as she tried to gouge the skin on her back with her nails. She threw herself onto the ground and rolled towards the fire. Her dilated pupils failed to focus on Mannie as he blew into her face but soon her gasps slowed. Mannie pulled Koba into a sitting position and made her drop her head between her trembling knees.

Before he could reach for water or buchu powder, she'd jumped up and grabbed coals from the fire, oblivious to their searing heat. She began to hurl them into the darkness.

'Go away you Pawed Things, you Cruel Cries in the Night. You will not have my meat. I will not sit and wait for you to harm me; not like the Mother Hills!'

The skin on the back of Mannie's neck prickled. What could she see that he couldn't? He scanned beyond the circle of firelight. Nothing. It must be bad memories then, he thought; the stuff she'd told him about from the Mother Hills. Jissus, two of them spooked, up on a haunted hill in the dead of night!

'Easy, take it easy, Koba, calm down. It's all right. You're safe. I got you.'

Koba's struggles stilled; her eyes shut, she seemed to sway. Mannie relaxed his grip on her but suddenly she was shaking violently again, her spasm moving both of them.

'Koba, Koba, stop it, man.'

He began to wonder seriously if his friend was possessed. He didn't believe in ghosts and spirits and things, but maybe . . .

When Koba went limp, lolling like a rag-doll in his arms, he began to worry. What should he do? Take her to his mother? He'd have to take along the powder she took. It was obviously some kind of drug. He remembered again what Koba has said about blowing in her face if she got sick. Jissus, now she was thrashing like a fish on a hook.

Mannie blew and blew and eventually Koba stopped shaking. She grabbed the water bottle Mannie offered her and drank the whole thing.

Why did her stomach hurt so, she wondered? Other parts of her body too. Had she been beaten? And why was it so cold? Where was her kaross and why was she sitting in front of Frog-boy with her chest exposed?

She crossed her arms tightly over her breasts and dropped her head. She had not seen any spirits — not even a steenbuck, let alone an eland. Nothing — no one had come to lead her to the other world where she might receive n/om. Zuma had been wrong — she was not going to be a healer.

'To trance you must have the courage to die, then come to life again,' Zuma had once said. 'There is pain along the path, and fear too, but if you can conquer these you will be worthy.'

Koba wiped her face and looked up at the moon. There was still a circle around it though it was getting paler.

She stood up and walked shakily over to Mannie, who stood hunched in a blanket next to the subdued fire. 'We must try again,' she said.

He shook his head. 'No way — you scared me half to death. I thought you were going to die or get taken over by the Devil or something.'

'Please-please.'

'NO!'

'I beg . . . '

'Koba-man, I'm bushed and my hands are sore.' He held out palms puffy and red from drumming.

'You don't understand. Now, when Great Star returns from his night's hunting, now is the most powerful time for drum-medicine dance. PLEASE!'

'It's all right for you; you can sleep for the rest of the day. I've got to go to school.' His headache was now beating like a bongo up the back of his neck.

'I will give you honey. I will catch you red meat. My heart walks on its knees to you. You must drum for me.'

'But what the hell is it all for, hey? You dance, you get crazy, you fall down. I help you get better . . . now you want to do it all again. What's the point?'

'Is for n/om — to get healing power to cure people.' She stood closer to him and, stretching up onto tiptoe, just managed to put her hand on his forehead. 'Maybe even your head-hurt.'

'How d'you know I had a headache?' Her hand felt as rough as a rasp, but he liked it. He felt his frown loosen. 'Ag, ok. I suppose a bit of drumming and dancing would warm us up.'

He picked up the drum and began to pat it, noticing that the tasseled tops of the grass were already sunlit.

Koba shuffled in the groove that her feet had worn around the fire. Her torso barely moved but under her lean flesh, her thigh muscles could be seen powering her forward. Round and round she moved, like an automaton.

'Mmm-mmm,' she intoned, 'music is heavy now. Will help n/om come.' She stared down at her dusty feet and began to babble to herself.

Suddenly Koba's movement and murmur ceased. Walking with the undulations of an underwater swimmer, she bent over Mannie.

He didn't like the look of her; her body was coated in a thick sweat again and her eyes looked crazy behind the bead curtain in her hair.

Koba's hands began to flutter near his forehead, like double-winged mopane leaves in a storm. A single note dribbled from her

slack mouth but once in the outside air it
swelled to a cry.

'Kaohididi!'

The shriek hurt his ears and made his heart
thump. Next to him Koba's legs were
trembling, the quivering spreading up her
body, making her pelvis and shoulders shake.
Mannie thought she was going to collapse
again. Then she seemed to control the spasm,
harnessing its energy. Her shaking stopped
and though her face was screwed up with
effort, her breathing was regular. She began
brushing Mannie's neck with her fingers.

'What are you doing?' he asked.

'Throwing out the sickness,' she panted.
'Your head hurt comes from tiny arrows shot
by the great god, G//aoan. I can pull sick
arrows into my hands and out — out here,'
she slapped her upper back.

Mannie was sceptical. Healing with just the
hands? She was no Jesus. As far as he knew
she didn't even believe in Him. He wondered
what his mother would make of this?

Time passed; he wasn't sure how much. He
could hear the guinea fowl begin their dawn
patrol far off across the veld. After a while he
stretched, raised his arms above his head and
glanced at the sky. There was green where the
yellow sunrise had mixed with blue sky.
Hmm, a person didn't often see that. Nice to

be up before it got scorching, he thought. Funny, he didn't feel so tired now.

And hey, his headache had gone!

He turned to tell Koba. But his friend wasn't dancing behind him; she lay asleep beneath the tree, curled like a comma under her kaross. And near her, even after he rubbed his eyes to make sure he wasn't dreaming, Mannie saw a young eland cow, grazing placidly, hundreds of miles from its natural habitat.

Chapter 16

Koba squatted on the riverbank and stared at the swirling brown water. The drought had broken. Floodwater from upcountry had turned the dry riverbed into a wild torrent. Koba watched a large nest sail into view. Probably a green heron's, she thought, as it whirled into an eddy before being trapped in a standing wave. That would be the place to cross the river — where a tree trunk held back the flow. She'd have to be quick though; the log might shift or her splashing might alert a crocodile. She didn't know the creature well enough to predict its habit in unusual circumstances — crocodiles didn't occur in the Kalahari and here she'd only seen them float, yellow-eyed and as inert as logs in calm water.

Koba knew she wasn't destined to be crocodile breakfast. Nor would she catch a buck on the reed island in the middle of the river. Not today. The oracle discs had predicted something else.

The discs had been Zuma's. She had slipped them into the kaross on the last day at the Mother Hills. Koba had forgotten them until Mannie shook the cloak out one day and they fell from the secret fold.

'What you keeping slices of old brinjal for?' he had said.

'Brinjal?' Koba looked puzzled. As he picked them up, Mannie realised they were made from hide, not eggplant, and they had faint markings scratched into the leather.

'Hey, are these oracle discs? Ma once told me Bushmen — sorry, Khoisan people — throw them before a hunt to see what will happen. Do you do that?'

Koba had shaken her head. She did read the discs but she didn't want him to know. He might think her stranger than he already seemed to.

Ever since the eland had appeared, she felt her friend stood a little in awe of her. She wanted to be just Koba to him — not Koba the magician, the Yellow One, the MaSarwa, or even the Khoisan.

Khoisan! She had once tried to explain that her people had no name for themselves and others who look and live like them. Why would they? They never met any others; there were too few of them spread across an area

249

too vast, she had learned from looking at maps with Mata. The only word they'd used for themselves was Ju/'hoansi; Harmless People was the closest translation she could think of.

But she saw that /Ton needed a name for her type of people. There was much in /Ton books and newspapers about labelling people. Still, if there had to be a title, shouldn't the people choose their name themselves? Mata agreed and asked which group name she would choose if she could.

'Bushmen.'

'But that word has always been used as an insult.' Mata had frowned an arrow line deep into her face.

'Yau, what's wrong with coming from the bush? We all do, here at Impalala.' Mata's eyes had grown very bright then and Koba had quickly said that from what she saw in the newspapers, the bush was safer than the city. Trouble in Cape Town, in Durban and then at a smaller n/ore called Sharpeville — the one that had made Mata cry so. And all because of Passbooks, Koba thought. What was this Passbook but a paper that said you were a person who had to carry a paper, or go to prison? Yau, the /Ton! Better to be a Bushwoman living in the bushveld. At least for the little time left.

Lately Zuma had been particularly present in the cave at night, mumbling on and on about chest-tappings and the need to heed them.

At first Koba had thought the old spirit was jealous of her closeness to these /Ton. But now she knew it was more than that; the fear snaking up her spine told her so. But running or hiding did not help. She'd learnt that.

Therefore she sat calmly next to the churning river, studying the reeds, noting their silent parting and closing as something dainty moved about in them. Just a little reedbuck or a duiker, perhaps, she thought.

She cocked her head, listening for movement in the undergrowth on the riverbank. Nothing yet. She resumed her leisurely observation of the island and saw a group of red bishops alight on the reeds, making them bow gracefully towards the water. The vivid males, puffed out atop the pale stalks, reminded Koba of flaming match-heads. Mannie regularly gave her boxes of matches. She loved the lion on the front and the convenience of one-strike fire — much quick-quicker than rubbing sticks together. She would take some with her, she decided. The Ju/'hoansi would be glad to have easy fire.

Koba then heard cursing as someone slipped down the muddy bank. Nyanisi,

251

youngest of Gideon's three wives, slid into view, scrabbling for a handhold to arrest her fall, her wide skirt rucked up almost to her waist, her beaded headband slipping over one eye. The other eye flashed angrily at Koba.

Perhaps she knows I sat here so it would be difficult to reach me, Koba thought. Her impassive nod gave away none of her amusement.

Without the traditional courteous pre-amble, without even bothering to rearrange her clothes, Nyanisi blurted out, 'People say you can talk to the ancestors.'

Even though she knew what was coming, Koba felt uncomfortable. For years Nyanisi had been her most hostile neighbour. Koba knew this regal beauty encouraged the piccanins to throw stones at her when she passed the kraal. If anything went missing, Nyanisi immediately suggested that the 'Ugly Yellow One' had stolen it. Koba found it difficult to feel well-disposed towards this woman. Yet she must accept the request Nyanisi was about to make. It was the start of what would be.

She forced herself to remain calm, scrutinising the string on her bow. 'Some-times I hear things,' she said quietly. She was taken aback when Nyanisi began beating her own breast.

'I am suffering,' the Tsonga woman cried. 'Six years I've lain with Gideon. Every time he comes back from the mines, he chooses my hut. I work with him on that mattress he bought me, every night. Hard work — he is an old man. I work harder than a new daughter-in-law pounding the maize. Bang, bang, bang. But still nothing.' She pushed her skirt down and showed her flat, brown stomach. 'I am empty,' she said tragically. 'I've visited three witchdoctors. I've put muti here,' she indicated her mouth, 'and here,' pointing to between her legs. 'Huw-ah, it burnt like fire.' She gazed at Koba with brimming eyes. 'What else must I do? Who else can help me? I'm suffering.'

As the woman's tears fell, Koba looked away. She heard a sniff before Nyanisi continued, 'The other wives mock me. Gideon pities me.' A longer sniff and then urgent fingers on her arm made Koba turn to Nyanisi again. 'Yellow One, you must ask the ancestors why I am without child?' Nyanisi's eyes were pleading. 'Perhaps your little voice,' Nyanisi lifted her lip in a sneer that showed her beautifully even white teeth, 'will not give offence and they might answer? Then you must ask what I can do to take this curse from me.'

'A curse? No.' Koba said quietly.

Nyanisi sprang up. 'It is! It is a curse. Why must this,' she yanked her breast from her bright yellow blouse, 'be used only to suckle a nearly toothless man?'

Koba looked away. Nyanisi had identified the problem herself. Gideon was old, his seed spent, but to tell that to a man as proud as that puffed-up korhaan? She'd have to think carefully about this problem.

'Intercede for me with the Old Ones, little sister. Please. I will give you many presents. Fish and salt and even money.'

Koba considered. Money she had no use for, but Nyanisi's loud mouth could do much to establish her as a healer for as long as she remained at Impalala. This would give her some protection from the Tsonga, but how could she achieve Nyanisi's goal without antagonising the headman? Unfortunately, her discs did not tell her that. For that, she sensed, she would have to use her intelligence.

'With my weak powers I will attempt to ask,' Koba said. 'But it will take time . . . and plenty of salt.'

Nyanisi nodded eagerly.

'Come in three days and I'll tell you what I have learnt.'

★ ★ ★

The news that the problem was Gideon's, not hers, did not please Nyanisi. 'He will not believe. He has proof of his strength — nine children with the other wives.'

'But Gideon is old now. His seed is not fresh and strong.'

'No. They will say I am insulting our man, our father. The other wives will turn him against me. Gideon will send me home and ask for his cows back.' She wrung her hands. 'I cannot shame my father so. My bride-price was the highest in our village.' She crossed her arms. 'I'm not leaving. When Gideon dies I want the hut that is mine. And I want children to look after me in my old age, like Selina. I want a son and a nice, quiet daughter-in-law. Not too clever and with a strong back.'

Koba hid a smile and said gravely, 'Then you must find another man to seed you.'

'Huw,' Nyanisi clapped her hand to her mouth. 'Gideon will kill me.'

'Gideon won't know.'

'But the other women will tell. Jealous-all.'

Koba had her plan ready. 'You can tell them you are working with me, who has the power to make you fertile where others have failed. They won't look for you on Pasopkop.' Nyanisi nodded. This was true enough — who wanted to roam around a haunted hill, even in the daylight? 'Anyway,' Koba continued, 'you won't be there, but out hunting for a strong young father for your child.'

Nyanisi lifted her chin and gave Koba a long-lidded look. A smile, almost lascivious, flirted around her lips. But she knew the problem. 'People will say I'm busy with witchcraft.'

'Tell them you are only using me to plead with the ancestors for a baby. They will understand.'

'Understand that I deserve pity,' Nyanisi said bitterly.

Koba shrugged. A little humility would suit those proud shoulders, she thought.

It was arranged that Nyanisi would leave the farm on afternoons agreed with Koba, who in turn would lie low on Pasopkop.

★　★　★

She saw Nyanisi several weeks later when the woman dropped off a cone of salt and several avocadoes she'd bought during her forays into the township. Nyanisi looked well, Koba thought. Like a woman getting lots of a certain kind of food.

'Not yet,' Koba warned, 'Not before Gideon comes.'

* ★ ★

Mannie tapped a cigarette from the packet of Lucky Strikes as he listened to the latest news on the Rivonia Trial. How dumb could people be? The guys arrested at Lilliesleaf farm weren't terrorists — they were just a bunch of naive Apartheid activists. Amateurs, like Pa said. Laughable to believe a nearby African state was going to send troops in gunboats. Yet the minute news of the raid broke, whites ran for their laager and tourism stopped.

Ma, of course, wanted to go to the trial. Pa put his foot down. There'd nearly been a riot in the court when that oke walked in waving his fist and shouting 'Amandla'. Ma could be arrested, just disappear, Pa said. True — everyone knew the Security Police could keep a person incommunicado for ninety days until they tortured information from them. Mannie took a quick, nervous puff on the cigarette. Did the police keep tabs on people even out in the sticks? Ma had been on illegal demonstrations a few years back, at the time of the Sharpeville killings. He'd wanted to go with her, but Pa wouldn't let him.

Mannie leant back in Deon's armchair and took a long drag on the cigarette. Nice, having the place to himself and not even any guests to worry about. Everyone's attention was focused on Pretoria; even Ma and Pa had gone eventually. They'd compromised. Pa would take the old girl to Pretoria to see her friend, Anna De Wet, if she promised not to attend the trial. Lekker, the way the folks were getting along these days! Walks in the veld together, holding hands under the stars when they thought he wasn't looking. Pa had a spring in his step when he led Ma out to the car yesterday — like he was taking his bride off on a honeymoon or something. Ag shame.

'Yau, you.' Koba stuck her head in through the open window.

'Hey, come in.' Mannie laughed as she sprang lightly over the sill. 'Have a beer.'

She shook her head so vigorously, her headscarf slipped down over her eyes. Impatiently she pulled it off. Mannie felt relieved. She looked like a housemaid in the doek.

'So, sit down. Cigarette?'

She helped herself then made straight for the rocking chair. It was her favourite piece of furniture. She loved the lull of riding it gently, but today she wanted speed. Gideon was home from the mines and it was time to put her plan into action. Just as well — Nyanisi had the glow of a pregnant woman. Koba felt she'd handled the situation well and she wanted to share her pleasure with someone.

'So, what you been doing?' Mannie asked.

She savoured her moment, slowly dragging on the cigarette then carefully exhaling a perfect smoke ring. Mannie did his frog impression, goggling his eyes at her. She giggled, then said smugly, 'I am helping Nyanisi be preg by Gideon.'

'Pregnant?'

Koba nodded.

'Ha,' Mannie slapped his knee, 'so the old cock's still got it in him, hey?'

'No, in Nyanisi,' Koba kept a straight face. 'But not Gideon's.'

Mannie exploded into laughter, 'Jis, Koba, you're getting too clever!' When he'd wiped his eyes he said, 'So, Nyanisi's got a lover, hey? Gideon'll kill her if he finds out.'

'That's why she's giving him my muti and saying it's made his seed strong again.'

'Maybe it has.'

'Bah — it's only jackalberry leaves. To make his tongue burn for whispering against me.' Mannie snorted a laugh. 'Gideon's seed is dead.'

'But he's fathered children with his other wives. Or aren't they his either?'

She shrugged.

'I bet you know. Your n/om animal has

probably talked with Gideon's ancestors and then trotted back to tell you.'

'Stop it,' she waggled her cigarette at him warningly.

Mannie laughed. 'Ja-jong, deny it all you like, but I saw that eland where it had no business being.'

'That was a gwa dream.'

'Ag, kak, man. I never smoked any of that druggie stuff. I just know what I saw. Like Shakespeare said, 'There are more things in heaven and earth . . . ''

'Horatio,' Koba said as she stubbed out her cigarette.

Mannie fell silent. He'd long felt that Koba should be studying now. She should write the matriculation board exam with him in December. She'd probably fare better than he would. But the education authorities had flatly refused her permission, despite Ma's efforts. What was going to happen to her, he wondered? Would they grow apart once he'd left school and gone away to study?

'You ever think of going back to find your people, Koba?'

'Soon.'

'What?'

'Not now, Frog-boy. Not that talk now.'

He stared at her. What was she planning? Why hadn't she said anything before? How could she look so relaxed? He felt all churned up inside.

Koba was sprawled in the chair, a slim arm and leg gilded by sun lazy in its leave-taking. He let out a long sigh. Jis, she was pretty!

Funny how in the beginning he couldn't wait for her to go. When had that changed, he wondered? And why hadn't he seen before how important she was to him? She'd shared the biggest events of his life. He felt a lump grow in his throat. He crawled across the floor towards her. 'Koba?' She slipped into his embrace.

This had been a long time coming and now it was here, she shook with excitement. Some dread too. A tapping had begun in her chest, but it was very faint and easily ignored. She lifted her face to nuzzle his neck. Beer, tobacco, /Ton boy . . . nice-nice. She offered him her mouth.

He sampled it, reverently savouring its guava-softness. Koba undid the buttons of her blouse then, arching her back like a bow, she offered him her breasts.

*   *   *

For days they wallowed in each other, discovering the tantalizing tastes and textures of another body. Mannie marvelled at each

261

new nuance of Koba — flesh and fluid. He found chamois on her thighs, peach skin on her bottom, the juice of new grass between her legs — fresh, herby, sour and sweet.

Theirs was a movable feast: on the lawn, under the fizz and pop of champagne stars; in the bath, where wet and shiny they slipped and slithered on each other, over and under, in and out, like a pair of otters.

In the oven of the afternoon they tiptoed into the shuttered master bedroom and played at being prison lovers as the sun fell in bars across their bodies.

Finally, drunk with loving, sore from fucking, careless of discretion, they staggered naked to the kitchen, desperate for food and drink.

Mannie wrenched open the fridge door, plunged his thumb through the foil top and glugged down half a bottle of cold milk. Koba declined. She was sucking at an icy cola bottle, pressing its curvy coolness against her cheek, her chest, the burn between her legs.

Mannie groaned. 'That looks so sexy . . . but I can't, I'm finished.'

Koba chuckled a deep-throated challenge and held his gaze with her almond eyes. Neither registered the tap at the door until it became a hammering.

Mannie grabbed a tea towel and held it

over his groin. Koba dropped to the floor, crawling out of sight.

'Hold on, will you?' he called.

'No, Master. Master must help me . . . ' One of the Tsonga women sounded frightened.

'I just have to . . . '

'Please, Master must hurry.'

Mannie yanked on the shorts Koba had tossed to him before opening the door a fraction. He saw Nyanisi, wringing her hands in front of her growing belly.

'I must speak with the MaSarwa.' She leaned into the gap, trying to speak around the door. 'Koba, Gideon thinks the muti . . . '

'Koba isn't here.'

Nyanisi took a step back and looked the boy up and down, slowly and insolently, her lip lifting slightly to show her matchless teeth.

Mannie stood with his arm blocking her way. Silently, he cursed her. This blerry woman was making him blush. After the two best days of his life, he now felt bad — like he'd been caught doing something dirty. He didn't want to think of Koba like that; now he was been forced to. Focking Nyanisi — spoiling everything because of her whoring.

'Gideon will hit me if the MaSarwa does not show this is his child,' she said.

'Well then, you'd better go find her.'

Mannie slammed the door on her furious face.

★ ★ ★

That last night they locked the house against the world. In the morning, Deon and Marta would return, Koba would resume her work as a healer and Mannie would go back to school. They knew all would be the same as before, but different.

They lay close in the big bed, Mannie's body curved around Koba's, arms enfolding her, hands cupped over her breasts — not to feel the thrill of her nipples peaking against his palms but to protect her and perhaps to assuage his guilt.

Ma had never discussed sex with him but he felt instinctively that she wouldn't approve of this. Because it was Koba, or because they were too young, or unmarried, he wasn't sure.

Married! There was a focking stupid law against it. Anyway, he didn't want to be; he was too young; maybe he'd never marry. He couldn't marry Koba anyway.

But then should he have slept with her? Had he taken advantage of her? No-way. He'd have left it at kissing; she'd started the other stuff. And he was so glad she had. It was so lekker. And she was so beautiful. Shit man, why was his life so blerry complicated? Okes got their rocks off all the time without torturing themselves about it, didn't they?

Mannie eventually fell into a fretful sleep.

Koba didn't. It was time.

If only there was somewhere they could go, somewhere they might be together, she thought. She'd wake her Frogboy and make him run with her now, before it was too late. But there was nowhere for people like them and this was the surest way to end it.

Zuma had been right all along. Little by little she was losing her skin here and she could delay leaving no longer. If she didn't have the strength herself to pull up the roots she had been warned against growing, she was going to have to do it the way the discs had shown — a cruel and frightening path, but one that would lead her home. She just wished the gentle boy sleeping next to her didn't have to be hurt.

She lay awake listening to the tappings in her chest. They seemed to grow more urgent with every heartbeat.

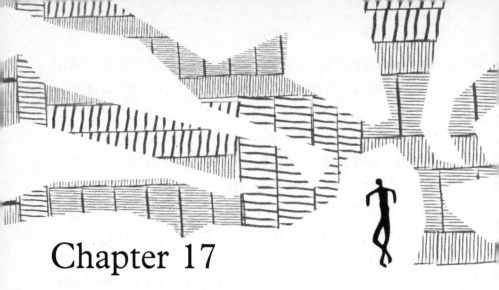

Chapter 17

With the new day came the sound of a van pulling up. Koba heard the dogs bark and then whimper. She shivered. Silence, then heavy footsteps trying to tip-toe quietly around the house. She lay unmoving in her lover's arms, hoping the tapping in her chest wouldn't wake him, reminding herself that Ju/'hoan strength lay in endurance.

The wooden shutters shrieked as the axe broke through them. Mannie sat up, fists flailing. Terror bulged out of his eye sockets.

A large policeman heaved and huffed through the window, cursing as the splintered shutter snagged his blue serge. A younger policeman was striding towards the bed from the doorway, smirking.

Koba kept her head on the pillow, eyes following him. He ignored her gaze and addressed himself to Mannie.

'We had a tip-off the maid was doing some

after-hours for you, Master. Let's see.' He ripped the bedcovers off the teenagers with a theatrical flourish.

'Liewe Magies,' the lumbering captain was now in the room, mopping the fat roll at the back of his neck with a dingy handkerchief. 'Not just a kaffirgirl,' he leaned across Mannie to peer more closely at the rigid Koba. 'He's doing it with a child! Sies. Bad enough you break the Immorality Act, but with a minor! Shame on you.'

The black policeman hovering in the doorway spoke up. 'Bushman, Baas. Small.' Message delivered he stepped smartly back into the shadows.

'Bugger-me. How old are you, girl?'

Koba just looked at him.

His face reddened. 'Don't just lie there making cheeky eyes at us, girlie. Get up. You're under arrest.'

The younger man grabbed Koba's arm and wrenched her off the bed. For a moment her slight brown body dangled in the air, limp as a rag-doll. Then she was chucked into the corner.

Mannie shouted and lunged at the smirker.

Smirk and his sidekick were ready for the boy. Quickly his arms were trapped and pinned behind his back, so tightly his shoulder blades cracked together. Still he struggled.

'Listen, sonny, don't make your situation any worse than it is, see. Just get dressed nice and quietly.' They handed him his underpants. In the heat of humiliation he tried to put two feet through one leg hole.

'That always happens,' the policemen guffawed as they stripped the bed, bundling the bottom sheet into a bag for evidence.

'You know, Captain, I read the other day that some Tukkies professor advised kaffirs against using sheets. Something about it being bad for the shine on their skins.'

'Don't believe everything you read, Jordaan. Now, we'll need your protection, son.'

Mannie stared aghast at the captain.

'You didn't use any, did you? Honestly, you kaffirlovers make me sick. D'you think there aren't enough blerry coloureds in this country? Liewe Magies!' He took his cap off and wiped the back of his porky hand across his moist forehead. 'Never mind, the District Surgeon can probably get all we need from inside the maid. Right men, just a quick look around in case we've missed anything . . . '

Smirk began ripping open drawers and flinging their contents onto the floor, not even pretending to look through them. The black constable got down on all fours and peered under the bed. Mannie noticed that the window was unguarded. Koba could

268

easily slip through it and take off. He could start a scuffle to delay the chase. She'd find a place to hide, knowing the farm as she did. He caught her eye, and with a glance pointed to the window. Almost imperceptibly she shook her head. Mannie's mouth hung open. What was the matter with her?

Then the search charade was over and they were shoved out of the room and into the back of the police van outside.

'Normally, we don't expect a white man to ride in the back with the kaffirs,' Smirk said, 'but under the circumstances . . . '

The grille banged shut and the van shot off, its acceleration throwing Mannie and Koba together against the sharp metal of the wheel housing. He wanted to grab her then and shout in that imperturbable face that she'd missed her chance of freedom. She'd rejected the only way he knew of to save her from what might lie ahead. But the ride was too violent for speech. They were being buffeted about, banged and bruised as they bounced down the dirt track.

Somehow, he had to get a message to his parents. He clung onto the back door, fingers through the grille like a desperate monkey. They'd soon be passing the Tsonga compound. That was their last chance.

Only one figure stood outside the reed

fence. She seemed to be waiting for the van. It was Nyanisi, upright under the enormous bundle on her head. But her face looked strangely misshapen, one eye swollen closed.

Mannie pressed hard up against the grille and bellowed, 'Police station. Tell the Mutari.'

Nyanisi smiled, revealing her broken front teeth.

Chapter 18

'Deon, I'm very grateful to you for taking me.'

Marta put her hand over his as it rested on the steering wheel.

He stared at it happily, not noticing how brown age spots blurred her delicate dusting of freckles. The five-hour trip was the perfect end to a damn good week, he thought. It had been years since he and Marta had taken a holiday; years since his wife had been this relaxed. Mind you, he thought, they'd both been busy: him establishing the rest camp, her getting all those drawing commissions from the publisher. Then there was her protest work.

Thank God she'd given up with the Minister for Education. What was the blerry point of alerting the authorities to Koba's presence on the farm just because Marta wanted her to have a certificate that showed how clever she was? They were breaking the law having Koba there at all. They were already up to their quota for African residents; they'd never get permission for another one who hadn't even been born there. But Marta insisted everyone should be able to take the exam they wanted to. She'd suggested Mannie refuse to take his, on principle.

Ja, Marta still got all flushed and fiery about principles and he still found it frustrating — and sexy as hell. Now they had time, he'd like to show her. Again. He'd like to stop the car right now and kiss her, make love to her on the back seat of the Vauxhall, right there, on the side of the road.

He placed her hand on his groin and raised an enquiring eyebrow.

Marta said laughing, 'I'm too old to be caught in a compromising situation on a national road, Mr Marais. Anyway, you've had quite enough for an old boy.'

Deon sighed theatrically and returned her hand to her with a gallant bow.

Marta smiled. The trip to Pretoria had been such fun: shopping, dinner-dancing at elegant Ciro's, going to the bioscope three times — a bioscope where patrons dressed up even though they'd be sitting in the dark.

Now, however, she felt guilty. This was a tense time for the country. Nelson Mandela was going to jail and grave injustice was being condoned by the highest body in the land. She should have been in mourning, not in evening dress.

'Will you look at that,' Deon said as they crested the last rise of the Highveld escarpment. 'A storm coming, at this time of the year!'

'No, it can't be. Not in the winter. Maybe locusts?'

'No. There's big weather up ahead, I'm telling you.' The sky darkened further as they began their descent to the Lowveld. Impalala was still more than an hour away and a warning wind was beginning to agitate the stiff leaves of mango and orange trees as they drove past orchards. Now the sky was an engorged purple. It pulsed with sheet lightning. Then a bolt zig-zagged down to the valley and crackled angrily up again, iridescently white. Marta counted to five before she heard the roll of thunder.

'Five miles away, the storm.'

Deon had to raise his voice because of another peal of thunder. 'No-way. It's just above our heads.' He smiled. 'My Ma used to say it was the angels moving their furniture.'

'That settee must be big enough to seat the whole host then,' Marta shouted back as a mighty rumble drowned out even the engine noise. Wind was buffeting the car, tree crowns looked like umbrellas blown inside out and the rain began to pellet down, the drops zinging into the bonnet like birdshot. The wipers fought to clear the veil of water across the windscreen, but when the raindrops turned to sticky hailstones, Deon pulled off the road and switched the ignition off. They sat, unperturbed. The car was a relatively safe place to be in an electrical storm and the rain would soon stop. With a squeak of leather, Marta shifted along the seat towards Deon. He put his arm around her shoulders. Through the steamed up windows they didn't notice the rain stop as suddenly as it had started. The sun began to steam the puddles off the tarmac.

★   ★   ★

Afterwards, Marta stayed snuggled in her husband's arms. 'I'm glad I'm going home; I'm not brave enough for subversive politics, like Anna-and-them.'

He stroked her hair. 'You're as brave as a lioness, Martjie.'

'No, I just write letters and demonstrate. Anna goes to court and visits detainees in jail. She says they use electric cattle prods to extract information from the prisoners. One died in custody, supposedly from hanging himself.'

'Himself, my eye! He would have had assistance from the ever-helpful security boys.'

'Maybe he did hang himself — to put an end to the torture?' Marta shuddered. 'Can you imagine?'

'Hell-no. Rather give me six rondavels with blocked toilets to deal with.'

She straightened up and began to button her blouse. 'Ja. Or twelve meals to cook.'

'Cook!' Deon laughed. 'Are you sure you wouldn't rather be tortured?'

★ ★ ★

An hour later the Vauxhall rattled over the cattle grid at Impalala.

'Tomorrow I must get started with re-thatching. Number five's the worst,' Deon said. He clicked his tongue in irritation. 'Will you look at that light, left on in the middle of the day? And what's the matter with the dogs?'

As soon as Marta walked into their bedroom she knew something was very wrong. Paper, powder, clothing were scattered everywhere, drawers were upturned.

Why had the bed been stripped? And what,

in Heaven's name, had happened to the shutters?

Heart hammering, she ran to Mannie's room. Tidy, and the bed unslept in.

Oh my God, he must have been in our bed when he was attacked.

She tore back to her room and cast about for signs of blood. Nothing. But the bedclothes were missing. Had the attackers used them to bundle the body up in? She must find them. Koba. Koba could help. Weren't her people the best trackers?

Marta ran from the room screaming, 'Find Koba!'

A pair of strong, brown hands halted her. 'Manana, the kleinbaas. They took him.'

'Who? Who took him?' she begged Selina.

'The po-lis.' Marta stared at Selina, her mouth wide but silent now. They both heard the uneven thud of Deon running into the house.

'What's the matter? W-who's hurt? What the hell happened?'

Patiently, as though talking to slow-learning children, Selina explained what she'd gleaned from a reticent Nyanisi.

'When did they take them? Where to?'

'How can Nyanisi know for sure?'

★   ★   ★

Deon pushed passed the sergeant hurrying out from behind the charge desk and burst into the captain's office. 'My boy, Manfred Marais, where is he?'

The captain rested his hand on the putter he'd been swinging.

'And you'd be, sir?'

'His father!'

'Well, sir, I'm sorry to inform you that your son has been arrested and will be charged under the Immorality Act. We caught him 'in flagrantas' with your little maid.'

'She is not a maid,' Marta hissed.

'I don't care how you caught him, take us to the children. Right now.'

'I'm afraid that's not possible.' The captain looked directly at Marta for the first time. He'd heard rumours she was a communist but to him she looked just like any other farm wife. 'Special Branch have taken the opportunity to question them. They're on their way to Special Police Headquarters where they'll be held under the General Law Amendment of 1963.'

Deon's face bleached. 'The Ninety Day Act?'

The captain nodded.

Marta crumpled into a chair.

★ ★ ★

At first they were too tense to talk as they drove with reckless speed back to Johannesburg, through valleys where the crocodile river ran mud brown after the downpour, up the mountain pass, two-wheeling round hairpin bends, Deon with his hand on the horn to warn unseen traffic. A long race back across the escarpment passing dusty fields around lone farmsteads, the odd copse of gum trees, wind-pumps that turned creakily in a listless breeze. Marta stared unseeing at the blood-red cattle behind barbed-wire fences, the kites perched periodically on the unending telegraph lines, raising and lowering their tales as they watched the ground intently. She didn't even blink at the black widow bird flying off across the veld, a snake dangling from its beak.

Please God keep them safe. Not the cattle prod, not cigarette burns on their genitalia, not their heads in suffocating bags. Please, please. It's my fault . . . if I'd never brought her to Impalala . . . I shouldn't have left them. They're just children.

Deon, meanwhile, gnawed at a knuckle, thinking it unlikely the security police would allow them to see the kids. Under the Ninety Day Law they weren't compelled to — they didn't even have to admit they were holding them in detention. He'd have to think of something, make a plan. And he'd have to get back to the farm soon. He couldn't expect Selina to keep an eye on things for long, even with no guests in camp. Man, he could do with a drink. He had been driving nearly all day. Nine, ten hours? He was dog-tired. Marta too, he shouldn't wonder.

'Deon, do you think those two, Koba and Mannie, have been er . . . lovers, for a while?'

'Hell-man, I don't know; can't say I'm too happy about the idea, though.'

Marta sat very still. She didn't want to hear this. Not now, when she needed his support to get through the trials ahead. Condemning the children morally was one thing. But politically? No, please God, not from this man she'd felt so close to just a few hours earlier on this very same stretch of road.

She spoke, hoping to pre-empt him, 'I ask because, if Mannie is sexually inexperienced, well, he might think he's in love.' She saw Deon's mouth move to form the words. She rushed on. 'Koba, I'm not so sure about. She's got a strong sense of her destiny, I suspect. I wouldn't be surprised if she could foresee certain things . . . you know, I mean it's not uncommon among the Ju/'hoansi. Not that she's ever told me anything like that, mind you. You know how private she is. Such a dignified little person.'

279

'Ja-no, but . . .'

'Ja-well, all I'm trying to say is, she'll know they have no future together and not just because of the law of this land. She's clever, but it's more than book learning she's got. It's like a wisdom she's inherited or something.' She turned her body to face him as an idea occurred. 'You know what it reminds me of? That thing they say about elephants — about how a new matriarch just knows where the water holes are, even if she's never been there before. She just knows what to do for the survival of the herd. Instinctively.'

'You're doing it again.'

'What?'

'You know. She-Tarzan, we plain-Jane.'

'I am not!' Marta turned away and stared at the empty road ahead. 'All I'm saying is, I think Koba knows her place is with her people. But Mannie?' She lifted her shoulders in a helpless shrug.

'One thing's for sure, it'll be hard for him to cope with the gossip there'll be about him,' Deon said. 'Socially, he'll be isolated. No self-respecting father's going to let our son date his daughter, is he?' Marta's lips became very thin. 'But the thing that really bothers me about this is, dammit-all,' he smacked the steering wheel, 'our boy, with *her!*'

Marta's heart sank.

'Jissus-man,' Deon pressed on, 'she's like a sister to him. I mean, it's practically incest.'

For a few moments Marta was stunned. Then she leaned across and kissed him.

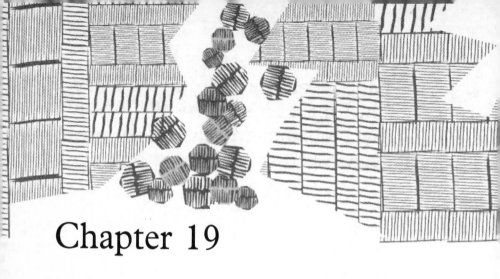

Chapter 19

When they got to Security Police Headquarters it was closed. The discreet entrance was locked, no uniformed policemen or even security guards in sight, no police vehicles, no blood stains on the pavement. Just a notice stating 'Hours: 8.30am to 5pm'.

Marta stood staring up at the building. Could this really be it — above a grocery store, she wondered? There were lights on in some windows, high above, but no bars that she could see. Perhaps the cells didn't have windows? Perhaps the children weren't even here? Where, where was she going to find them? Where could she begin to look? She turned to face the road. Traffic droned passed in an indifferent stream.

How could all these people, with children tucked up safely in bed, driving out to dinner or the bioscope, not care? Didn't they know the danger they and their children were in?

The evil being done in this bland building they drove by every day? But the truth was the occupants of the cars and their families were all safe. They were white. She wanted to run into the traffic, screaming and screaming and screaming.

★ ★ ★

They checked into a boarding house nearby and were served supper. They didn't notice the twice-boiled meanness of the boarding house soup, or the stickiness of the oilcloth beneath their cracked bowls. That night they lay in bed, holding hands, staring at the neon light shining through the threadbare curtains. 'Vacancies' it flashed.

★ ★ ★

At 8am the next morning they were outside the grocery store on the main street. To its left an entranceway led to a small lobby with a three-person iron-grille lift and a staircase. They chose the stairs and had to join a sedate ascension of ordinary-looking business men in suits and ties, distinguishable as security police only by their uniform short-back-and-sides haircuts.

The headquarters was already open for

business, the long wooden bench in the barely furnished waiting room holding three occupants: two black women who held hands, and a young man.

Marta went straight to the desk, gripping it with both hands. 'We'd like to speak to someone about the detention of our son . . .'

'And another minor,' Deon added.

From an open office door they heard a command barked, 'It's the Marais boy and the Boesman girl; came in last night. Give them the next-of-kin letter.'

Marta sat down. Hard. The impact jarred her spine all the way to her neck. She heard herself sob.

'Tula, tula,' she heard one of the women whisper in comfort. But there could be none. A man emerged from the open door. He wore a short-sleeved shirt and a kind smile.

'Mrs Marais, is it?' He stopped in front of Marta. 'Captain Steyn, Security Police.' He put his hand out. Deon hurried over to take it. 'Now don't you worry; your boy's quite safe. Just want to ask him a few questions and then . . .'

'But where are they, the children?' Deon interrupted.

'If you'd take the time to read the letter the clerk has provided you with, Sir, you'd see they are being held at Jeppe Street station, no

284

more than two miles from here. A nice modern facility, cells on one side, charge office on the other. Even a little courtroom.'

Marta's breathing felt constricted. 'Can we see them?' she managed.

'I'm afraid that won't be possible at the present time. But you can leave fresh clothes for them with the sergeant at the desk, and food. No news materials of course.'

Deon gripped Steyn's tanned forearm. 'Captain, please. We are both men of the world. My boy having, er, sexual congress with . . . ag-man, it's hardly a matter of state security, is it?'

Steyn withdrew his arm as if from an open sewer. 'I'm afraid that the General Law Amendment Act prevents me from discussing the case with you at the present time, so if you'll excuse me . . . '

* * *

As they hurried down the staircase, they heard heavy footsteps behind. The larger of the two black women had followed them from the waiting room.

'Sew; the madam must sew a letter in the shirt,' she panted.

'Excuse us?' Deon said.

'For the boy; you' son. They never will let

you see, but po-lis, they give the clothes. We put the letter, small-small, in the collar of the shirt and sew closed.'

Marta recovered herself and addressed the woman in Zulu. It was a lucky choice. She was from Natal but had been in Johannesburg for a month trying to secure the release of her son, Jabu Zondo, arrested under the Sabotage Act. She had recently received a letter from him saying he was well and being fairly treated. She pulled it from her bra and, unfolding it carefully, showed it to Marta. The handwriting looked shaky.

'That is not his hand,' Mrs Zondo said. 'Jabu would never go out of the lines like that. He was my first-born. He was very good in school. Since he was that high.' She pinched three fingers and held them at knee height. 'Now I want to know, what have they done with him? When is he coming home?'

Captain Steyn appeared at the top of the stairs. 'Mrs Zondo,' he barked, 'I haven't got all day you know.'

★   ★   ★

The uniformed policeman at Jeppe Street station confirmed that one Manfred Marais and a Bushman female, name unconfirmed, were being held in custody there. 'Separately,' he sniggered, 'in solitary.' Marta and Deon would not be able to see them.

* * *

Back outside, Deon said he was going to telephone someone — an old hotel chum who'd gone into the police force. 'You coming?' he asked Marta.

She shook her head. 'No. I'm going to buy a shirt for each of them, and a needle and some cotton. I'll see you back at the boarding house.'

But Marta found she couldn't just walk away. She wanted to stay near the police station and walk around the building, just in case.

In case of what, she thought, on her fourth circuit? Would she be able to catch their bodies if they were pushed out of a window? Could she shout, 'Mama's coming' when she heard them scream? There were no screams, only the sound of cars, buses and motorbikes buzzing by in an unending, unknowing stream.

Eventually she went off to make her purchases.

* * *

Back in their room, Deon found her unpicking the collar of a school shirt. 'Myburg will do what he can, but he's not optimistic. He says our best bet's someone in government. I know it's a long shot, but we could ask Lettie. See if she keeps up contact with any of Etienne's old party choms?'

'Ja-ja, go call her.'

* * *

Though they hadn't seen Lettie since their visit to Sukses, they'd stayed in touch. Marta was a conscientious letter writer while Lettie preferred to telephone. Marta was sure that everyone on the Onderwater district party line was glad of Lettie's preference. Her sister-in-law was still famously indiscreet.

'Wragtig, what a scandal!' Lettie said on hearing the news. 'But I can't say I'm surprised, Deon. It's mos what you must expect if you insist on treating them the way Marta does. Give a kaffir an inch and they take a whole yard.' Deon heard a collective whisper of sympathy from the listeners-in.

'But, ja-no, children are such a worry, hey? There's my André with hair down below his ears.' Deon found himself gripping the receiver very tightly. 'Dankie tog his father isn't here to see it.' She sighed dramatically.

'Anyway, no good crying over spilt milk, hey? Look, I'll have a think about what I can do. If I can help to keep the Marais name out of this, I will.'

Deon stepped through the door of the first bar he passed on his way back to Marta. He sat down, willing himself to order only a cola. If he started on brandy it wouldn't be for show. He must get back, but he needed a few minutes on his own. Marta would understand. She needed him strong now.

His eyes sought his reflection and found it behind a battlement of bottles stacked in front of the mirror. He smiled sardonically to see his old stalwart, Klipdrif brandy, in such close proximity to his mirrored mouth. Klipdrif — Stone Ford. And what was that English expression? Between a rock and a hard place. Ja, that was how he felt now.

He ordered a cola.

★   ★   ★

By the next morning, Lettie had sprung into action. She called Deon to report her progress. 'I spoke with Denis Bezuidenhout . . .'

'Denis?!'

'Ja, a rooinek Bezuidenhout, but toemaar, his heart's in the right place. He's an MP

289

— Nationalist, of course. He did a lot of shooting with Etienne. Etienne always called him 'Anyone-for-tennis-my-name-is-Denis' — ag, you know how funny Etienne could be. Shame-man, Denis was very kind when Etienne died. Came to the funeral. All the way from Cape Town, hey? You remember him? Tall, handsome man and he's got a good chin. His wife died not so long ago — thyroid. I sent a lovely tribute: carnations, red and white. Denis remembered and said . . . '

'Lettie! What did he say about getting the children out?'

'Ag-no-what, it can't be done. Parliament's got no say over the Security Police. But he says old Senator Bosch is your best bet. The man's very big on Bushmen.'

'D'you know him?'

'Ja-well-no, not actually. But I did sit next to him once. Magies, he was boring! Talked about Separate Development all night long. But I don't think he'll remember me. Didn't even want to dance, and anyway, he and Etienne didn't see eye to eye. He thought Etienne shouldn't have any tame Bushman on the farm. Send them all back to the desert, he said. It's their homeland.'

Deon felt a glimmer of hope. 'He's the one, Lettie. He's the man we've got to talk to about Koba. Can you do it?'

'Ag-no, I don't think so.'

Deon thought for a minute. 'What about if Denis Bezuidenhout helps you? I mean, maybe you wouldn't mind speaking to him again and arranging a meeting?'

'Ooh, naughty boy,' Lettie giggled.

'Sorry, Ousus, I know he's a rooinek, but I just thought it might be a good excuse for you to get away from the farm for a bit? I remember how much you enjoyed your trips to Pretoria when Etienne was alive.'

'Ja, it was sooo lovely. He'd take me to Ansteys for a cream tea and buy me a new dress at Finelady's. We'd walk in the garden at the Union Buildings and all the jacaranda blossom would be falling on our heads, like purple confetti.' She began to sound tearful. 'He was a good man, that brother of yours. Why did he have to be taken so young?' She began to snivel. 'Christmases are very hard for me and André.'

Deon saw the need for party-line sympathy. 'Poor Letjie. You've been very brave all these years. If he were here, Etienne would think it high-time you had a treat. Come to Pretoria, Ousus.'

She sniffed loudly. 'I've got so much to do here. It's the Women's Federation meeting next week and I've promised to bake for the church bazaar. Then André . . . '

'And of course I'll pay.'

'Oohh, it would be sooo nice to stay in a hotel and be waited on. I could do a bit of shopping at Finelady's.'

'I'm sure the budget could stretch to that.'

Dinner at a hotel near the Union Buildings was arranged. Denis would be invited, Lettie would wear a new outfit and Deon would get a chance to present his case.

★ ★ ★

Marta, meanwhile, had delivered two parcels to the police station — a shirt, dried apricots and some biltong in each. Sewn into the collars of the thin cotton shirts were long narrow notes written in light pencil, which she'd agonised over, trying to fit as much love and encouragement onto the strip as she could. She was sure the children would get the shirts, but would they think to unpick the collars? Her only hope was they would notice an unusual stiffness around the neck, something the sergeant who inspected the contents of each parcel had failed to feel. Koba might notice the stitches and think they were better now than all those years ago in the storeroom at Sukses. But would she also wonder why they had been unpicked and resewn?

Marta crossed her fingers and prepared to wait.

★ ★ ★

Marta devised a routine for herself; small ceremonies she could perform daily to control her rising sense of panic. She rose, having hardly slept, splashed cold water onto her face, stared into the fly-shit spotted mirror and told herself it would be alright. Then she set out to patrol the perimeter of the Jeppe Street station. Four times round the block — four was lucky. She'd had no further bad news about the children, so four was hope.

Later, she'd step into a public phone booth. She tried her friend Anna De Wet. Anna was oddly abrupt, but they arranged to meet outdoors, in a place Anna described cryptically as 'where we had that picnic'. It could only be Joubert Park, Marta thought, remembering one of their sunny outings from just a few days ago. She made her way there.

The news wasn't good. Anna warned that their telephone was being tapped and for all she knew, she and her civil rights lawyer husband were being tailed. 'I was very careful coming here. I'm sure no one followed. But for Mannie and Koba's sakes we shouldn't be connected. Last thing you need now is an association with suspected 'Commies'.'

They made an arrangement to keep in touch via public call boxes. Anna said there was talk of the so-called Ninety Day Act being extended to 180 days without trial. She also said that Jabu Zondo was likely to be released soon if his mother had received a letter from him.

'Lately, they make them write one of those letters so if the detainee accuses the authorities of torture when they get out, they can produce a copy of the letter to disprove it.' Marta looked white. 'Don't worry. I'm sure they won't be torturing Mannie. He's just a child.'

'Jabu's only seventeen,' Marta replied.

★   ★   ★

Afterwards, Marta went back to the phone box near Security Police Headquarters. Let them keep an eye on her all they liked she thought. From here she could watch them too.

She opened the telephone directory and began to work her way down the list of government departments: Prisons, Justice, Education, Mental Health. She argued with telephonists, secretaries, aides, deputies and, once, a minister, all the while frantically feeding the hungry coin box. They told her to put it in writing, to call back the next day, next week, next month. When Deon found her, she was standing with her forehead pressed against the glass.

'Never mind. Lettie might help.' Marta pulled a face. 'No, really. She's got a good heart . . . '

'I know. And she can't resist a good drama.'

'Ja, especially if she can star in it in a new outfit.' Marta nodded. A smile was more than she could manage.

⋆ ⋆ ⋆

The next day she was back in the phone booth. She didn't lift the handset. There was no one else she could call. She just wanted to stand there, in that cramped, defaced, urine-stinking box.

'They might be like this, their cells,' she explained to a puzzled Deon. 'No bigger than this; the smell might be the same if they only have a bucket to use.'

'But you're getting cold, Marta. You're shivering.'

'They might be cold.'

Deon had to leave her. He went to see if he could secure them an interview with Steyn at

Security Police Headquarters. Marta stayed in the booth, emerging only when the irate tapping of someone wanting to use the phone roused her.

She headed for a bakery where she bought a big box of doughnuts. She carried it, unopened, to the non-European entrance at the Jeppe Street station. She wasn't allowed inside but the black women, who waited there every day, trickled out eventually. She enquired after a Mrs Zondo. Someone told her she'd returned to Natal because her mother was sick. Jabu had not been released. At Marta's insistence, and tolerated because she was that most unusual thing, a white woman fluent in a black language, they helped themselves to a 'Sugarbun'. Might be the only food some of them had all day, Marta suspected.

As the days passed and she became a familiar sight with her box of buns, they talked with Marta — always about their missing children; how they'd never let them out of their sight again when they got them home; how they would cook them their favourite dishes and make them concentrate on their school work. Never about how they'd bury their bruised, broken bodies.

★　★　★

296

Deon sat through an insufferable meal with Denis Bezuidenhout and Lettie, listening to a shot-by-shot account of the man's recent tennis victory. 'The old bugger just would not give up,' Denis said. 'Eventually I had to resort to disguised topspin and sneaky drop shots. Not exactly cricket, hey, but all's fair in love and war, what?' He winked at Lettie.

Neither of them seemed interested in raising the issue of Koba with the Senator. Deon left frustrated. He hoped that 'Tennis Denis' would too.

★ ★ ★

Another week passed with Deon increasingly concerned about expenses. With no money coming in and a stream of bills to settle from Lettie's expensive hotel, he needed to get back to work. He must re-open the lodge, do some advertising, get customers back in. And the publisher might have sent some work for Marta. Shouldn't they leave Johannesburg for a while, he asked?

'You go if you must. I'll stay.'

'But Martjie, you can do nothing here. At home there'll be things to take your mind off . . .'

'I do not want my mind taken off the children. Can't you understand that I can't go back to normal? There is no normal when governments can do this to their citizens.'

'Ja, but money's getting tight and . . . '

'I'll sleep in the doorway at Jeppe Street if I have to. I don't care. I am not going to betray the children by . . . '

'Betray the children? Is that what you think I'm doing just because I've pointed out that we have to have money? I resent that, Marta. I really do.'

Deon left and didn't return to Johannesburg for three weeks. Back on Impalala he worked like a Trojan, setting the lodge to rights, making deals with travel agents to get customers in, trying to keep Mannie's whereabouts secret from those who asked. When he returned he brought fresh clothes for Marta, avocadoes from their tree, and a commission from the publisher. Marta didn't even open it.

Deon said nothing about how empty the farm was without her and the children, nor how tempting the bar in town looked. He couldn't fail Marta. Not again.

That night they lay against each other, forced to by the dip in the boarding house mattress, but they didn't hold hands.

As soon as Deon left for the long drive back, Marta resumed her new work.

She was collecting details of the detainees from their families and preparing a petition to send to the Minister of Justice. That was all she wanted to talk about, even when Anna called her. 'This is something I can do, Anna. I'm not a revolutionary, after all. Just an administrator.'

'Ag, Martjie, you don't have to make a grand gesture. I once heard it said the best contribution to 'the cause' that people could make was inside their own homes, in their own families. You and Deon treat the people who work for you fairly; you've brought your son up to have no prejudice about blacks. Quite the opposite.'

Marta began to laugh.

'Ag sorry,' Anna giggled, 'I didn't mean . . . ' But now Marta was laughing so hard she had to hold onto the sides of the phone booth to support herself. It was part hysteria, she knew, but when she'd wiped away her tears and said goodbye, she felt better.

Chapter 20

Senator Bosch met them in the waiting room of Security Police Headquarters. He looked every inch the patrician, with his full head of silver hair. He stood tall and sure, as though he felt he had God and the government on his side. Steyn wore the sulky expression of a man who had been outranked and outmanoeuvred.

Marta could still hardly believe that Lettie's coquetry had opened doors that had been firmly shut on her pleas and on Deon's persistence.

All dimples and country charm, Lettie had been working the government cocktail and dinner party circuit, eventually engineering a meeting between Deon and the Senator. Once Senator Bosch understood that Koba was an opportunity to show the Homeland Policy at work, he'd written the necessary letters.

Marta, wan and crumpled, was beyond caring who was making mileage out of the situation — as long as the children were freed. She bowed her head gratefully when the receptionist hung an identity tag around her neck.

They were ushered through a reinforced glass door to a hospital-green office. Seats were proffered, but it was a crush. Steyn stepped behind the desk and without looking up said, 'I've prepared all the documentation for you. If Mr Marais would just sign here . . .'

Deon knocked the pen off the desk in his haste to comply. While the officer scrabbled around on the floor for it, the Senator proffered his gold-nibbed fountain pen.

Then it was done and with mixed feelings Marta watched Deon's humble gratitude when Steyn said they'd be dropping all charges and weren't interested in questioning any other members of the family 'at the present time'.

The Senator nodded gravely. Then came a respectful knock on the door and a uniformed policeman stuck his head into the room. Steyn beckoned and seconds later the policeman pushed a boy into the office.

Mannie stood there blinking. He looked pale and very young in khaki school shorts and an open neck shirt. His feet were bare. Marta leapt out of her chair. 'Liebschen, Liebschen!' Her eyes swooped, searching his exposed skin for injury. He seemed blemish-free, but his eyes held a sorrow she couldn't bear to see. She made to pull him to her, but the rigid way her son stood, as though the tightening of his tendons was all that was keeping him upright, stopped her.

Not in front of these people, his haunted eyes begged.

Marta watched Deon clasp their son's thin shoulders and smile at him too long.

'You've grown, son,' she said. Then she had to fall silent as the Senator delivered a lecture on the importance of Afrikaner youth 'keeping pure'.

Marta quivered with suppressed rage.

★ ★ ★

They were then escorted back to the reception area. 'Koba? Where's she?' Mannie asked.

'The Bushman female is being loaded now. She'll be taken to the station and put on a train back to her homeland, courtesy of the government of the Republic of South Africa,' Steyn intoned, 'after the Senator's press conference.'

'But where's she now?' Mannie's eyes were wild, his feet stamped with impatience.

Marta grabbed his cold hand. 'I think I know, son. Come.'

Outside the non-European section, they saw a small figure, swathed in a blanket, being bundled into a police van. Mannie broke away and ran. By the time he reached the vehicle, the doors had been shut. He banged on the grille. 'Koba, is that you?'

'Yau, you.' He heard the words spoken softly by the small, shackled shape.

Then he was shoved aside by a black policeman who barred his view.

Mannie felt himself being pulled backwards. Behind him he heard noise: the babble of black women, a soup of Xhosa, Zulu, Sotho words, and his mother's voice, greeting them. Rough hands stroked him, patting and congratulating. Over the bereted heads of smiling women, he saw Koba's white wire cage shudder as the van started up.

'Thank you, thank you Sissie. Yes, this is Mannie — yes, my first-born. Many thanks. Yes. And may your wait soon be over. May Sipho soon be home safe. And for Mrs Zondo, for her Jabu, I am praying, please tell her, Mama.'

Marta tried to detach herself from the group. She felt as though she'd cheated.

She'd acted like one of them, been accepted as a fellow-sufferer, but clearly she wasn't. Even here she was privileged, advantaged, thanks to her race. Should she have refused the Senator's help? She knew none of these women would have expected her to, but it didn't make her feel any better.

She stared over the beaming faces to look at her son. There was desperation in his bloodshot eyes. 'Please, please, we must go,' she said to the women.

'Ladies,' it was Deon, pushing politely through the crowd, 'if you'll excuse us, our,' his eyes caught Marta's, 'our daughter is in that van. We must follow.'

The crowd parted. Women clapped. A voice called in Zulu, 'You, you sir, and the Sugarbun family, hamba kahle.'

Marta kept her head down as Deon led her away.

★ ★ ★

Lettie was waiting for them round the front, under the 'Whites Only' sign. She was trim in a baby-blue crimpelene suit and matching hat, and stood talking animatedly to Denis Bezuidenhout. To Marta, she seemed dressed for the official opening of Parliament. Lettie tripped forward and kissed the air near

Marta's ear. Then she patted her sister-in-law's cheek with a gloved hand. 'Don't you worry, Martjie, there's nothing here that a good oatmeal face pack won't fix.'

Marta's neck blotched, her eyes glittered dangerously. Deon stepped between them. 'Come ladies. We must get to the station. There's going to be an official send-off. With photographers.'

Lettie's eyes danced under the wide brim of her hat. 'I'll drive,' she said. Blithely, she set off up a one-way street, against the flow of traffic. Facing cars hooted at her Mercedes. 'Oops,' she giggled and grating the gear into reverse she tried to back up the street, tacking right, then left like a sailboat. Denis tensed. 'Ag, I'm sorry, it's this hat.'

'Take it off then,' Marta hissed.

'Ag, even if I take it off, the hairdresser's used so much spray, I feel as though my head won't turn on my neck.'

'Watchit, er, Lettie-liefie,' Denis said, his foot pressed hard against the floorboard on the passenger side.

'Oopsie, was that the curb?'

Deon groaned as they heard the scrape of hubcap and Marta had an overwhelming urge to laugh. She groped in her handbag for a handkerchief and held it to her mouth. Inappropriate, she knew; it must be the relief.

After six of the worst weeks of her life, her son was back with her, safe and sound. He was thinner, filthy and so much older in his eyes, but he was alive. And so was Koba.

Mannie craned forward on the long back seat. He felt as though he'd walked out of prison and onto the set of a 'Carry On' film. His auntie, dressed like the Prime Minister's wife, was using a Mercedes Benz to wreck parked cars; his mother, who looked ten years older than she had a few weeks ago, was killing herself with laughter; his father, whose Sunday-best suit seemed to have grown too big for him, was agreeing with the complete stranger in the front seat that the 'Boks had the best rugby side anywhere in the world; and all the time Koba was leaving.

Had the country gone mad while he'd been in prison? How could it be that a world of muffled screams, slamming cell doors, sobs in the dark and literally shitting one's pants under interrogation could seem more normal than this?

It was insane. He wanted no part of it. If Koba was going back to the Kalahari Desert then so was he. There they could live away from this lunacy. There they could love each other without fear and shame.

★　★　★

At the station, Lettie parked with maximum fuss. Mannie drummed his filthy fingers on the backrest of her seat. Deon stilled his agitated fingers. 'Thanks very much, Ousus,' he said to Lettie before she'd turned off the engine. 'We'll see you inside if that's okay?'

'Ja-ja. You go. I've got to powder my nose. I won't be long; I've got a compact so I don't need to go to the little girl's room.'

'Lettie-love, this is, er, an official occasion,' Denis said, plumping up his cravat.

'I know, I know. That's why I don't want shine on my nose.'

'Yes, well, er, we don't want to miss the Senator's statement — Separate Development and all that. Very important, being seen to practise what we preach. Good opportunity with this, er, Khoisan girl. Quite a find, what? So, er, you powder and I'll just run along in the meantime.'

'No wait, I'm ready.' Lettie dimpled. 'But I'll just go make sure Mannie doesn't get his picture taken by those nosey newspaper men. We don't want a scandal.'

However, Mannie was long gone, thrusting through the crowd in the station concourse.

But it felt weird. Like stepping into a pinball machine: blaring noise; flashing signs; constant movement; people and their baggage obstructing his route at every turn. Which was his route? He stopped, bewildered. He felt giddy and sick. He longed for his dark cell. He'd take more beatings, even the kicks in the balls, if they'd just let him back in.

Then he felt a strong hand on his forearm, steadying him. 'Come on, son. It'll be this way.' Deon led him through a doorway marked 'Non-Whites'. They were at the bottom end of a long platform. Above the 'Whites Only' barricade, uniformed porters pushed trolleys of matching luggage for white passengers. Men in suits and hats, women in floral dresses and gloves. Down below the barricade it was every man and woman for themselves as people scrambled to load bundles, boxes, babies and cardboard suit-cases into the dingy carriages. Mannie spotted a phalanx of serge-blue uniforms. But they were above the barricade in Whites Only.

'She must be there.' His parents watched him race away, ricocheting off people in his path. When they caught up, Mannie was arguing with a young policeman.

'You can't go any closer, sonny. That's a Senator there talking to the press.'

'Fock the Senator. That's my girl . . . '

'Hey, you watch your . . . '

With a waft of L'Air Du Temps perfume, Lettie was among them. 'If you'll excuse me, officer.' She inserted herself between Mannie

308

and his adversary. The policeman stepped back to avoid her hat brim. She tilted her head back and dimpled up at him. 'I'm supposed to be there next to the Senator for the photos, but it's such a crush I can't get through. I'm counting on a big strong man like you to help me.' She tapped his shoulder with her pale blue gloved hand. He immediately shoved his broad shoulder into the tightly packed crowd of onlookers and forced a path through.

Mannie took his chance and ducked through the crush. He saw her at once, very small next to the Senator, her face impassive, her hair wild. Koba didn't flinch as the Senator placed his hand on her head and flashbulbs popped.

Mannie wanted to run to her, wrap her in his arms and take her away from this. But the five feet separating them seemed like miles. He hesitated. He felt afraid. Not because of the police presence but because of the way Koba was gazing past him, her eyes focused on some point on the distant horizon where the railway lines converged.

He smiled and raised his hand to waist level, waving surreptitiously. Koba ignored him.

Lettie arrived with Denis in tow. She slipped one hand through the arm of the

Senator, the other through Denis's. The Senator looked disconcerted. Lettie flashed a dazzling smile at the cameras.

When the photo opportunity was over, the Senator, his phalanx, Lettie and Denis all left. Koba, handcuffed to a black policeman, was pushed towards the Non-White section. 'Koba,' Mannie hissed, following her. She didn't look over her shoulder. The policeman lifted her up the carriage steps onto the train. It juddered into life as the engine started.

Mannie stood stunned. He knew she'd heard him. He'd seen the muscles at the top of her back tense. Why wouldn't she acknowledge him? Did she blame him for their imprisonment? What had they said and done to her in there? Didn't she love him like he loved her? He felt his heart tear.

'You have to let her go, Liebschen.' His mother was beside him, aching to hold him. He swayed. He felt tired, so tired, but he squared his shoulders.

'Ma, have you got sixpence for me?'

Marta looked surprised, but taking out her purse she handed him the small coin.

'Thanks.' And he was off, running up the platform, under the barricade and out of sight.

Koba, installed in a window seat on the train, watched him run away. It surprised her.

She'd felt the pain of his heart in her own. It had cost her all her remaining strength to keep her eyes from his when she saw him at the front of the flashing crowd. Now her Frog-boy was running away. Well, perhaps it was better like this.

Marta tapped on the glass. The policeman lowered the window and indicated that she could lean out.

'Oh my girl, my girl, are you all right? Ag, I'm so sorry for what happened. For everything, you know; from the beginning.' Marta wrung her hands. 'I probably didn't do right by you, Kobatjie. I think I made it worse, the way I kept you on Impalala. Deon was right, all along. He always saw you clearly, like I never did.' Marta was crying, tears coursing over her spots like floodwater over pebbles.

Koba touched her hand as it rested on the window edge. 'A good person who follows their heart can't stray too far from the path, Grandmother says.'

'Ah, I would have liked to have known your grandmother. I'm sorry I never asked about her. So many things I didn't do — would have liked to have done . . . ' Marta raised her hand and placed it on Koba's hair.

'I should have let you braid,' Koba said softly. The carriage jerked as the brake was released. Marta stepped back and stood next to Deon. He took her hand, then he lifted his hat to Koba. She smiled at him. 'I still have your gift.' She took out an old pocket-knife from her returned possessions, the one he'd left outside her cave so many years ago.

As the engine began to gather power Mannie appeared, vaulting over the barricade and sprinting toward Koba. She leaned further out of the window and he thrust a packet at her.

'Here,' he panted. 'Not mongongo nuts. But they are salted.'

Koba peeped at the peanuts and felt her resolve beginning to melt. She lowered her face to his. Timidly, he cupped it in his hands. He saw her lids close and tremble like satiny brown butterfly wings. Two small tears became trapped in her upturned lashes. He reached for her lips with his, but Koba pulled back.

'No.'

Mannie sprang away, his features a mosaic of misery. Now he knew for sure; Koba didn't want him. Even if she had been given the choice, she would have gone back to her people. She had told him, long ago. He just hadn't listened properly.

He balled his fists up in the pocket of his shorts. Why had she let him love her? Why had she let him believe she loved him? What the hell had he taken all those beatings for? Every time the Security Police told him to admit she was just a whore and promise he would never see her again, he'd screamed he loved her and would marry her.

But Koba didn't need him or want him. She belonged to her tribe and he never could. His mouth set as he took a last look at her face. That gentle, concave profile. It was beautiful but it was strange.

Koba drew her head back into the carriage. She felt like a bulb too long uprooted — dry, sour, beginning to shrivel up, draw inwards. She couldn't have kissed Frog-boy. She had no juice left to give.

I've been exposed too long, she thought. There has been too much of me for Clawed Things to tear at.

By now word had spread around the packed carriage that there was a prisoner on board. Curious passengers craned their necks to see the black girl so precious to whites that she had to be guarded by a policeman. She felt their stares. She didn't care what they thought — a train and its occupants no longer terrified her. But she was frightened of what lay beyond this journey, of people who would look at her with more than idle curiosity. Would her kinsmen accept her or reject her?

The driver gave a short blast on the horn and the train jolted into motion. She steadied herself. There was nothing she could do now. She had chosen this path when she chose to remain for the nights with Frog-boy. She could have heeded her tappings, taken money from Mata and gone away by herself — before the policemen came. But she knew, even after all the torment of prison, that she could never have left Impalala of her own free will. The place and the people had grown into her, slowly reaching into her heart like a fig tree forcing its way between rocks. Uhn-uhn-uhn, the roots were deep.

She sighed. It was no help to have the sight and foresee that it would end with sorrow. Neither Grandmother nor the discs had told her how much Frog-boy's hurt would cost her.

She leaned back out of the window. 'Mannie!'

He started. She'd never used his name before.

'You gave me salt. I gave you honey. It was not nothing. Don't forget.'

As the train pulled out she kissed her palm and blew across it towards him.

Glossary

Bakgat	Marvellous, great!
Basie	Young boss
Biltong	Air-dried strips of salted, boneless meat
Bioscope	Cinema
Bliksemse	Swine/bastard
Boep	Belly
Boereperd	A gaited horse
Boerewors	Traditional South African sausage
Boesmanne	Bushmen
Boet	Brother
Boetie	Diminutive of brother
Boetie-boetie	Butter up
Braai	Barbeque
Brak	Mongrel dog
Bundu-bashing	Travelling over rough or difficult ground
Chaffing	Teasing (in context used)
Choms	Chums
Dankie tog	Thank goodness
Doek	Headscarf; traditionally worn by black South African housemaids

Dominee	Minister of the Dutch Reformed Church
Dongas	Gullies
Dopping	Boozing, usually spirits
Eina	Ouch
G//aoan	God
Gaats	Exclamation of surprise or dismay
Goef	A dip, as in swim
Guarri	Shrub
Gwa	A hallucinogenic mixture of plants
Hamba kahle	Go well (*In Zulu*)
Hxaro	The San custom of giving and receiving gifts with designated exchange partners
Jaap	Country bumpkin
Kaffir	Derogatory term for a black African
Kaffirboetie	Derogatory term for 'black African lover'
Kaffirmeid	Derogatory term for a black African maid
Kaross	Cloak made of animal hide
Klaar	Finished
Kleinbaas	Small boss
Kleinboet	Small brother
knobkieries	Fighting stick/club, usually with a knobbed head

Koaq	A respectful demeanour
Koeksisters	Plaited doughnut dipped in syrup
Koppie	Hillock
Korhaan	South African bustard
Kori	Very large bustard
Kraal	A cluster of huts occupied by one family or 'clan'
Kussed out	Passed out/ asleep
Lekker	Nice, pleasant, enjoyable
Liefie	Love
Liewe	Dear . . .
Makulu	Big
MaSarwa	Pejorative term for San/ Khoisan
Meidjie	Diminutive for maid
Mielie	Corn
Miesies	'Missus'
Moerova	'Helluva'
Mos	In fact; actually
Mutari	Boss
Muti	Traditional African medicine
n!a'an	Respect word
n#ah	Type of fruit found in the Kalahari Desert
n/omkxaosi	Owner of medicine
N/ore	Home
Opsaal	Saddle up
Ouboet	Older brother

Ous	Fellows
Outa	Respectful address to an elderly black man
Padkos	Food for a journey
Pasop-jong	Beware, young one
Piccanins	Small black children
Poes	Obscene word for vagina
Pronk	Curvet characteristic of displaying springbok
Rooinek	Red-neck (an Englishman)
Rondavels	Circular house with a conical thatched roof
Sjambokking	Horsewhipping
Smaaked	Fancied
Sprog	Youngster
Stoep	Open porch
Thundersticks	Rifles
Tickeys	Small coin. Equiv. of 2,5 South African cents
Toe	'Closed up'; impenetrably stupid
Toemaar	Never mind
Tokoloshe	An evil spirit
/Ton	White person
Takkies	Laced canvas shoe
Velskoens	Rough shoe of untanned hide
Voetsek, jou	Be off, you fucking mongrels

Focken brakke
Voortreker   A Boer pioneer
Vrek   Die
Wragtig   Exclamation of incredulity

(Note: majority of definitions taken from *A Dictionary of South African English*, Branford, J. with Branford, W. (1991). Cape Town. Oxford University Press)

Background information
by Candi Miller

History of the Ju/'hoansi

As political fashions waxed and waned, the groups of southern African hunter-gatherers, small in build with light brown skin and 'oriental' eyes, have been labelled Bushmen, MaSarwa, BaSarwa, Khoisan and San by researchers. However, these people had no collective name for themselves, although the tribe I write of have always used 'Ju/'hoansi', translating as 'harmless' or 'ordinary people'.

From their perspective, the world was a hostile place. Not only were they surrounded by natural predators but their oral history records their persecution by invading pastoralists, both black and white, for centuries. They were not blameless however, provoking attack from the pastoralists by poaching their livestock and stealing the goods of returning migrant workers. It became common practice to shoot 'Bushmen', abduct their children and use them as indentured labourers on settler farms in what was then German South-West Africa.

320

Modern times have seen no let-up in the problems faced by these nomadic tribespeople. Fences impede the migration of vast antelope herds they depend on for meat. Various governments have expropriated large sections of their traditional hunting grounds for game reserves, forbidding them to hunt there. A quote from Dumba, an elder of the Kxoe San community, illustrates their feelings: *'In the old days we lived as hunters — with a bow and arrow and an assegai. Then the law came that we couldn't hunt. Now we are unsure of our lives . . . '*

Mysticism
To this day, the Ju/'hoansi use a trance dance ceremony for healing purposes. Ju/'hoansi shamans claim to derive their healing power from spirit guides, usually antelope, whom they meet in a mystical world when they trance. Some Shaman say they have an ear for the voices of their ancestors, who might make their presence felt in the form of mini dust tornadoes, or 'dust devils'. Some members of the Ju/'hoansi tribe are able to heal many physical ailments using their knowledge of medicinal plants.

Language
Only in recent years have linguists devised a

way of representing the unusual click consonants in San languages. These are made when the tongue is drawn sharply away from various points on the roof of the mouth. Here's a guide to pronouncing the ones you'll find in this book:

Dental click, as in /Ton, white person. (Sounds like mild reproach: 'tsk tsk'). Place the tip of the tongue immediately behind the top front teeth and pull gently away.

Palatal (alveolar) click, as in N#aisa. Similar to above, but made by pressing front of tongue to roof of mouth, (on the ridge just behind top front teeth.) Withdraw tongue quickly from ridge.

Lateral click, as in Kh//'an. (Similar to the sound one uses to urge on a horse.) Suck one side of the tongue sharply away from the alveolar ridge.

Gutteral (Alveopalatal) click, as in !Xam. A popping noise made at back of mouth, by drawing end of tongue away from curve where the alveolar ridge meets the hard palate.

/'h This denotes long aspiration of the dental click, as in Ju/'hoansi. The apostrophe indicates a check of breath.

Like most cultures who've relied solely on oral communication, the Ju/'hoansi language is rich in wordplay, metaphors, euphemism and vocables. Conversation is entertainment for these people and consequently they are skilled storytellers and mimics. Idiophones litter their dialogue — e.g. '!khui!' for the report of a rifle.

The Ju/'hoansi have a term, 'n!aukxui', for the process of inventing new words to fit new situations. It's more complex than semantics and more fun, producing words like 'iguana fingers' for 'fork'.

They also have a tendency to repeat phrases. This is used to suggest sustained action e.g: Zuma in her story-telling. Then there are 'respect' words for difficult circumstances, e.g. a feeling of dangerous unease is called 'lion's walking' — understandable in their environment.

'Respect' words can also enhance the politeness, prudence or delicacy of chat — 'meat' or 'food' for sex; a giraffe, valued as a bountiful meal, is respectfully referred to as 'Tall Elegant Person'. Tallness is also an accolade from people whose average height is five foot. Baboons, with their lethal bite, are 'placated' with the name: 'People who sit on their Heels'.

You'll read 'what's up-front' as the term for faces and territory is 'tree-water'. Water, unimaginably soothing as it slides through an oesophagus perpetually sand-blasted in the

Kalahari, is simply, 'soft throat'.

I could go on and on but this is not a dictionary. A Ju/'hoansi/English dictionary was compiled by Patrick Dickens and produced in 1994. Researchers like Megan Biesele in her book, 'Women Like Meat', do much to celebrate the vivacity of the Ju/'hoansi language.

Acknowledgements

I would like to acknowledge the work of the charity for tribal people's rights, Survival International, not just in southern Africa, but all over the world. You can learn more about their campaigns at:
www.survivalinternational.org.uk

Also, grateful thanks to those who helped with the research for this book: George Bizos, Gaye King, Andre Kritzinger, officers of the Nyae Nyae Foundation and the Ju/'hoansi people living in that particular area of Namibia. They tolerated my company and were gracious enough to myth-swap with me around their campfires at night in the Kalahari.

Invaluable advice was obtained from experts in their respective fields: Prof. M. Toolan and Gary Travlos — thank you. For years of support and help, my eternal gratitude to Bev Wilson Schram, and may I express my appreciation to my willing readers and wonderful editors: Betty Chicken, Maeve Clarke, Tamar Hodes, Rob Johns, Dina Lewis, Penny Rendall and Uma Waide.

Myra Miller and Crystallo Travlos — couldn't

have done it without you two stepping in to care for my family while I was buried in the book — and to Louka, Xanthe, Yiannis and my mother, Myra, thank you for patience beyond the call of familial duty.

Also a big thank you to every writing student I've ever had. I've learnt so much from all of you — and it's been fun. And finally, in memory of my first creative writing teacher, Lionel Abrahams.

Candi Miller

We do hope that you have enjoyed reading this large print book.

Did you know that all of our titles are available for purchase?

We publish a wide range of high quality large print books including:
Romances, Mysteries, Classics
General Fiction
Non Fiction and Westerns

Special interest titles available in large print are:
The Little Oxford Dictionary
Music Book
Song Book
Hymn Book
Service Book

Also available from us courtesy of Oxford University Press:
Young Readers' Dictionary
(large print edition)
Young Readers' Thesaurus
(large print edition)

For further information or a free brochure, please contact us at:
Ulverscroft Large Print Books Ltd.,
The Green, Bradgate Road, Anstey,
Leicester, LE7 7FU, England.
Tel: (00 44) **0116 236 4325**
Fax: (00 44) **0116 234 0205**

UNSTOLEN

Wendy Jean

The thing about being the unstolen one is that you'd better not rock any boats: people who can't take any more stress in their lives depend on you. And because, after all, you weren't taken, you'd better be grateful for everything you've had — your brother sure didn't get anything . . . Bethany Fisher has always lived in the shadow of her missing brother. Four-year-old Michael was abducted when Bethany was a baby, and no trace of him was ever found. Now a college graduate with a small son of her own, Bethany's life is thrown into turmoil when her mild-mannered mother suddenly snaps . . .

WEEKEND

William McIlvanney

A group of lecturers and students arrives on the Scottish island of Cannamore for a study weekend. Away from his wife, David Cudlipp feels free to seduce one of his students; Harry Beck seeks distraction from his stalled writing career; whilst Andrew Lawson rests from caring for his bed-ridden wife. Among the students, Kate Foster plans to lose her virginity and Jacqui Forsyth to recover from a break-up; while for Vikki Kane, it's a chance to shed her inhibitions. Then there's Marion, the 'Mouse', who plans only to observe everyone else. But nothing turns out quite how anyone expected . . .

THE TWISTING VINE

Margaret Muir

In Yorkshire, Lucy Oldfield works as a maid at Heaton Hall. But when Lord Farnley's daughter dies, a shadow is cast over its future . . . Feeling insecure and unable to overcome temptation, Lucy steals an expensive French doll from her dead mistress. When the Hall is put up for sale and the staff dismissed, Lucy returns to Leeds. There, she falls victim to the deceit of an admirer, finding herself with a child to support. And then a chance meeting with a gentleman on a train leads to an offer that appears to be too good to be true . . . But will Lucy find herself subjected to even more heartache?

BETWEEN, GEORGIA

Joshilyn Jackson

Nonny Frett understands the meanings of 'rock' and 'hard place'. While her husband is easing out the back door her best friend is laying siege to her heart in her front yard. Working in the city, she's addicted to a little girl deep in the country. Nonny has two families: the Fretts, who stole her and raised her right, and the Crabtrees, who lost her and can't forget they've been done wrong. Now in Between, Georgia, population 90, a thirty-year-old stash of highly flammable secrets is about to be ignited — and Nonny is sitting in the middle of it . . .

AFTER MICHAEL

Betty O'Rourke

Fiona Latimer learns that her husband Michael has died of a heart attack alone in his London flat. She is shocked but not devastated; they had led separate lives for some years. Two people arrive at the funeral, each with considerable influence on future events. Anthea is a girl who knows more about Michael than she will admit, and Simon is someone from Fiona's past, whom she now realises she should have married instead. Gradually, secrets from Michael's past are uncovered and the final, shocking betrayals are revealed. Fiona now discovers her life with him was not at all what it had seemed . . .